D0594772

ORENDA

CURSE OF
IMMORTALITY

PEARL BEACON
ELIN PEER

Copyright © 2022
By Elin Peer and Pearl Beacon
All rights reserved.
No part of this book may be reproduced in any form
without written permission from the author, except for
brief quotations embodied in articles and reviews.
ISBN: 9798836962753
Orenda – Curse of Immortality
First Edition
The characters and events portrayed in this book are
fictitious. Any similarity to real persons or organizations
is coincidental and not intended by the author.
Cover Art by Miblart
Editing Martin O'Hearn

BOOKS IN THE ORENDA TRILOGY

For the best reading experience and to avoid spoilers, below is the order of the Orenda books.

#1 Curse of Immortality
#2 Betrayal of Blood
#3 End of Eternity

All characters are fictional and any likeness to a living person or organization is coincidental.

To be alerted for new book releases and discounts, sign up to our lists.
www.pearlbeacon.com
www.elinpeer.com

DEDICATION

We would like to dedicate this book to you, our reader.
We appreciate you suspending rational thought for a
while and letting us take you to a magical place.

We hope that you bring back a bit of the magic to your
everyday world.

Love
Pearl and Elin

CHAPTER 1
THE FATE OF A WITCH

Most childhood memories blur in your mind with time. Others stick like glue to your subconscious where they hide until they occasionally come back up to remind you that they are still there. The memory might as well have been yesterday because you can still smell the air, see every vivid detail, and most of all you can feel the emotions as if you are still that young child. These types of memories can stick with you until you are eighty years old, or in Maeve's case, five hundred years old.

Back when Althea and Maeve were born in the early sixteenth century, most days looked alike in the small English village, Abingdon, that they called home. People were hard-working and woke up with the sun, ate breakfast, went to work, did chores, ate supper, and went to bed to do it all again the next day. Like any typical morning Althea's and Maeve's father, John, had already left for work before their mother woke them. Old Janet who lived next door had stopped by to chat as she did so often, and breakfast consisted of porridge.

Today, however, wasn't any other day. Many of the villagers would be late to work because they were hurrying down to the square. The loud shouting from outside made the five-year-old twin sisters Althea and Maeve look to the windows in their small house where their mother, Anne, and old Janet were pressing their noses at the glass to see what was going on outside.

"Oh, look at them marching down the street. They've all gone mad, they have," old Janet muttered.

"What's going on? Can we see?" Althea asked in her young high-pitched voice, but old Janet was quick to refuse, "No. This is not for children."

Still sitting by the wooden table, the young twin girls felt left out. Althea followed Maeve when her sister pushed the clay bowl away and crawled up on the bench to stand tall enough to catch a glimpse of the action outside.

"Why are they shouting?" Maeve asked feeling unsettled by the angry noises from the people marching through the narrow street in front of their house.

"They're on their way to the market square to hang the witch," Anne said and received a reproachful glance from her older neighbor.

"There's no need to tell them that. They're only five," Janet whispered in a disapproving tone.

"Why wouldn't I? They'll see it with their own eyes," Anne argued and dried her hands on a cloth before hanging it back on the small nail on the wall. "It's good for children to know how the church protects us."

Janet shook her head and made a small step to the side for Anne to pass her in the tiny kitchen. "John won't like it. You know how angry he got when you brought them to the hanging last year. Remember how it gave the girls nightmares for months?"

It was rare for Anne to use a sharp tone with old Janet, who was kind enough to help them so often. But it was as if the anger from the people outside seeped under the doorway and made her hiss, "John won't find out because we won't tell him."

"But..."

Anne ignored Janet and waved her hand for her twin daughters to come with her. "Your father asked that you spend the morning with him at the stables. So that's where we will go after we take a quick stop."

Althea and Maeve didn't question their mother's instructions when she swung the wooden door open and popped her head out.

As the noise from outside became louder, so did the voice in Althea and Maeve's heads telling them to run and hide under their bed. They remembered all too well the last woman they saw murdered.

"Hold my hands and don't let go," Anne instructed her daughters before she rushed them out the door and into the angry mob of people.

Althea turned her body and looked back at old Janet, who stood in the doorway with an expression of deep concern on her face.

"Come along, child." Anne squeezed Althea's hand and pulled her along.

Althea and Maeve had played in this narrow street for as long as they could remember, but it seemed narrower and darker now that it was crowded with people. Their heads turned from side to side as they tried to recognize the grown-ups around them. Maeve thought she recognized the tailor that her father sometimes talked to, but his face was so distorted from the shouting that she couldn't be sure.

Althea and Maeve had to run to keep up with the fast pace of their mother and the others in the sea of people. Once they got to the center of town, the crowd was enormous, and Althea was sure that there were far more people present than the last time their mother had brought them to a hanging. Above all the shouting from the crowd, a soul-ripping scream from a woman grew in volume.

Althea and Maeve couldn't see with all the large grownups around them, but Anne kept pushing her way up front and tugging them along with her.

The woman's desperate cries for help burned into the hearts of the two terrified young girls. Althea had a

3

tight grip on their mother's dress and when they got up front, she refused to see another hanging. Instead, she closed her eyes shut and buried her face against her mother's hip.

Maeve, on the other hand, felt paralyzed and with her unable to look away she saw everything. Wherever she looked, angry people were spitting, shouting vulgar things, and throwing rotten eggs, onions, and tomatoes in the direction of a woman who stood under the large oak tree with a noose around her neck. She was dressed in nothing but her white nightdress, which was torn in places, and full of stains from the rotten eggs and vegetables that had been thrown at her. Standing with bare feet, she had her hands tied in front of her, making herself small as she looked down and sobbed. In some places, her hair was wild and unkempt, and in the front, a rotten egg had smashed on her skull leaving the sticky substance to run down her sobbing face.

Maeve blinked her eyes when she recognized the woman to be Ellen, the daughter of the miller. It shocked her to see the young woman bleeding from scratches and with angry red streaks running down her jaw and neck as if someone had hurt her. A large onion hit Ellen hard on the shoulder and made her scream again, followed by more heartbreaking sobs and cries for help.

Maeve wanted to look away or hide against her mother's body the way Althea did, but she couldn't.

None of this made any sense to the five-year-old. Witches were supposed to be scary, but Ellen had once watched them while their father helped the miller, and Maeve could still remember how she had plucked a flower and handed it to Maeve with a gentle smile.

Anne yelled with the others for Ellen to go to hell and it made the young, frightened woman roll her shoulders forward and bow her head, making herself even smaller as she continued sobbing.

"No," Maeve shouted in her small, child's voice when a large, bulky man with a crooked nose and close-set eyes jerked Ellen's body and adjusted the rope around her neck.

Ellen must have heard the small protest because she raised her head and found Maeve in the crowd, looking straight into her eyes.

"No!" Maeve repeated as her voice cracked from the ball of emotions in her throat and tears began streaming down her cheeks.

Ellen kept her eyes locked on the innocent child and somehow Maeve understood that Ellen needed to look at someone who wasn't mad or screaming at her.

When the man pulled at the rope that hung across the thick branch of the big oak, the yelling of the crowd turned into cheering. A gasp escaped Maeve's lips, and her small body froze in place when Ellen's body lifted from the ground and hung helpless with her hands tied in front of her. She witnessed the woman's desperate kicking of her legs in death spasms until she didn't move anymore. Maeve was instantly overcome with guilt for not stopping the execution. Ellen had looked at *her*, and for a long moment, they had held eye contact. Though Maeve had wanted to run up and tear the rope from Ellen's neck, she had stood frozen and watched Ellen take her last breath.

"Burn in hell, witch," Anne spat as all around them, the crowd celebrated seeing Ellen's body dangling lifelessly from the rope.

The sensation of needing to throw up pressed at Maeve's throat, preventing her from being able to talk. She squeezed her mother's hand tighter as tears wouldn't stop streaming down her red cheeks. Maeve couldn't tell how long they stood watching Ellen's dead body before her mother finally pulled at her small hand, leading them away. The image of Ellen would forever be burned in her mind and the powerlessness of not being able to help the poor woman stayed with her as well.

Maeve walked close to her mother, but her mind was clouded from the intense connection she had felt between herself and Ellen. All the way, their mother talked about how satisfying it was to see good conquer evil, but Maeve struggled to find any good in the situation. All she was left with was a deep sadness that weighed heavily on her small body and heart.

Once they were outside the village, everything was quiet except for the sound of birds chirping. Seeing the manor and the stables in the distance made Maeve speed up. She longed for a big hug from her father, who always calmed her when she had nightmares.

"Can we run?" Althea asked and their mother was quick to agree.

"Fine. I don't have time to walk you all the way to the estate anyway. You know the way to the stables, don't you, girls?"

Althea nodded her pretty little head.

"Remember what I told you. If your father asks, you came straight from home. Don't tell him that I let you see the execution of the witch. That has to be our secret." Squatting down, Anne looked her girls over and adjusted Maeve's dress. "Remember to be good and do as your father says."

Maeve nodded and sucked in her lips before building up the courage to ask her mother, "Why did they kill Ellen?"

Anne let out a sigh. "You know why. She was a witch."

"But how do you know that? She didn't look like a witch," Maeve inquired.

Anne straightened her daughter's hair and used a serious tone. "Looks can be deceiving. Ellen put a spell on the carpenter. He was completely bewitched and wanted to leave his wife and children to be with her. But his wife suspected something was wrong and followed Ellen one night and saw her talking to the devil."

Maeve's eyes grew large. "Really?"

"Yes. We've discussed this before. You remember what happens to witches, don't you?"

"Yes, Mum," Maeve answered and looked away.

Anne brushed her daughter's cheek, recognizing the fear in her eyes. "You two are such good girls, and I want more than anything for you to experience the eternal bliss of heaven with me and your father. That's why it's so important that you stay away from the devil's work. That *witch*," she spat the word out as if it was poison to her tongue, "she was evil and will rot in the depths of hell."

Anne rose to her full height and brushed her long dress that was so dreadful to wear on such a warm summer day. "Run along, girls, I'll see you tonight."

Althea and Maeve nodded before they sprinted towards the nice manor where their father worked for the rich Clifford family.

The dirt road was long and their little legs soon tired from running. When Althea slowed down to catch her breath, Maeve did the same. It was typical of the girls to do things in unison because even though the girls were so young, Maeve and Althea shared a bond, much stronger than many who'd been friends for decades. Often it felt as if they could read each other's minds.

"Why did you look at the witch when we said that we wouldn't look again?" Althea blamed her sister because, after the last witch trial, the girls had made a pact to keep their heads down.

"I didn't mean to. It just happened. I saw the whole thing," Maeve said in a tone so sad that it made her sister take her hand.

Althea's gaze fell to the ground as her thumb ran circles on her sister's hand.

With a loud sniffle, Maeve said, "She was the lady who played with us when Dad helped the miller."

"Oh." Althea's face visibly sank. "I liked her. She was nice."

Trying to make sense of everything, Maeve concluded. "Well, she must've been pretending to be nice since Mum was certain she was a witch. They had to kill her... to protect us," Maeve said in the hopes that she could convince herself. But the truth was that witch or no witch, what had happened made their stomachs hurt and their eyes water.

The air hung heavy between the sisters as they silently carried on walking down the dirt road until they saw their father, John. He stood outside the stables, stacking hay in his brown pants, worn leather shoes, and a shirt that had once been white.

Althea and Maeve were overcome with excitement to see him and once again set off into a run. Of course, their father spotted them long before they reached him. With the sun beaming down on John's sweaty face he watched his beloved daughters run toward him. Their locks of bright orange hair flew in all directions matching the summer sun perfectly, like an extension of its flames.

John was a devoted and protective father who loved his daughters deeply. Anyone who knew him would say he was a kind man known to be warm and helpful.

He waited patiently, and when the girls finally reached him, he got down on one knee to embrace his young daughters in a tight hug. "I've been waiting for you. What took so long?"

"Mum let us run to you because she had something important to do," Althea explained, dodging his question while using her hand to cover her eyes from the bright sun.

But seeing Ellen executed weighed heavily on Maeve, who craved her father's comfort. Despite their mother's instructions not to mention it, Maeve blurted out, "They killed another witch again this morning."

His eyes narrowed. "I'm aware, but you didn't see it, did you?"

Althea bit her lip before admitting, "I closed my eyes, but Maeve saw everything. It was Ellen from the mill."

John was upset with his wife, Anne, for allowing their daughters to witness something as cruel and horrible as another execution. They had talked about it and he had been clear with Anne that he didn't want the young girls to catch a glimpse of the hanging. That's why he had made her promise to bring the girls straight to him after breakfast. He was well aware that Anne thought she was protecting their girls by showing them to be careful of witches, but John wasn't a superstitious man and didn't for one second believe that Ellen had been a witch. The whole situation saddened him and brought back unwanted memories from the night his sister was accused of witchery. As far as John was concerned, witches were a made-up construct by the church to scare people. He wished he could speak openly about the healing powers that ran in his bloodline, but in these times, it was better to keep those sorts of abilities a secret and blend in.

"Girls, why don't you take some hay to Henry and go say hi to him?" John suggested. With the subject of the witch hanging feeling like a knife in the stomach to him, he needed a moment to find the strength to comfort his daughters.

Maeve grabbed her sister's hand again and headed into the stable where Henry, the brown horse lived. Both girls loved it when they got to visit their father at work. Unlike the other five horses under their father's care, Henry was old and calm with a friendly personality.

9

While the other horses were down at the large pasture, Henry had a leg injury that required him to stay in the barn.

"Hello, Henry," Althea greeted the old horse while separating the hay in her hand, giving half to her sister and the other to the horse.

The girls stood on both sides of the large animal petting it with the tender hands of five-year-old girls. Maeve was careful to do as her father had instructed and laid her hand flat for the horse to eat the hay from. She was already having a hard day, so when Henry sniffed Althea's hair and nuzzled her arm instead of taking the hay that Maeve offered him, she felt rejected and hurt.

"Come on, Henry, let's go outside," Maeve said and untied the rope holding him.

"What are you doing?" Althea yelled after her sister when Maeve led Henry out of his stall. Running to catch up, she added, "He's not your horse. I'm his favorite person."

"No, you're not. I am," Maeve yelled as she guided Henry outside in the warm sun. John was on the other side of the stable and didn't hear how the girls were bickering at each other. It was a silly argument to get so riled up over but when Althea grabbed Henry's face and pressed her own against it, Maeve pushed at her sister, shoving her away from the horse.

Henry moved and gave long and loud neighs when the girls' yelling turned into screaming. Using words to express your emotions takes time to learn and being only five years old, yelling into each other's faces with their eyes closed was as good as it got for Althea and Maeve.

The sound of Henry running off reminded the girls what the argument had been about. Alarmed, they both opened their eyes and stopped screaming. Althea jumped back when she saw red flames running up the stable and scattering around her and Maeve. Henry, who had gotten scared from the screaming and the fire, was now far out on the fields.

It was summer and everything was dry and dusty. The flames caught the hay and when John came sprinting around the stable, the fire was already spreading fast.

"Get away from there," he shouted, and the girls were quick to run and hide behind him. Moving them to a safe distance, John gave them firm instructions. "Stay here."

What the girls saw made no sense to them because as their father ran to the stables, his hands flew through the air extinguishing some of the flames as if invisible water had been poured onto the fire.

He disappeared into the smoke and reappeared with his arms full of saddles. Four times, John went inside and brought out more things, but the fire had reached the roof now and roared with such strength that loud cracking sounds told him it was a matter of time before the building would collapse.

Coming to find Althea and Maeve, John pulled them into a tight hug and asked them, "What happened?"

"We didn't do it," Althea hurried to explain. "We were screaming at each other and when we opened our eyes there were flames all around us."

John closed his eyes, knowing that his daughters had powers they didn't understand. Ever since he found out that Anne was pregnant, he had prayed that his daughters would be born as humans, like their mother. But despite wishing on every shooting star John had seen, it seemed Althea and Maeve had been born with the abilities that ran in his bloodline.

For a long moment, John stared at his frightened daughters. Thankful that they weren't hurt and that no one had been there to see what had happened, he sank to his knees and began to cry. Althea and Maeve had never seen their father cry before, and it left them quiet and feeling unsure about what to do. What they didn't understand was that in that moment, John's world collapsed as he understood that he couldn't keep his daughters safe in the village. Their powers would make them a target and he couldn't allow them to end up like Ellen or the other poor souls accused of witchcraft. It was of paramount importance that the twins learn how to control their powers and he couldn't teach them that without them accidentally setting everything on fire and their mother finding out. It broke his heart that keeping his daughters close would be to risk their lives. Faced with the only option available to him, John sobbed for the first time since the night his sister had been accused of witchery and his whole world had collapsed for the first time.

Even Henry came back to investigate the strange noise that his beloved caregiver was making and tried to comfort John with loving pushes. Pulling his daughters closer in his lap, John kissed their red hair and for a long moment, he held them tight while crying and rocking them back and forth.

With no other choice left, John made the decision he had tried to avoid at all costs. Rising from the ground, he worked fast. Getting the strongest and fastest horse from the pasture, he put a saddle on the large stallion. The girls asked many questions, but it was as if John couldn't hear them because he was so lost in his thoughts.

Picking up the girls, he placed them on the horse before hoisting himself up and riding off. The Clifford family and their servants were spending time in one of their other houses by the seaside, but the fire was large enough that it would attract people from the village. John had to get away before people came to ask questions.

There was only one place for him to bring his daughters to safety and he had no idea how to get there.

Quieting his mind, he sent out his request for guidance to Zosia, praying that the spirit of nature would lead him and his girls to his sister.

He knew his request had been accepted when the birds in the trees began to communicate with him and lead the way. Galloping through the forest, he prayed that Rose wouldn't be furious with him for what had happened the last time they'd seen each other six years ago.

CHAPTER 2
DEEP IN THE FOREST

The details would blur in their memories with time, but Althea and Maeve would always remember the confusion and sadness that weighed on their stomachs when their father rode the giant horse as fast as it could run through the woods. They had given up asking questions many hours ago because all John would say was, "It will be alright."

It was the first time that Althea and Maeve left their village in the countryside of England. Traveling required time and money, which their parents had little of. While their father worried about the repercussions of borrowing a horse from his employers and how to explain everything, Althea and Maeve sat in a trancelike state holding on to the mane of the horse. As the hours passed, the horse and the girls became exhausted, but John was wide awake, internally focused on following the group of sparrows that seemed to show him the way. As the woods grew denser, he got off the stallion without waking the girls and walked for miles until he picked up on a lovely scent of freshly baked bread. Soon, they reached a clearing where wildflowers grew and a house that had seen better days stood welcoming them.

In the window, he spotted the face of his sister, but despite his relief that he had found Rose, his face was still paralyzed into a stern exterior when he finally announced to his daughters, "We're here."

The girls blinked their eyes open to see that they were deep in the forest. It had been mid-morning when they left their home, but the sun was already below the treetops and would be set in a few hours. Its golden rays shone through the tall trees and their green leaves. Althea squinted her tired eyes and took in the small cottage in front of them.

With a tree that poked through the corner of the roof, it was like no other house Althea and Maeve had ever seen. Either the cottage had been built around the tree, or the tree had grown through the cottage. The whole place looked worn down. And with moss growing on the uneven roof that had several bird nests lying around with chirping hatchlings inside, it was as if nature had taken over an abandoned house. The smoke coming out of the brick chimney told another story though. Someone lived here and took great pride in the small vegetable garden that was protected by a fence, and a small creek that ran along with the garden and passed the house. As they got closer, it became clear that the vines growing on the façade of the house were tamed and didn't cover the open windows. But the biggest sign that someone lived here was the delicious smell of food that made Althea's stomach growl.

John helped his daughters off the horse and for a moment all three of them took in how the evening sun gave the house a golden tint. All the colorful flowers on the ground and the walls stretched out towards the light to get the last glimpse of the sun for the day.

"Where are we?" Maeve asked. "And who is that woman?"

They all looked to the woman, who appeared to be around their father's age. She stood in the doorway watching them with an expression of disbelief on her face.

Without meeting his daughters' eyes, John instructed, "Take the horse to the creek and give him some of the apples from that tree over there. He needs to rest so let him graze while I go talk to Rose. If you're

15

hungry, eat as much fruit as you want, and feel free to play out here until we're done talking."

The girls complied and went to greet a black cat that lay on its back in the grass. When they looked back at the cottage their father had gone inside.

At first, there was a long and awkward moment of silence between John and his sister. They hadn't seen each other since before the twins were born and the night that they separated had been distressing to both of them.

"I'm glad to see you found safety," John said and took the seat that Rose offered him.

"Yes. I've moved around a lot, but two years ago I found this abandoned cabin and made it my own. I sell produce in the nearest town to support myself."

Over the next twenty minutes, John told his sister the whole story in a rambling way.

Rose sat with her hands folded in her lap and her gaze hanging low. With grief and sorrow in her tone, she sighed. "I can't believe they killed Ellen. She would never hurt a fly."

"Please, Rose, I love my daughters and I need you to keep them safe. You can teach them to control their powers and maybe in time they can have normal lives like me."

Her head snapped up as she locked eyes with John. "You mean to learn to hide who they are?"

"Yes."

"There's nothing normal about hiding your gifts from the world."

"No, but with everything that's going on, we have no other choice."

Rose stood up and clasped both hands on the back of the chair she had just been in. "The cottage is small, but I'm sure we can make it work for the four of us."

John dried his eyes and avoided his sister's gaze as he slowly spoke, "Althea and Maeve deserve to know who they are, but I can't teach them about their powers. Not when we live in the same house as Anne, and I don't want to think about what would happen if she ever found out." He shook his head. "You know how she is. She wouldn't understand." He paused when he saw how his sister flinched and removed her hand from the chair before pulling back a little.

"Anne has already lost so much. I can't leave her too. But I know that my girls are no longer safe, so, Rose, I beg you, please protect my daughters and raise them as your own."

In truth, Rose had felt lonely over the years. She had all her animals whom she loved dearly, but she missed the family she had grown up with and had always longed to be a mother herself. She was a kindhearted soul and there was no way she could turn her back on her young nieces.

"I will love them and care for them, just as our parents did for us," she promised.

"Thank you." John was so quick to get up from his seat to hug her that his chair fell over.

When he released her from his tight hug, she looked up at him and asked, "What will you tell Anne?"

John's face turned solemn again. "I'll say that they were playing in the barn while I went to check up on the horses in the farthest pasture. I wasn't there when the fire started but by the time I reached them, the girls had both died in the fire."

"People will wonder where you went for so long."

"I'll explain that I didn't know how to tell Anne, so I stayed in the forest all day."

Rose's gaze lowered. "She'll be devastated. To lose one's children in a fire..."

"It's horrendous." John finished her sentence in a grave tone. "But I'd rather comfort my wife through her grief while I know my daughters are safe than to see them murdered as witches one day."

John took a last glance around the cottage that his daughters would call home from now on. The walls were slanted and the windows crooked. In the corner was a kitchen with a table that held jars and cooking supplies and over the table hung lavender and rosemary. A fireplace stood in the center of the wall with a fire heating a large pot of something that smelled amazing. On the walls hung pots and pans and flowers hanging by their stems.

"You must all be hungry," Rose said and went to light a few candles now that the daylight had almost disappeared.

"Yes. Very. And I'm sure the girls are curious to meet you." He turned to the opposite side of the room where a tree grew through the house and up above the roof. It seemed as if the branches served as steps that could be crawled up on. Walking over to see for himself, John discovered that on top of the roof amongst the thick branches of the tree was a terrace that Rose had built for her to sleep on. It was big enough for Althea and Maeve to sleep with her, and it offered blankets to keep it soft and cozy as well as thick branches above to keep it dry.

As Rose opened the front door that was an inch shorter than herself, she turned to her brother and asked, "Will you stay for the night?"

"No." John snatched an apple from the bowl on the table. "I should get back to Anne as soon as possible, I know she'll be worried sick. She might think that all three of us died in the fire. But I'll take a bit of bread for the journey home if you have some to spare."

Rose made sure to give him a big chunk of the bread she had pulled out of the oven an hour earlier. "Take anything you want from the garden. The plums are ripe and delicious." She gave her brother a last smile before they walked outside to Althea and Maeve, who sat on the grass patiently waiting.

The girls looked up at their father as he spoke. "This is my sister, Rose, your aunt."

Maeve frowned and looked at the woman, who had wild, curly, brown hair and dirt on her arms. "You've never told us we have an aunt."

"No, I haven't, and I'm sorry for that. But Rose is one of the kindest people you'll ever meet and from now on, you two will be living here with her."

"Why?" Althea cried.

"For your safety."

"No, I don't want to," Maeve blurted out at the same time Althea asked in despair again, "Why?"

"I wish I could stay and explain everything, but I *have* to get back. Rose will tell you what you need to know." He got down to his knees to be at the same level as his daughters who stood small, fragile, and confused in front of him. "I need you two to understand that I'm only leaving you here because I love you more than anything. I wish it didn't have to be this way, but for now, it's what's best. Be kind to your aunt; she is a good woman and I know that she will love you just as your mother and I do."

Sobs escaped the girls as they clung to their father, but in the end, no plea or tight hug could make him stay. John left his daughters in the middle of the woods with his sister. As he rode off, he had every intention of coming back and visiting them, but in the end, it would be the last time Althea and Maeve ever saw him.

Rose felt the children's pain as her own. She too had lost both her parents and still grieved over the tragic events of that fatal night.

Putting a hand on each girl's shoulder, she offered, "Why don't we go inside and eat some of the soup I made for dinner? I'm sure your heads are full of questions, but we'll have to take one answer at a time until you understand everything about what it is to be an Earthen."

"What's an Earthen?" Althea asked.

Rose smiled. "We are. Come on. Just like humans, we still need to eat."

CHAPTER 3
THE SECRET SPECIES

It was dark and cold outside, but the candles and fireplace made it warm and toasty inside the small cottage. Althea was braiding Maeve's long, red hair in the candlelight, while Maeve sang to the sleeping cat in her arms. Nothing warmed Rose's heart more than to see her two girls happy and healthy.

Standing in the kitchen kneading dough for bread, she let her hands work while enjoying the sound of the melodic wind chimes that accompanied Maeve's beautiful voice. It was as if the wind listened and wanted to sing along.

Rose's mind was going over the ingredients for the soup she would make for tonight's dinner when she heard a distant noise coming from outside. Dusting flour off her hands, she walked over to the window and stood for a moment letting her eyes adjust to the darkness outside. Her eyes narrowed a little and her gaze centered on the tiny light flickering in the distance.

"Shhh." Stretching her hand out, Rose shushed Maeve to get her to stop singing. No one ever visited them out here. Acute worry made her spine straighten as the light came closer, confirming her fear that it was people carrying torches. There were many of them and they were moving closer at a fast pace. Unsure what to do, Rose felt sweat form on her forehead. She remembered this scenario all too well. Last time it had been torches carried by a different group of people, but a mob of people was dangerous to Earthens no matter what village they came from.

Rose couldn't understand how they had found out about her abilities. She had last been to town four days ago and although she was well aware that some of the people probably found her strange, she was always so quiet and careful not to draw attention to herself. Never had she offered to heal anyone.

With the town being at least an hour away, she must have stirred up suspicion amongst the humans to make them march all the way out here and that could only mean one thing: the time which she had feared more than anything had come – they wanted someone to burn.

"Stay inside and hide," she told the girls with a shaking voice before she walked outside, shutting the door behind her.

Trying to hide her fear, she kept her voice friendly as she tried to calm down the angry crowd. But her words were no use. They kept moving closer, yelling accusations and cursing at her.

"Please, I haven't done anything! I would never hurt anyone!" Rose defended herself and held up her hands to stop them from coming closer. But when they were within arm's reach, they did not forcibly grab her and tie her with rope as she feared they would. Instead, a short man with a long dirty beard grabbed her outstretched hands and threw her down on the wet and dirty ground.

Confused, Rose looked up at the mob surrounding the cottage.

"We're here for the witches," an old woman said with a sadistic smile on her wrinkly face. Rose stared in horror as the woman pulled a cloth from her pocket and lit it on fire using her torch.

"No!" Rose yelled and hurried to her feet before she was shoved down into the mud once again. "Don't!" she cried.

The woman didn't hesitate before she hurried to the door that a man held open and threw the burning cloth inside.

In desperation, Rose fought to get up. Ignoring the taste of mud in her mouth, she screamed with terror as others threw burning sticks through the window.

"They're just children," she cried and felt a pure sense of desperation. This had happened before and the last time it was her parents that lost their lives. The sound of banging fists on the door tore Rose apart and she wailed when she caught a glance of Althea and Maeve clinging to each other before the whole house lit up into flames, devouring the girls inside.

Her only thought was that she would rather die with them than live to grieve them. Sobs escaped Rose as she got to her feet and fought to get past the mob, but the people wouldn't budge. No matter how much she hit, cried, and fought, there was nothing she could do to get through the wall of angry villagers celebrating what they saw as a victory. Falling to the ground in defeat, Rose curled herself into a small ball and sobbed as the laughter and cheering from the mob grew louder and the screams from the girls died out.

"You're a failure. Did you think you could protect them from us?" someone mocked her, and it silenced the crowd. Rose's heart skipped a beat when she opened her eyes to see that everyone was standing in a circle around her and her former best friend. Anne stepped forward and stopped in front of her. She didn't look a day older than the last time she'd last seen her. Still a beautiful young woman with angry eyes, she hissed, "You couldn't save my mother, nor could you save my daughters." As if her tongue was a dagger, every word from Anne cut deep as she hissed, "You are a failure and a fraud. How could you think that I could *ever* love you?"

"Please, Anne, I kept them hidden for all this time. I love them and I would have given my life to save them; I would have died for them," Rose whimpered in her defense, but it didn't stop Anne from walking closer and spitting on Rose's dress.

"You are a witch, and the world is better off without you," she said with an icy gaze in her eyes and her lips pressed into a fine line.

Frightened, Rose felt strong hands pull her to a pole, where someone tied her hands to it. She should scream and cry, but no words escaped her trembling lips.

The villagers were booing and cursing all around her, and amid the crowd, Anne stood with a large torch and a hateful expression on her face. Without saying a word, she walked to stand in front of Rose again. Keeping intense eye contact, she stabbed her torch against Rose's body and smiled with satisfaction when her clothes caught fire.

The last thing she saw was Anne standing in front of the fire, her face orange from the large flames. "I could never love you," she said again before the flames were the only thing Rose could see and feel.

Waking with a gasp, Rose sat up and saw that she was on her terrace with wet blankets surrounding her from her excessive sweating.

She placed a hand on her wet forehead and tried to steady her breathing while reminding herself that it had only been a dream.

For minutes, she listened carefully for any sound of people approaching, but there was nothing. All she heard was the heavy breathing from Althea and Maeve sleeping peacefully higher up in the tree on their terrace.

It had been nine years since the girls had come to live with their aunt and while the girls had grown into beautiful teenagers, Rose's constant nightmares, and worries about losing her nieces, had created deep lines that made her look twenty years older. Althea and Maeve were used to Rose waking in the middle of the night in a sweat and gasping for air. It was the same type of dream that had tormented her throughout the years. Sometimes the fear of having nightmares once again prevented her from falling asleep, but as she lay under the clear night sky with hundreds of stars to count, she reminded herself that being this far out in the forest and away from civilization, the girls were safe. And yet, this time, the dream had felt more vivid than usual, and she couldn't shake the feeling that it was an omen of something awful to come.

Unable to fall back to sleep, Rose climbed down the tree and into the cottage. The sky was still dark and offered no light, other than the sparkles of the stars. She had only just lit one candle when she froze, and the sweating started once again. With her eyes glued to the small orange flame, she had just lit, flashes from her nightmare came back to Rose – the terrifying sight of Althea and Maeve burning inside the house had her reach for the back of a chair for support. The candle's flame flickered and now showed Anne standing in front of Rose with hatred in her eyes watching her burn. These images had lived inside her head and had haunted Rose for years. Forcefully blinking her eyes, she snapped herself out of it.

Knowing that it's much easier to distract your mind from the thoughts you try to keep at bay when your hands are busy, Rose began baking bread and cleaning the house – just like she did on many sleepless nights.

"Good morning," Maeve said with a yawn and rubbed her tired eyes when she crawled down the tree a few hours later.

Rose had been aggressively mixing berries in a bowl and became so startled by Maeve's voice that she nearly dropped the bowl.

"How long have you been up?" Althea asked as she stepped down from the last branch.

Rose looked at her nieces and blinked her tired eyes three times when she noticed it was already light outside. "A little while."

Fourteen-year-old Althea approached her aunt, who was now a little shorter than herself and gently took the bowl out of her hands. "You look tired, Aunt Rose. Why don't you go and rest while Maeve and I take care of breakfast?"

Althea put the bowl of berries down and took her aunt's hands while Maeve hugged Rose from behind and kissed her shoulder. This was the first time that Rose had been able to relax since she had awoken from her night terror. However, just the thought of it made her heartbeat speed up. "No." She sighed and pulled the girls into a hug where she kissed them both on the head. "I would rather get started with the day. Go take a seat, breakfast is almost done."

Althea and Maeve set the table and took a seat in the creaky wooden chairs, but they kept a close eye on their aunt and worried for her. The girls didn't know about the anguish Rose had experienced and how it haunted her, but they knew that she didn't get enough sleep and that much of the time she looked like she was in another world. They worried for her. However, Althea and Maeve never knew the worst of it since Rose always felt the calmest when she was in their company. The three of them were close and rarely got into arguments, which made their lives peaceful.

The morning sun shone through the windows as they sat at the small table eating their breakfast and chatting about what to do with their day. Rose was just about to take another bite of her bread when the sound of a bird landing on the windowsill made her turn her head.

"Maeve, I want you to listen to what she's saying," Rose instructed. Althea had mastered communicating with animals when she was ten, but Maeve often struggled.

"I know you excel when it comes to making potions but communicating with animals and listening for the flowers that hold the healing rootling is closely related."

Maeve groaned because somehow her hearing wasn't as sharp as her sister's after all the years of practicing. It frustrated her whenever Althea would stand in a meadow with wildflowers and listen for only a brief moment before searching out the one flower among thousands that held a healing rootling in its root.

"There's no need to groan. You're superior when it comes to making potions. But you'll need those rootlings for the most powerful ones so you'd better practice listening," Rose insisted, giving a supportive nod.

With a look of concentration, Maeve focused on the small bird, trying to understand its message. When that didn't help, she closed her eyes and listened again. All she heard was chirping.

With a sigh of defeat, Maeve threw her hands up. "I have no clue."

"Darling." Rose tilted her head and gave Maeve a tired smile. "The more your mind demands to understand the bird, the more you're separating yourself from it. Remember that you and the bird are one, just as we all are. It takes practice, but as soon as you accept that and stop trying to force it, it will come."

"Let me try again." Maeve stood up from her chair and walked over to the bird. When she stretched her pale hand out, the small bird hopped onto it and continued chirping. Closing her eyes, Maeve imagined herself and the bird melting together, and loved the bird as if it were her own eyes and ears.

When mental images appeared in her mind's eye, her lips pursed up in a smile but when she recognized the image her smile disappeared. "I see a small girl who is much too pale and tired."

"Wonderful, Maeve, well done," Rose praised her and elaborated on the bird's message. "The girl has been sick for some time, but she's not getting proper treatment because the priest has told her family that she is possessed."

Althea and Rose had both understood the bird's message the moment it entered their home. After thanking the small bird for its message, Rose faced the girls. "I wish there was something we could do, but the world has turned its back on us healers. We can't risk offering our help."

"Rose?" Althea's expression was pleading. "We can't just let her die. Isn't there something we can do? What if we came with you? We are safer in a group, and we have to learn how to heal and care for humans eventually."

Rose's throat sank to the bottom of her stomach. She knew that Althea was right, in theory. An Earthen's role had always been to heal and care for all living beings and the truth was that it was far overdue in the girls' training. Rose herself had worked with her parents to learn from them as she grew up. Althea and Maeve were already of age to be healers, but she hadn't been able to teach them to heal anyone but each other and the animals and plants in the forest. Her priority had always been to keep the girls safe and hidden in the forest and away from civilization. Rose couldn't bear the thought of losing them just as she had lost everyone else whom she cared for.

The small voice of her father whispered inside her that a life of hiding from your destiny is not truly living at all.

"It's not that I don't want to help the sick girl that the bird is telling us about. But we can't risk it just yet."

"But then when?" Maeve asked with her hands falling to her sides in defeat. "I'm dying to see something other than this forest."

Rose scratched her shoulder and looked away. The subject always made her nervous. "Maybe I can take you to town one day, but not until you have full control of your abilities."

"We do," Maeve claimed. "You can test us if you don't believe me."

Rose wanted to end the argument and decided to give a test so difficult that the girls wouldn't pass. "Alright. Follow me," she instructed and walked out into the small field behind their home. Althea and Maeve eagerly followed and once they stood beside her, she knelt and pressed her palm a few inches above the dry summer grass. When a small flame lit and began to spread, she rose back up. "Extinguish the fire."

Althea and Maeve looked at each other with large eyes. Rose often challenged them when it came to learning but controlling the elements was an advanced skill, especially at the age of fourteen.

Rose didn't tell the girls that despite being a fast learner herself, she hadn't mastered the control of fire until she was seventeen.

Rose would rather give her nieces a life of hiding from their destiny than for them not to have a life at all.

"We blow out candles, so maybe we should try to use air," Maeve pondered out loud as she got down to her knees in front of the small orange flame.

Both girls placed their hands in front of the fire and visualized wind flowing through them. When nothing happened, Maeve bit her bottom lip and looked at her sister.

"Maybe it will work if we channel our energy together." Althea scooted closer to Maeve so that they were shoulder to shoulder. But once again no wind emerged from their efforts.

Althea's face filled with freckles turned in the direction of her sister. "We need more emotion. Remember what Rose said a few years ago when she taught us about the elements? She said that we set off the fire in the barn because of our emotional outburst. If emotions are the way to control the elements, then we need to find strong emotions within ourselves somehow."

Maeve looked over her shoulder to their aunt, who was carefully watching them. "Yes, but how?"

"What if we sing our favorite song? The one we always make Rose sing for us," Althea asked, knowing that songs were like art that brought out intense emotions. And this song brought out more emotion in them than any other.

"Okay, just concentrate on creating wind," Maeve instructed before the girls began to hum the soft melody that always brought up nostalgic feelings from their childhood.

To you the world is dark, there can be no light.
Although you try to run, you can never hide.
The fear within your heart is a dreadful cage.
Your feet carry on, at a fast pace.
Hmm-hmm-mm-hmm

When the earth opens up and buries you deep.
You lie in the dirt, swallowed by fear.
You'll never escape, for the shadows are here.
They live in your heart, where you carry them, dear.
Hmm-hmm-mm-hmm

A scared and fearful heart can see no light.
But I see you, lying in the ground.
Take my hand, I'll help you out.
The shadows are near, but I have no fear.
Hmm-hmm-mm-hmm

The world is dark, and evil lies near.
Your angry heart carries that fear.
You don't see how the sun shines down.
Your back is turned, with your gaze on the
ground.
Hmm-hmm-mm-hmm

Take my hand, I'll show you the light.
My shadow is near, but I have no fear.
Feel the love that shines from my heart,
For I choose to turn to the sun and the light.
Hmm-hmm-mm-hmm

Take my hand, you're never alone.
I love you, dear, so have no fear.
Together we'll face the world as it is.
The good and bad, we'll still be here.
For even in the dark, the sun will be near.
Hmm-hmm-mm-hmm

As the girls sang each verse with gentle voices, a breeze suddenly emerged from their palms. It made Maeve jerk her body back in surprise.

"Stop," Althea said, lowering her hand. "The wind is only making the fire bigger."

"Then what about water?" Maeve asked, looking at the fire that was slowly starting to become bigger.

The girls raised their palms once again and began to sing the song their aunt had sung for them since they were five years old.

The palms of their hands became moist and soon small droplets of water separated themselves from their wet hands. Althea and Maeve continued singing their gentle song as they held their hands above the fire and let water fall onto the flame. Slowly but surely they extinguished the flames.

With her mouth dropped open, Rose watched with amazement. She felt proud of her accomplished nieces, but her throat tightened, knowing what she had promised them if they succeeded. Being a woman of her word, meant that she would have to bring Althea and Maeve with her to the village.

After the horrific night of terror she'd had, she had a strong feeling that nothing good would come of this.

CHAPTER 4
FIRST TIME IN THE VILLAGE

On Saturday morning, Rose brought the girls with her to the local town, Lerwick. The contrast between the girl's bubbly excitement and Rose's quiet concern made it a strained conversation as they walked to the marketplace where they would sell produce just like Rose had done for years.

"Remember not to talk to anyone," she ordered for the tenth time. "You are there to observe and as soon as we have sold the flowers and vegetables, we're leaving."

"Yes, Rose." Althea nodded before sending her sister another glance with suppressed excitement and her eyes glistening.

To others, the small, English town would have been a dull experience, but Althea and Maeve had been isolated in the forest for nine years. At fourteen they were longing to see more than trees, moss, animals, and clouds in the sky.

As they reached the outskirts of the town, Althea fisted her hand into her skirt feeling the need to hold on to something as they ventured into danger. It all felt forbidden and scary at first, but things changed the moment they walked down the street among houses, people, chickens, and children laughing while chasing one another. Memories from their childhood rushed back and overwhelmed both Althea and Maeve while Rose kept her head down and hurried Tobias along. The horse moved in a slow walk, carrying the heavy burden of leeks, carrots, apples, plums, and rhubarb in buckets tied across his back.

For years, the girls had imagined the town to be a place of danger and now that they were here, they saw ordinary people going about their day. A man greeted them with a friendly smile, raising his hat before passing them.

"Morning, ladies,"

Maeve smiled and greeted him back, but that made Rose whisper a warning.

"You're drawing attention to yourself. Don't meet their eyes and don't greet them back. Humans may look kind, but they are unpredictable and can turn on you fast."

Once they reached the town square other merchants were already setting up their products on display. While Althea helped Rose unload the buckets from Tobias's back, Maeve stood taking everything in.

There was a lovely scent from the left where a woman sold freshly made oat cakes. A butcher was calling out to some passers-by to come and test a sample of his juicy ham.

A young man who was no more than a teenager himself was red-faced from carrying wooden boxes with bottles. He was the son of the brewer and helped his father sell beer and cider.

Maeve couldn't take her gaze off him because the young man was the first person her age that she had seen in nine years.

"Look," Maeve whispered to Althea and showed the direction with her eyes.

Althea stood with four apples in her hands and turned to see just as the young man set down a heavy box and rose to stretch his back. When he saw Althea and Maeve staring at him, his eyes widened a bit at the sight of such beautiful girls, and he quickly found a better posture, pushing out his chest to make himself appear bigger.

"Don't just stand with the apples. Put them with the others." Rose's instructions broke the moment and made both girls refocus on their aunt.

But youth is a tricky thing and so is curiosity. Despite the warnings from their aunt, both girls kept exchanging glances with the brewer's son, and by the time the sun had reached the church tower, he found the courage to approach them.

With color on his cheeks, he came with a bottle. "Ehm... my father and I were wondering if you would trade some of your plums for a bottle of our finest cider."

Maeve lit up and stepped closer, but Rose pulled her back and answered him. It frustrated both girls to miss out on an opportunity to talk to the young man when their minds were full of questions.

With twelve plums in return for his bottle of cider, the young man sent a last shy smile toward both Althea and Maeve before walking back to his father.

"He looked nice," Althea said but only received a warning glance from Rose.

Rose was tempted to tell the girls that it was her childhood friend whom she had loved and trusted that had one day turned against her and caused her to lose everything. But she had kept that secret from them so far because there was no need to speak ill of their mother, Anne.

For a moment, Rose got lost in dreadful memories from the night she fled from the angry mob and her ancestral home burned down. Her parents had been killed because of Anne's betrayal. It was a wicked twist of destiny that Anne believed she'd lost her daughters in a fire and now they lived under Rose's protection.

"Of course, I'll be happy to carry them for you."

Rose snapped out of her sad memories when an old, frail-looking woman handed Althea coins for the produce she needed.

"Aunt Rose, you don't mind, do you?"

"Pardon?" Rose wasn't sure what Althea was asking her.

"This lady asked for my help carrying her basket to her house. It's too heavy for her." Althea was looking at Rose, who felt torn. The old woman needed the help as she was moving slowly with a walking stick to support her. But letting Althea walk through town alone wouldn't do, and neither would leaving the girls in the marketplace by themselves work.

"It's not far," the old woman said and gave a smile that revealed a missing front tooth.

Althea picked up the woman's basket, which was heavily loaded with rhubarb, onions, potatoes, and apples. Smiling, she said, "Lead the way."

"I can take the basket," Maeve offered, clearly eager to venture off and see more of the town.

Picking the lesser of two evils, Rose declared, "No, I will do it. You two will stay here. Don't go anywhere."

Walking away from the girls made Rose feel like she was being stretched too thin. She kept looking over her shoulder until the old lady led her down a street and away from the town square.

It should have been a short walk, but the old woman was talkative and painfully slow. Once they reached her house, she asked Rose for the kindness of carrying the basket inside and unpacking it. Despite her suspicion and lack of trust in humans, Rose was a kind soul, and it was in her nature to help.

"It's no fun getting old," the old woman said and struggled to lift her feet over the tall doorstep. "I used to be strong like you. Had fourteen babes in my time, but sickness took eight of them in one cursed winter."

"I'm so sorry to hear that," Rose said with deep-felt empathy. Losing family was something she could relate to and with her frequent nightmares of losing Althea and Maeve, she felt awful for the old woman who had survived eight of her children.

"You have beautiful daughters."

"Thank you," Rose uttered and didn't tell the woman that she was Althea and Maeve's aunt and not their mother.

"My son is kind enough to let me live here with him and his sons. They all work at the mine. I try to cook for them and keep the house, but with my hands it's difficult." The old woman sank to a chair and looked at her hands, which were swollen and deformed with contractures making her fingers close. Shutting her eyes for a brief second, Rose tried to tell herself that it was too dangerous to help, but the healer in her was tortured for not being able to ease the woman's pain. After unpacking the basket, she walked over and kneeled next to the woman.

"My grandmother used to have hands like yours. She said it helped her to feel the heat from a friend's hands. Would you like me to give you some of my heat?"

The woman sighed. "That's kind of you, but I'm not cold. Just in constant pain." Her gaze fell to Rose's hands. "What I wouldn't give to have young hands like yours again." Reaching out she took Rose's hands in hers.

The heat started immediately as Rose felt the rheumatoid nodules on the old woman's hand. Easing suffering in others was what she was born to do.

But the old woman let go of her hands and sighed. "Oh, don't you bother soothing an old woman. I'm sure you have better things to do."

Getting up from the floor, Rose stepped back. "Will you be all right?"

The woman nodded and raised a hand in a small wave. "Thank you for your kindness."

At the market square, the brewer's son, Marcus, had taken the opportunity to go and talk to Althea and Maeve now that Rose was gone.

"I haven't seen you here before. Are you new in this area?"

"We're just visiting our aunt," Althea said, sticking to the story Rose had asked them to use.

Another man in his early twenties stopped to buy flowers and stayed to talk to the sisters. He introduced himself as Frederick and was most charming.

Male attention was unfamiliar to Althea and Maeve but strangely exhilarating. Frederick and Marcus were quite competitive when it came to offering the girls compliments.

"Since you're visiting, maybe you would like me to show you around the area," Marcus offered. "There's a small castle no more than a twenty-minute ride from here and the ocean is only a short walk away from there."

"That's a great idea. We could all go swimming," Frederick suggested.

Giving a shy smile, Althea admitted, "I love swimming."

Frederick's face lit up. "Then I'll be honored to take you."

The brewer's son was quick to agree, "Yes, we should all go."

Maeve's eyes were glowing as she looked at her sister. It sounded like an amazing adventure, and she was dying to have some fun.

Biting her lower lip, Althea shifted her balance. "I'm afraid we'll have to decline. We have so few days visiting our aunt that we couldn't possibly."

Maeve groaned in protest because she was tired of hiding in the forest.

"Oh, but don't worry, it'll only be for a few hours. We promise to treat you with the utmost care and respect," Frederick assured them. "I'm sure your aunt would encourage you to have some fun while you're here."

A bird landed on the bucket with apples and while Maeve was distracted by the flirting with the young men, Althea heard its message loud and clear. The little sick girl it had told them about a few days earlier still needed help. She was close and suffering.

Althea didn't notice how her facial expression turned grim and her posture changed, but Maeve mistook it for fear of Rose.

Leaning close, she whispered to Althea. "What is she going to do? Honestly, if we kept it a secret, she probably wouldn't even notice us being gone for a few hours. Come on, Althea, I want to go swimming with them."

Althea's gaze kept darting to the bird, who lifted from the bucket and flew to sit on a small fence. It called for her to follow, but she stood as if paralyzed by all her aunt's warnings playing tug of war with her instinctive need to help the little girl.

"What's wrong with you?" Maeve elbowed Althea, who snapped out of her focus on the bird. "Why don't you answer him?"

Blinking her eyes, Althea looked at Maeve and the two young men, who were all watching her. "Pardon?"

"I asked if you would like to go on a stroll with me through the village?" Holding the flowers he had bought from them in one hand, Frederick smiled with an expectant look.

"Ehm... Maybe another time."

"I'll do it," Maeve said and stepped forward.

"No. We promised Rose that we wouldn't go anywhere," Althea protested and quickly whispered to

39

Maeve, "The bird came back asking for our help with the sick girl."

Maeve's eyes widened. "It did?"

"Yes. She must be close."

"What are you two whispering about?" Marcus asked but Althea and Maeve were focused on searching to see where the bird had gone.

"There!" Althea pointed discreetly to where the bird sat watching them.

"So, are we going swimming tomorrow then? It's Sunday and we could go after church." There was so much hope in Marcus' tone of voice.

When the girls turned to respond they saw Rose come toward them with long strides and a troubled expression on her face. She was so focused on getting to the girls that she didn't pay attention to where she was going. Her hands had yanked up her skirt to avoid the fabric touching filth in the street, but she still stepped in some of the horse manure that the street team hadn't removed yet.

The way she scowled at the two young men when she reached them made the situation awkward.

"Did you need anything?" Rose asked in a dismissive tone and while Marcus took a step back, Frederick, who was a bit older, was brave enough to state his request.

"With your permission, madam, I would like to take Maeve on a stroll. I understand the girls are new to the area, and I would love to..."

Rose cut him off with a hard "No. That won't do."

For a moment they stood caught in a power struggle with Rose staring at Frederick with an arched eyebrow, and him staring back at her with annoyance. It was evident that he found Rose too overprotective and wasn't used to being refused.

"I think my father might need my help," Marcus mumbled and with a polite nod to both Althea and Maeve, he walked back to help sell beer and cider.

Frederick averted his gaze from Rose and gave Maeve a sugarcoated smile. "What a shame. I was merely trying to be welcoming. I hope to get the pleasure of meeting you again another time."

Only when he walked away did Rose relax her stance. Turning to Althea and Maeve, she complained. "I knew it was a bad idea to bring you here. You are far too pretty to go unnoticed and infatuated young men rarely take no for an answer. We can't have them sniffing around to find out where we live."

"We told them we were here for a short visit," Althea assured Rose, but Maeve felt cheated of an adventure and crossed her arms.

"You didn't have to be so rude."

"Yes, I did, Maeve. Didn't you see the entitlement in his eyes? Men like him are dangerous."

Maeve pouted. "Just because you had a bad experience with some humans doesn't mean that they are *all* dangerous. In this town, people might be different."

Althea who was always the peacemaker, mediated, "Rose is just worried that they might confuse us with witches. Isn't that right, Rose?"

Rose threw out her hand and looked into Maeve's eyes. "Oh, trust me, there are many ways a man like that can ruin a girl like you."

Being a teenager, Maeve didn't appreciate that Rose was being protective and coming from a good place. Her natural longing to break free of the suffocating and limiting fear she had grown up with made her hiss low. "I wouldn't know since you never allow us to go anywhere."

"Maeve!" The warning in Rose's tone only provoked Maeve further and in a fit of immature anger, she ran off.

"Maeve. Maeve, come back here."

The more Rose shouted the faster Maeve ran. She wasn't scared of these people. She was scared of missing out on life. Running in the direction of the bird, she told herself that she needed to help the sick girl, but of course, that was merely a way for her to justify her poor behavior toward her aunt.

Show me the way, she told the bird without uttering a word.

It lifted from the fence and flapped its small wings, taking off in the direction of a narrow street. Maeve didn't think, she just followed the bird for every turn it took until it stopped on top of a sign with a hat on it.

Coming to a halt, Maeve took in the house in front of her. There was a display of hats in the window of the small shop. On the second floor, two windows were open and as she listened, she heard the sound of a woman crying.

Maeve's heart was pounding in her chest as her heart and mind warred. According to the bird, there was a sick child in this house that needed help. Maeve had no experience with healing humans, but she had healed plenty of animals and was eager to help if she could.

With the resentment she felt toward her aunt at that moment, Rose's warnings of staying away felt cowardly to Maeve. They were Earthens and born to heal.

Disregarding her aunt's order to stay away from humans, Maeve took a step forward and placed her hand on the door to the shop.

A discreet bell sounded when she pushed it open, but no one was inside. The sound of the woman crying intensified and pulled Maeve past the rows of hats in all colors and shapes to a wooden staircase.

"Hello?" she called softly. For a second, she listened and realized there was more than one voice. A low muttering told her a man was upstairs as well.

Taking a tentative step up, Maeve called out again, "Hello?"

When no one answered, she continued until she stood upstairs in an open loft with two beds against opposite walls. A woman lay head down on one of the beds, sobbing. Her feet were still on the ground and looking closer, Maeve could tell she had buried her head against a girl who had her eyes closed. Next to the bed sat a man on a wooden chair with his head down and his hands tearing into his hair.

The low mutter came from a man in black who stood with his back to Maeve. Although Maeve had been only five when she left her village, she understood that he had to be a priest, and it made her throat tighten. Priests were the leaders of the witch hunt and the ones posing the biggest risk to an Earthen like her.

It was as if the people in the room were completely absorbed at the moment and didn't register Maeve's presence as she stood with her hand on the banister unsure what to do.

"She's in heaven now with our Lord and creator," the priest said and walked over to place a hand on the grieving mother.

This time a heartbreaking sob came from the father.

There was nothing Maeve could do, and she knew she was in the wrong place at the wrong time when the priest declared, "I'm sorry for your loss. These are grim times indeed when innocent children are targeted by the dark forces."

In that moment, Maeve wished she was one of those Faders that Rose had told her and Althea about. If she could have turned into a mouse and run down the stairs, she would have done so. But it was like her legs wouldn't

43

co-operate, and childhood memories of Ellen dangling from the noose came back to her in full force. She remembered how Ellen's frightened face had turned red from the tight rope around her throat that cut off air from entering her lungs. But now, as Maeve stood frozen, it felt as though she was the one who couldn't breathe.

Any second now, the priest and the grieving parents would turn to see her standing there, completely out of place. How many times had Rose emphasized that humans weren't strong enough to carry the burden of grief? Instead of consoling the poor parents, the priest called their daughter's death an act of evil to distance the God he served from the unfair tragedy of losing a precious child. Of course, he had to blame dark forces, or his parishioners might turn on God.

Despite her numbing fear, Maeve managed to move her left foot back. The creaking of the floorboard under her sounded as deafening as church bells in a small room. Without blinking, Maeve stared at the grieving people in front of her as if they were three separate heads of the same dragon ready to attack her at any time.

It felt like the turning of the priest's body happened in extra slowness, giving Maeve a small eternity to face her mortality. She was fourteen. Too young to have experienced much but old enough to stand trial if the priest found it convenient to cast the blame on her.

The priest was younger than she imagined. He had stubble and looked gray and tired, but he couldn't be much older than Rose. For a moment, he looked stunned and blinked as if his sleep-deprived eyes were trying to make sense of her standing right there without speaking.

"Who are you?" The sniffling voice came from the mother, who was now watching Maeve as well.

Run Maeve screamed on the inside and as soon as the priest took a step toward her, her body finally listened.

As if Satan himself was on her heels, she ran down the stairs and out of the house. The streets felt narrower and scarier than when she followed the bird, and every corner she turned brought her onto a new street. With her mind in a state of pure panic, she was panting and having trouble with her balance. It was like she was trapped in an endless maze.

She remembered being five and squeezed in between adults with hatred marring their faces as they walked to Ellen's execution. When two women called out to her, Maeve's lips quivered, and she began to cry.

"Are you hurt?" one of them asked, but Maeve kept running. Taking another turn, she stopped when the road split into three. She was utterly lost and couldn't think clearly.

"Maeve."

Her head snapped up at the sound of her name. There, coming toward her, was Althea. With the sun behind her, her curly orange hair glowed like a halo, and it made Maeve cry with relief.

"Where were you?" Althea scolded, but her tone quickly turned soft. "Oh, no, what happened?"

Grabbing onto her sister's wrist, Maeve looked back over her shoulder. "I went to see the sick girl, but she had already died. They're going to blame us for her death if we don't get away right now."

The disturbed expression on Althea's face turned to a look of pure determination. Taking Maeve's hand, she moved at a fast pace leading Maeve back to the market square where Rose waited. Tobias was already prepared to leave with the buckets tied across his back. With one glance at the state of the girls, Rose ordered, "Keep your heads down and follow me."

All three of them walked in long strides without speaking. The worst things possible were running through their heads as fear followed them like poisonous honey sticking to their backs. Every little outburst from a child or neigh from a horse made them tense up and hold their breath.

Reaching the edge of the forest felt like reaching land after swimming with sharks, but they still walked fast to get further into the safety of the trees.

In Maeve's mind, she had barely escaped getting hanged from a tree like Ellen.

Rose didn't know about Maeve's encounter with the priest. In her mind, she had made a terrible mistake by exposing the girls to the persuasive powers of young men.

Being an empath, Althea picked up on all the angst and dread and decided that Lerwick was the last place she wanted to go back to.

"Are you alright, Rose?" Althea asked.

"Yes. Don't worry about me," she replied but the truth was that she was alarmed at how close she had come to heal the old woman's hand. She should have never taken a chance like that.

Leading Tobias through the forest, Rose's thoughts went back to the time she had to flee for her life.

CHAPTER 5

BETRAYAL OF A FRIEND

15 Years Earlier

Where most Earthens had fled to live in isolation, the Nash family stayed in their small forest cottage clinging to the hope that the humans they had helped over the years wouldn't turn on them. As a midwife and healer, Matilda had helped more or less all of the villagers at one point or the other. And every farmer in the area knew to consult Paul when it came to understanding the health of their crops.

At nineteen, John was one year younger than his sister Rose, but not half as gifted when it came to working as an Earthen. She knew the names of every herb she saw, and she had mastered complicated recipes long before John.

Both of them had grown up learning to care for animals and humans with compassion and patience, but still, John sometimes questioned if he wanted that lifestyle for himself.

Their parents often said that Earthen's greatest strength was the kindness in their hearts, but there were days when John didn't feel kind at all. He resented Rose for how easy everything was for her. And he resented himself for finding it hard to look at her. Eventually, the two siblings drifted apart as John found it easier to avoid his sister altogether.

Rose wondered about her brother's reserved attitude toward her and wished things had been different between them. But despite that not being the case, she wasn't lonely. She had her parents, who were kind and loving, and she had her best friend, Anne, who lived in the village.

Anne was a few years younger and the daughter of the baker in town. Growing up, the girls had become close friends despite how different their families were. One afternoon in early spring Rose finished work early and headed into town to see her friend.

In many ways, Anne and Rose looked much alike, with their brown hair and eyes, but Rose was well aware that Anne's symmetrical features and well-shaped eyebrows and lips made her much more attractive.

Once, Rose had complained to her mother that she'd been unlucky in her heredity, getting the worst from each of her parents while John got the best. Her mother had replied that the most amazing trees in the forest weren't those that were most symmetrical and pretty. "The most beautiful ones, in my eyes, are those that generously provide a safe home for birds, squirrels, and other animals. Especially those that are so deeply rooted that even though a storm broke off branches and made new ones pop out in odd places the tree didn't fall. They may not be symmetrical, but they are by far the most beautiful because of their strength and greatness. It's the same with people, honey, and to me, you'll always be beautiful."

One afternoon when Rose came to visit Anne, she found her hanging up sheets outside her house. Instantly, Rose was hit by the sad state of her friend, who had red-rimmed eyes with dark circles under them. As soon as she saw Rose, Anne's drooping lips quivered.

"What's wrong?" Rose asked and held Anne, who threw herself into a hug.

"It's my mum. She's sick. She's been coughing for four days straight and this morning I found bloodstains on her sheets." Anne's voice was brittle. "That's why I'm washing them."

With her brows lowered, Rose rubbed Anne's back. "I'm so sorry. I can tell that you're exhausted. Has anyone else in your family shown symptoms?"

Looking back at the small house behind the bakery, Anne shook her head. "No. The little ones are fine for now and my father has always been an ox of a man. It's just that with my mother down, Lola and I are left with all the housework."

"Here, I'll help you." Rose bent down and grabbed a wet pillowcase to hang it up for drying.

"It's a good thing that you and your family never seem to get sick," Anne pointed out. "Even that time I had the chickenpox you didn't get it."

"Oh, I don't know. My dad had a bad case of pneumonia last year," Rose said and felt bad about lying.

"How's your brother doing?" Anne asked and picked up the empty basket to put the clothes in.

"John? Well, he's good, I suppose. I haven't asked him recently. You know he doesn't speak to me unless it's necessary. My mother and father are good as well. All in good health." Although Rose had answered, she had missed the small spark of love in Anne's eyes when she spoke John's name.

"I need to get water." With a tired gaze, Anne looked at a large jug made of burned clay that stood close to the door.

"We'll do it together," Rose offered and went to pick up the jug.

The two young women walked through the village passing people they knew. The dirt roads were still a bit sticky from the rain that morning, making it impossible to avoid mud on their shoes. The smell of horse manure and urine assaulted Rose's sharp senses when she steered around a fresh pile. She couldn't wait to get out of her shoes that she only ever wore around humans.

49

Despite Rose's attempts to cheer Anne up, none of the usual subjects of chatting and gossiping got her attention.

Turning her head, Rose looked into the eyes of her friend. "You're really worried about your mum, aren't you?"

Anne stopped to let a man on a horse pass. "What if she dies? I'm scared someone cast a curse of bad luck on my family. Last month my father couldn't get flour for two days and my little sister tripped and broke a tooth on Friday."

Rose stopped walking and took her friend's hands. "Anne. Not you too. There's no such thing as curses. People get sick but that's normal. Let's hope your mother's cough isn't contagious. How are you feeling?" Without asking, Rose felt her friend's forehead with the back of her hand but there was no indication of a fever.

"I feel alright. But I'm young so I probably won't get it."

Rose didn't tell her tired friend that if that were the case, no children would ever die. Taking her friend's hand, she suggested, "You should come with me to my house, I might have something that could keep you from getting sick."

There was a moment of hesitation from Anne, who looked back toward her home. "I need to get back to check on my mum."

"We'll walk fast, Anne. I just really don't want you going back inside without a mixture of herbs that will strengthen your lungs."

It was rare that Anne came to Rose's home, and only a few times had she been inside. With all the herbs and natural remedies inside the Nashes' home, a human could become suspicious and quickly jump to conclusions. That's why the Nash family had long ago made a rule of no human visitors unless necessary. But

Rose was so focused on protecting her friend from whatever disease that had her mother coughing up blood from her lungs, that she didn't stop to think. No one was home to remind Rose that it was best if humans didn't see all the bundles of dried flowers and herbs hanging from the ceiling. Or the shelves full of bottles and jars that Rose went straight for, letting her right index finger run over each bottle before she stopped abruptly. Fishing out the small flask with purple contents from behind other bottles she gave it to Anne, who watched the whole thing in confusion.

"Drink this," Rose instructed.

Anne looked unsure but when Rose gently pushed her hands with the bottle in them towards her lips, she chose to trust her friend and chugged down the contents. The sourness bit Anne's tongue, causing her face to scrunch up. "What was that?"

Rose didn't answer but took the bottle and said, "Stick out your tongue."

When Rose saw the bluish discoloring on Anne's tongue her fear that her best friend had been infected was confirmed. Thoughts spiraled as she went over all the potions she knew in her mind. Rose had been a healer long enough never to take a sickness lightly, especially not one that made you cough up blood; she knew she had to act quickly to save her best friend and her family.

"I can fix this," Rose muttered and turned back to the large shelves to search for the right remedy.

"Fix what? Am I sick?"

"You will be if we don't get you some medicine fast."

"How can you be sure? Is it the same illness as my mother?"

Rose ignored her friend's question and worked with concentration. With precision, she mixed the right ingredients making sure to follow the steps her parents had taught her.

Anne moved closer and stared as Rose ground up green herbs in a stone mortar, only to scoop up the paste and roll it into a small ball. Grabbing a jar of honey, Rose dipped a small spoon in and placed the green ball on top of it.

"Put this into your mouth and let it dissolve; it will prevent you from getting sick."

Anne had been long enough in the cottage for warnings to enter her mind. She knew that Rose's family were healers, but it had never concerned her until now. Staring at the wooden spoon in front of her, doubt crept in. Could this be something devilish?

"Do it, Anne, please," Rose encouraged. "It will help you."

With a tiny shake of her head, Anne pushed away all hesitation. This was her friend Rose, who was the sweetest and kindest person she knew. Rose was the kind of person to pick up injured porcupines and carry them home to heal them. There was no way she would poison her.

Opening her mouth, she bit down over the spoon and swallowed the concoction.

"You may wake with a sweat during the night but that's just the sickness leaving your body."

Anne sunk to a chair. Looking around, she warned, "Rose, you have to be careful. With the way you and your family live, some might think you do witchcraft here. I don't want to see you hurt."

"We're not a danger to anyone. On the contrary, we help and heal."

"I know, but..." Her eyes darted around taking everything in as she fiddled with her brown skirt. "You could still get accused of doing the devil's work."

Rose sat down next to Anne. "The devil isn't real, Anne. And I'm not a witch."

"Yes, he is real. Father Morgan says so himself. I'm not saying that you're a witch, but what if..." Again her eyes glided across the bottles, jars, and pots with strange ingredients. "I mean did you ever question where your parents learned all this from? What if it's witchcraft and you just don't know it?

"What are you talking about?" Rose asked, not liking the way Anne spoke to her as if she were talking to a delusional person.

Eager to wash away any dangerous misunderstandings about her parents being witches, Rose grabbed Anne's hand and confided in her friend the secret that her parents had forbidden John and her to ever tell a human. "We're not witches, Anne. I was born an Earthen. But there's nothing evil about Earthens. We are pure-hearted healers and protectors of nature."

Anne moved back a little. "You're making that up."

Shaking her head, Rose felt desperate to prove that she was telling the truth.

"Look." Raising her hand, she showed how she'd mastered the element of fire by creating a small flame in the midst of her palm.

At first, Anne looked scared, but then her expression changed, and she leaned in a little closer. Fascinated and sure that it was some kind of trick, Anne reached out and touched the flame with her finger, only to be burned. Anne's pretty brown eyes widened in shock as her gaze flew to Rose. "It's real?"

"Yes. We Earthens learn how to control the elements of air, fire, water, and earth. I can also communicate with animals." With eagerness, Rose pointed to the shelves. "And I can make medicine to heal the sick, like you and your mom."

"Are the rest of your family Earthens too?" Anne asked.

Sensing disapproval in her friend's tone, Rose protected her family. "No, it's just me. But there are other Earthens out there."

After looking thoughtful for a moment, Anne asked in a hopeful voice, "Can you heal my mother?"

"I can try. But we'll need more herbs. It will go faster if you help me collect them."

Moving fast, the two friends headed into the forest, which was still damp from the night of rain. It was early spring, and the tall trees were showing off their gorgeous green leaves. As they gathered the right plants, Anne suddenly said, "You know, Rose, I think it's sad that you've never been in love."

Love was one of Anne's favorite subjects to gossip about, but it often made Rose feel awkward and uncomfortable. Keeping her gaze on the ground, she answered, "I wouldn't say that I've never been in love."

Anne stopped in her tracks and stared at her friend in disbelief. "You never told me you liked someone. Do I know him?"

Rose's cheeks flushed red because Anne did know the person Rose loved, but it wasn't a man. Unwilling to tell Anne that her crush was a pretty girl with brown hair and brown eyes who had been her best friend since childhood, Rose did something she'd promised to only ever do if she was left with no other option – she lied.

"No, you don't know him, I met him in another village when I went with my father to heal an old lady."

When Rose didn't volunteer more information, Anne turned the conversation back to herself. "Oh, alright. It's just that I never hear you talk about him. I think about my future husband and the children we will have all the time. I can't wait to start my own family," Anne rambled on. It never occurred to her that Rose might be in love with her and so she was unaware of how, to Rose, her words felt like daggers to the heart.

"I want a large family and I know exactly what I'll name my children."

Knowing this was a future they could never share, Rose hid her emotions and asked, "What will you name them?"

"Margaret and Jane for my girls." Anne bent down to pick up a wild yellow flower and put it in the basket that Rose carried. "And Peter and Simon for my boys. What about you, Rose? What will you name your children?"

Rose, who loved children, was painfully aware of how they were made, and the thought of sleeping with a man disgusted her. Still, she had fantasized about motherhood and said, "I once had a dream that two young girls with the same orange hair color as my brother and mother sat in front of me and they told me their names were Althea and Maeve. Althea means healer, and Maeve means the intoxicating one. I thought those were beautiful names. So, I suppose if I had two daughters those are the names I would choose."

"Maeve and Althea." Anne tasted the names and gave an approving nod before brushing her hands. "Do we have enough now?"

Looking down at the basket in her hand that was filled with wildflowers, mushrooms, leaves, bark, and herbs, Rose nodded. "Yes. This is plenty. Let's head back."

Walking side by side, they tried to avoid the mud holes and yanked their dresses up when needed. When their paths separated, Anne sighed. "I'd better get back to help Lola with my mum and the little ones."

Rose rubbed her friend's arm with soothing strokes and assured her, "I will prepare the remedy for your mother and bring it as soon as I can." For a moment she stood watching Anne walk off. Her heart hurt for her friend, whom she loved deeply. Anne's mother coughing up blood was a bad sign, but as long as she was alive there was still hope.

When Rose got home, she hurried to make the strongest medicine nature gave access to, but quickly realized they were running low on a few items that weren't found locally nor did they have very many rootlings left. Sprinkles of a crushed-up rootling mixed into a potion were one of the strongest substances and one that should only be used carefully by an Earthen. But rootlings grew underground, protected in the root of certain flowers, and it was time-consuming to find and harvest them. It took her father a long ride to collect Mullein Weed and her mother worked with her into the wee hours of the night chopping, extracting, and mixing every ingredient until Rose fell asleep at the table.

When she woke up in the morning she went back to working on the medicine and by late afternoon it was finally ready. With no time to waste, Rose hurried to Anne's house with the small flask in hand. Excitement made her strides long because this was her chance to prove to Anne that Earthens were kind-hearted healers. Anne's hints that Rose's parents might be performing witchcraft had been particularly hurtful because, for years, Rose had feared that Anne wouldn't want to be friends anymore if she found out how different Rose and her family were. Over the years, Rose had had nightmares about losing her best friend. Curing Anne's mother would no doubt bring them closer, and it would be a relief to Rose that Anne knew her healing powers and she didn't need to hide them.

Hurrying down the narrow Bakers' Street, Rose sniffed in the lovely scent of baked goods that always hung in the air around Anne's house. She made a right turn and walked through the gate to get to the outbuilding of the bakery where Anne lived with her family. With a smile on her face, Rose was just about to knock on Anne's front door when she heard a giggle coming from the other side of the house. Recognizing it as her friend's voice, Rose walked around the corner to show Anne the medicine that she and her parents had worked on all night long.

The moment she turned the corner and saw her closest friend, her smile vanished. It was a strange thing that a person's life could crumble in a mere second, but that's what happened when Rose saw the girl whom she was in love with kissing a red-haired boy she knew all too well. When Anne opened her eyes and saw Rose staring at her she quickly pushed John away and dried off her mouth to remove the evidence of her betrayal.

John had a look of confusion until he saw his sister standing behind them. For a moment the three of them stood there waiting for someone to break the silence, and then John said, "We'll speak later." He leaned in and gave Anne a quick kiss on the cheek. "Best of luck to your mother." Leaving with his head down, he didn't greet his sister.

When John was gone and Rose broke the awkward silence, her throat felt as dry as if she had tried to swallow the flour from the bakery. "How long?"

"A few months," Anne answered honestly.

"Why didn't you tell me?" Rose tried hard to suppress her feelings. The girl she was in love with was with her brother and hadn't told her about it despite them supposedly being best friends.

"I tried to." Anne's gaze was glued to the ground, and she quickly changed the subject. "Did you make the medicine for my mother?"

Rose answered by lifting the basket with the flask. Following Anne into the house where her mother lay in her bed coughing, Rose tended her as well as she could. Her body was burning hot, and her throat was torn up from the inside because of all the coughing. For hours Rose nursed Anne's mother, healing her and cooling her body down with the elements of air and water. Sadly, it proved difficult to give her the medicine because of her constant coughing. And with her advanced state of sickness Rose doubted it would have helped much anyway. The poor woman had sadly been without treatment for too long.

Eventually Rose told Anne that there was nothing more she could do.

"Will my mum be alright?" Anne asked with glassy eyes.

Rose sympathized with Anne and wished she had better news, but she wouldn't lie to her friend no matter how much she wanted to tell her that her mother would be fine. Sucking in her lips, she shook her head.

First Anne stared at her and then she burst into tears. With an accusatory tone, she thundered, "You… you… *lied to me*. You said you could heal her!"

Rose looked down. "I eased your mother's pain and she's sleeping now. But you should get the others and stay close because she doesn't have long, Anne." Sadness dripped from Rose's tone, but it was as if Anne couldn't see reason, and instead, she directed all her sorrow and fear onto her friend. With eyes wet from tears and her voice blazing with anger, she sneered.

"Get out of our house. I know what you are. I should have never let you come close to my mum, *witch*."

The shock of hearing her best friend call her the feared word had Rose stumbling back. "What did you say?"

"You heard me." With her eyes narrowed, Anne repeated the horrible word. "*Witch!*"

In shock, Rose hurried to leave without saying another word. All the way home, she cried with her heart breaking more for every sob. It was difficult for Rose's parents to understand what had happened because she couldn't finish a full sentence without her voice breaking and sobs disrupting her speech.

"Come, my love. Let's make you a cup of tea," Rose's mother said while her father held her in a tight hug.

With their comfort, love, and patience, her parents got Rose through the following weeks where she tried to come to terms with her strong grief over losing both her best friend and the girl she was in love with.

Her brother John never learned the truth about his sister's feelings for Anne. The two siblings weren't close and when he fell in love with her best friend, things happened much too fast for him to stop and reflect.

First, there was the awkward encounter when Rose found him and Anne kissing, and then there was her futile attempt to save Anne's mother.

Anne was devastated and not knowing what else to do, John had comforted her the best he could. Soon her siblings fell ill, and that's when the rumor spread that buying bread from the baker was bad luck.

John stayed loyal and tried to tell Anne that things would get better, but she kept mumbling about her family being cursed by a witch.

It created a deep conflict within John, who feared for his family whenever talk about witchcraft surfaced. But he was stuck. Being young naïve kids in love, John and Anne had done something that was only supposed to happen inside a marriage. On the morning before Rose found them kissing, Anne had shared the news that it had been seven weeks since she'd last menstruated. With her pregnant, John had felt trapped between protecting his parents and sister or his unborn child. When he confided his dilemma to his parents, they told him to do right by Anne.

He wanted to, but it scared him how Anne changed over the five weeks it took from her mother's death until her father and four siblings had all died as well. Anne, who had been playful and untroubled, became cynical and mean.

Still, he married her and did his best to cheer her up, but it didn't help much. Over the next months, Anne turned her grief into a battle for revenge and decided that Rose was to blame for the sickness in her family.

John desperately tried to reason with her, but grief and fear are enemies of logic and common sense. Anne wouldn't listen when he reminded her that Rose was most likely the reason Anne was still alive. After all, it was Rose who had protected Anne from the disease with her herbal medicine.

Neighbors and friends of the Baker family joined forces with Anne and one fatal night it came to a confrontation between the village and his family.

If only John had had a horse that night, it would have given him more time to warn his family and things might have ended up differently. All he had were his two feet that carried him as fast as he could run from Anne's house to his family's home on the outskirt of the woods.

Banging the door open, John ran straight for his sister's bed and shook her shoulders until her tired eyes opened and looked up at him. "Rose, come on!"

His father, Paul, called out from the small alcove where he and Matilda slept. "What is it, John?"

Rose sat up and stared at her brother with puffy eyes full of confusion.

"It's Anne and the villagers. They're accusing you of having placed a curse on them." John pulled at his sister's arm. "I'm serious, Rose. You have to leave right now before they get here. The whole village thinks you're a witch."

"Anne and the villagers are coming here?" Their mother's bare feet made the wooden floor squeak as she ran from her bed to look out the window.

"I saw a large group marching this way. They're coming to get you. I'm so sorry, I tried to stop them."

Convinced this was a dream, Rose stared at her brother in denial.

"Didn't you hear me, Rose? You have to hide!" John yelled and tried to drag her out of the small bed.

When Matilda gave a loud shriek, John joined her by the window where their mother stood pale and frightened.

"They're already here," John breathed and watched in horror as a mob of people came toward them with burning torches and angry shouting. Rose and her father moved to the window as well and now all four family members stood closely together facing what they had feared all along.

"Give us the witch or we'll burn down the house," a man from the mob yelled in anger.

"That's Roger, the carpenter from East Street," Matilda muttered. "I know him."

"Don't go out there," John warned his mother when she reached for her shawl.

"We don't have a choice," Matilda said and took a second to caress Rose's chin before she gave a nod to her husband. Paul walked outside with Matilda, who faced the angry group of people.

"Roger McBree, your tone is certainly different from the night you fetched me to save your wife and daughter's life. Have you forgotten how much you thanked me then? And you, Maureen. We both know you wouldn't have survived giving birth to your twins if Rose and I hadn't helped you. How dare you all march to our house in the middle of the night, calling our daughter a witch? Have you been so blinded by fear and superstition that you can't see that we are healers? There's nothing dangerous here. You can all go home."

"I don't believe you. My wife died in labor nine years ago and you refused to save her," an old man with a hunched back growled. "You and your daughter are both evil witches."

"Liar," Paul called out and pointed to the man. "Matilda did try to help, but your poor wife gave birth to sixteen children in less than twelve years and we warned you after your last set of twins. You knew that she wouldn't survive another pregnancy and you still put a child in her belly. Matilda didn't kill your wife – you did!"

Paul's defense of his wife and daughter didn't help calm down the group of angry people.

Roger spat on the ground and muttered vile words that should never be spoken among neighbors.

Holding up her palms, Matilda tried to calm the mob, but a woman with a missing front tooth held up her torch and demanded in a shrill voice, "Give us the witch who cursed the Baker family."

"We have no witches here," Paul yelled back and pulled Rose behind him.

To Rose and her family, it felt like the ultimate betrayal when Anne stepped out of the shadows and into the light of a torch. "I saw it with my own eyes." Her lips quivered, and her wet eyes were filled with hatred towards the person she'd once loved as a sister. "Rose claimed she could heal my mother with her medicine, but it was a trick for the devil to claim my poor mother's soul. After she drank that repugnant stuff Rose made for her, the devil himself came at night to claim her and when I woke up the next morning there was nothing I could do. My mother was dead." Anne pointed her finger at Rose. "You killed her."

To Rose, it all felt bizarre. Holding on to her father's sleeve with her fingers fisted tightly together, her knees felt like they might give in. Everyone knew what happened to women accused of witchery. But the mob of people sending her death glares was the same people whom she had always treated with kindness and had tended to when they were sick. Surely, they couldn't be serious about wanting to kill her. It was like being caught in a nightmare, and Rose couldn't fathom that Anne and the others could turn on her like this. She stood frozen while people kept shouting. Her heartbeat was so fast she could hear it thumping in her head like a heavy clock swinging back and forth. Everything became blurry and tears filled her eyes, as Rose stared at the girl whom she had been so deeply in love with that she hadn't been able to dream or think of anyone else. Anne's unfair accusation that Rose had killed her mother made it hard for Rose to breathe. It was difficult to understand how Anne could change so drastically since she had always called Rose the kindest person she knew, and now she wanted her dead. Killing clashed with everything Rose stood for, and Anne might as well have kicked Rose physically in the stomach because with her face twisted in anger and disgust, it hurt all the same.

Rose gaped when Anne continued her betrayal with one hand on her pregnant belly and the other one pointing at everyone as she spewed out, "I'm telling you all that Rose is a witch who stole the soul of my mother and gave it to the devil."

"This is a misunderstanding." John stepped forward to stand shoulder to shoulder with his father, shielding Rose from the angry mob that was moving closer.

"She has poisoned his mind," Anne said and looked around at the others. "John is a victim of his sister's wicked ways. He doesn't understand what he's saying."

The mob moved closer and the old woman with a tooth missing sneered a warning. "Protecting a witch is a crime too. Maybe the whole family is a group of witches."

Paul backed Rose away from Roger, who stabbed his torch in her direction and spat onto her nightgown.

Pressing his nose into her dark, curly hair, Paul whispered to his daughter, "Rose, listen carefully. When I let go of you, you need to run as fast as you can. I know it's far but go to the old hunting cabin by the waterfall."

"I'm not leaving you," she protested but just then a large man threw a torch onto their thatched roof.

"Do as he says," John hurried Rose but when she still hesitated, it was Matilda who grabbed her hand and squeezed hard. "Run, Rose. Run as fast as you can!"

CHAPTER 6
PRINCE ON A WHITE HORSE

Althea and Maeve had promised each other long ago to never keep secrets between them. But childhood promises can be hard to keep, and as they grew into women, Maeve began hiding certain things from her sister.

At the age of twenty-two, the few memories Maeve had from before she went to live with her aunt had become blurry. She didn't remember much about her parents, other than the fact that her mother had been human.

After the dramatic visit to the local town when the girls were fourteen, Maeve had felt so sure she had come close to death, that for years she hadn't rebelled against Rose's orders for her and Althea to stay away from humans.

"All humans are dangerous, and some are even evil. They can seem like your best friend and still turn on you," Rose would warn them.

But Maeve still remembered her mother's smiling face, and she vaguely remembered being tucked in and being kissed on the forehead by both her parents before drifting off to sleep. That wasn't an evil face she'd seen smiling down at her. Maeve often wondered about her parents, and she sometimes thought about the two young men she had spoken to in the market square when she was fourteen.

As she grew older, Maeve insisted on foraging alone because it gave her time to herself and a place to think without interruptions. But as she wandered the woods, searching for herbs and rootlings, she crept closer and closer to the few villages she could reach by foot. Sometimes she even dared get close to Lerwick, the town where she had come face to face with a priest.

Now at the age of twenty-three, she often sat at the edge of the forest and watched humans from afar. But she never left the safety of the forest because of fear that she might end up like Ellen if she got too close. Sometimes when she closed her eyes, she could still hear Ellen's screams and cries as the executioner hanged the young woman for witchery. Eighteen years had passed but Maeve still remembered how she had felt suffocated by the large angry adults around her.

Nowadays, as she watched the humans from a safe distance, she often fabricated stories about them in her mind. Perhaps the old man riding a horse through town had been married three times but had no children. And maybe the woman carrying a child in her arms was in a hurry because she was having company later that day. In Maeve's mind, some were good people and others weren't. Sometimes hours would pass when she sat against a tree and wondered how different her life would have been if she'd been born as a normal human. It was in those moments she found forgiveness for her father who had abandoned her and Althea in the woods with Rose. His need to fit into a community wasn't hard to understand and Maeve didn't blame him.

Maybe it had been different for Earthens in past generations who had been bonded with and surrounded by other Earthens, but for Maeve, she could relate to her father's longing for connection.

She was tired of living an isolated life and watching humans interact showed her how much she was missing out on. Her secret desire to experience love and friendship wasn't something she could share with her sister and aunt. Rose would be petrified if she knew how close Maeve came to humans, and Althea would worry that she was miserable. But Maeve wasn't unhappy with her life as an Earthen, she was just curious and wanted to see more of the world.

A few times, Maeve had been close to telling her sister when they lay watching the stars at night. But Maeve knew that though they were twins with the same orange hair color and same strong abilities, they were very different from each other. It was not only in appearance, where Althea had many freckles, beautiful blue and green colored eyes, and large wavy curls in her hair whereas Maeve's hair was straight but also in personality. It was because they were best friends, and Maeve loved her sister dearly, that she didn't share her fascination with humans. Althea seemed content and Maeve didn't want her to develop the same kind of longing that she battled daily.

It was a warm and sunny afternoon as she sat in the shade between the trees. She had already been gone for too long, but her eyes were glued to the young couple that walked hand in hand around the outskirts of the town Lerwick where Rose sold her produce on Saturdays. Love felt like a myth to Maeve, something she only ever heard about in stories. She knew her parents must have been in love because they had decided to marry. But with the few blurry memories left from her childhood, her parents' fondness for one another was not one she could remember.

On the rarest occasion, she saw a discreet kiss on the cheek or a couple holding hands when she watched the humans, but she'd never seen love up close or felt it herself.

When the couple snickered and ran hand in hand to the woods, Maeve hid behind a tree and discreetly watched with one eye through a gap between some branches. Sucking her full lips in between her teeth she forced herself to keep quiet. They stopped not far from her and wrapped their arms around one another in a tight hug. She was so close that she heard the moans when their lips touched in a kiss. Maeve placed a hand on her stomach, not liking the ache that attacked her without warning. The jealousy and envy she had felt over these past years when watching humans laugh with their friends or go about their daily life paled compared to how she felt in that moment. She was overcome with a deep sadness from seeing the couple kissing and knowing it was unlikely she would ever experience anything as wonderful herself.

The young couple only stayed a few minutes before they left again. With a sigh, she rose from the ground and gave the tree she'd been resting against a hug before she headed back home.

Walking through the forest her thoughts kept wandering back to the couple until something else caught her attention.

Maeve's gaze flew up to the sound of a soft melody. It would be easy to miss for anyone, but Maeve was a trained Earthen and knew the song of a healing rootling when she heard it. She stepped carefully on the ground, to keep her footsteps quiet so that she could hear the melody and track down the flower protecting the rootling. When she found the little purple flower, she knelt before it and thanked it. Gently humming the same melody back, she informed the flower that she meant no harm. She had only just dug the plant up and pulled the roots apart to get to the rootling when a voice startled her.

"Pardon."

Maeve turned her head to see a man on a large stallion watching her. He was far enough gone that she could run, but with him having a horse, he could catch up to her in no time.

"Are you alright, miss?" he asked and moved closer.

Maeve quickly extracted the blue healing rootling from the roots of the flower and stuffed it into a pocket on the side of her skirt. Her heart was galloping in her chest, but as she rose to her feet and faced him, she tried to look as if talking to strangers was an everyday occurrence to her.

"I'm fine, sir," she answered and mustered a polite smile while watching him with both fascination and trepidation.

He was handsome and confident in his movements as he got off his horse and made his way toward her. Taking in Maeve, he was struck by her innocence and loveliness. Her high cheekbones and full lips made her a classic beauty and her bright orange hair reminded him of shining gold. But the thing that fascinated him the most about this surprising jewel of a young woman was her pretty, large eyes, which added such softness to her.

Maeve herself was unaware of her beauty. Up until now, she hadn't been close to a human since she was fourteen. And so, the only other girl she had to compare herself to growing up was Althea, who was also a natural beauty. "Are you lost?" the man asked.

"No. I'm just out for a walk." Maeve shook her head with shyness. Bowing his head, the handsome man gave her a charming smile and introduced himself. "It's a pleasure to meet you. I'm James Lanchester."

Maeve wasn't used to the sensation of excitement making butterflies swirl in her stomach. She had often imagined what she would ask if she met a human again. She'd even rehearsed the conversation in her head. But being so close to James made her mouth go dry and it felt like she had forgotten how to respond.

"What is your name?" James asked.

"Maeve," she answered softly as if trusting him with a precious gift that she should keep to herself.

His lips split into a smile that showed his teeth. "I should have known that such a beautiful girl would have a beautiful name."

Maeve's cheeks flushed red, and a shy smile spread on her face.

Tilting his head, James narrowed his eyes as he looked at Maeve's dirty hands and the flower that had been dug out of the ground. His puzzled expression finally made the words she'd struggled to find fly out of her mouth. "I found it like this. Poor thing. I was just replanting it when you came along." Maeve got down to her knees and looked up at James, who took the opportunity to get closer to her and squatted down next to her.

He didn't think too much about Maeve's strange behavior but assumed that she was well aware of who he was and like many other women, she was shy to be conversing with a man of his wealth and status.

Offering his help, James's hand brushed against Maeve's as they planted the flower. Their brief skin contact made her cheeks heat up and with each kind smile he gave her, she eased up a little more.

"Do you live in town?" Maeve asked James.

He stared at her, surprised she didn't know. "No, I live up at the Felton Hill Estate."

Tilting her head, Maeve asked. "Where is that?"

"Oh, it's about two miles from here. It's a manor, idyllic really, with a gorgeous park and the most breathtaking view of the ocean."

"Is it your parents' house?"

James chuckled before answering softly. "It was but when my father passed away some years ago, I inherited his title and took over the management of the estate, as well as the responsibility for my mother and two younger brothers."

Tilting her head to one side, Maeve watched James and asked. "Do you have children?"

His tone turned a bit playful as he gave a charming smile. "Not yet. But I do intend to marry and have a family if I can find the perfect woman."

Maeve asked many questions. Most he found strange and obvious. But that was because James didn't understand how little she knew about humans. Maeve made him laugh several times with her naïve questions, but it only made him like her more.

When a crow flew over their heads and cawed, Maeve feared her aunt was looking for her. "I'm sorry, I must be heading home."

"Please allow me to escort you?" he offered and got to his feet.

Maeve hesitated for no more than a second before she took his outstretched hand and let him help her up from the ground. "No thank you. It's quite far away, and my aunt and sister don't like company."

"I see." He nodded as they walked side by side back towards his tall horse. "May I at least see you again?"

When the horse pressed its muzzle against her hair and made sweet noises, Maeve smiled and caressed it back.

"That's strange. My horse isn't fond of people in general, but he seems completely smitten with you," James looked on in fascination as the horse moved closer to Maeve. "I like animals and they like me," Maeve said and caressed the large stallion.

"Will you meet me here tomorrow at noon?" James asked.

Maeve knew she should say no, but her strong longing for an adventure made her agree, "I'll meet you then," she promised and walked the other way with a beaming smile on her face.

That first meeting between Maeve and James became the first of many. James found her entertaining, and she always seemed so eager for him to tell her about his life. It suited his self-absorbed personality to brag about his travels, importance, and life in luxury and see her swallow it all up like the gullible country girl she was. Over the next fourteen months, Maeve and James met in the woods, but always in secret. She wasn't proud of how she sneaked off to see him, but James made her feel alive in a way she'd never felt before. He made her heart flutter, and it seemed the world was a lovelier place to be when he was around. James knew about distant places like London and Paris and told her tales about grand balls and theatres. He promised to show her the world and Maeve fell deeply in love with him.

Maeve never spoke about James to Rose and Althea, but they still felt the change in her. And though they often asked her where she went on her hour-long excursions, she was quick to brush them off. People do incredible things for their first love, and for Maeve it included lying to those she loved most.

One summer afternoon, Maeve and James lay on a blanket that James had brought and talked about their future.

"I hope we have many children when we get married," James said and caressed her shoulder.

Maeve smiled, as their dream of marrying was a recurrent topic between them. "I would particularly like a boy with your handsome face," Maeve said in her angelic voice as her eyes glowed with love.

"Yes, we will have plenty of boys," James agreed as he lay on his side propped up on his elbow with his head resting in his hand.

As she lay on her back looking up at the leaves on the swaying trees, Maeve's mind took her far away from her dull life in the forest. She was visualizing her future with her and James enjoying the life he had promised her with an abundance of parties, experiences, and love.

"You're the most beautiful woman I've ever laid my eyes on," he repeated for the hundredth time since they'd met and leaned in to plant another kiss on her soft lips.

Maeve giggled as their kissing intensified. The melody of the birds chirping overhead felt like their personal ensemble of musicians and nothing could have made the moment better. She liked it when James ran his hands up her body and groaned into her ear, but when he pushed up her skirt and opened his pants, she laughed and pushed at him.

"Stop it, James."

"Why?" he asked in a hoarse tone, nibbling at her earlobe.

"Because we're not married yet, and you said yourself that a woman who lies with a man outside of marriage is a whore. You said you liked me because of how pure and innocent I am."

"But darling, we might as well already be married, I've already committed to you, and you've committed to me. Now it's just a matter of time before you become Mistress Lanchester. There's no need for us to wait any longer." James leaned back in and began to gently kiss her throat.

"When?"

"When what?" He looked into her large, beautiful eyes.

"When will we be married? You only ever say it'll be soon, but you've been saying that for some time now, James."

With a deep sigh, he tilted his head and pressed his lips together. "I just need to get a few practical details in order and then I'll take you far away from this life of poverty that you live. Soon the rest of the world will see

73

that the most beautiful woman in the world is mine. You will be the most stunning and best dressed lady at all the balls we attend. And I will cover your beautiful skin in gold and the finest jewelry. You will be happy, my love, I promise." He picked up her hand and traced kisses up her arm. "Every man will hunger for you and every woman will be intimidated by your beauty. But you'll be mine, Maeve. No, you *are* mine. So why should we wait till our wedding night? I've already promised you everything, and I'll keep that promise."

Eager for the life with him that he painted so clearly, Maeve trusted James' every word and let him pull up her skirt and roll on top of her. She had seen plenty of animals breed over the years, but although she was deeply in love with James and his touch released butterflies in her stomach, she was surprised by how painful the act was. It didn't last more than a minute or two before James rolled off her with a deep sigh and then looked over at her with a satisfied grin.

Maeve wasn't disappointed because she'd had no expectations for sex. To her, all this act meant was that James had proven his love and commitment to her. Maeve didn't give him much time to collect himself before she leaned over to him and began to kiss his lips.

They hadn't been kissing very long before the sound of a gasp made Maeve sit up and turn her body to see Rose staring at her.

CHAPTER 7
CAREFUL WHO YOU TRUST

Rose had sensed how Maeve's mind often seemed to wander, and she'd suspected that Maeve was keeping secrets. But Rose knew her niece was a good girl. At least that's what she told herself every time the mistrustful thoughts crept in.

Maeve had been gone for many hours and Rose was beginning to worry as she so often did. After sending two birds out to find her and receiving no reply, she grew more worried and headed into the forest to find Maeve herself. She tracked her footsteps and used her abilities to find her niece. When she turned the corner of three large moss-covered boulders, she came to a sudden halt and stared in disbelief. The sight of Maeve and a human man lying on the ground kissing was so unexpected that a loud gasp escaped Rose's lips. Suddenly everything clicked into place, and Rose felt stupid for not catching on to Maeve's strange behavior sooner. But then again, even her most suspicion-laden thoughts hadn't predicted that Maeve would ever converse with a human let alone be intimate with one.

Stepping backward, Rose nearly lost her bearings as she tripped over a branch. Just then Maeve looked up at her and as their gazes locked, Rose felt the same overwhelming betrayal she had felt when she'd discovered Anne and John kissing. She realized now that Maeve had taken after her mother in more ways than just her looks because Anne too had lied and betrayed Rose's trust.

Back then, Rose had reacted with anger, but this time she remained calm. She was well aware of how fast things could escalate. The sight of the stranger next to Maeve watching her flooded Rose's memory with images of the night when a mob came to find her. In her head, she heard her parents yelling for her to run.

"Rose?" Maeve's voice was shrill as she pushed her dress down and sat up.

Turning her back from a sight that would haunt her in her nightmares, Rose ran.

"I'm sorry, James, I have to go." Maeve hurried to her feet, but James reached out and grabbed her wrist.

"Who was that?" he asked.

"No one. Please, I have to go." She placed a quick kiss on his cheek before hurrying after her aunt.

"What's wrong?" Althea asked when Rose flew through the front door. But Althea received no answer because Rose was too baffled to speak as she paced the room.

Moments later, Maeve entered the small cottage with her cheeks red from running. "I'm sorry, Rose. I didn't mean for you to find out this way."

Althea, who had been mending a dress, stood up and asked with confusion in her tone, "What is going on?"

Maeve turned to her sister, and like a river, the truth flowed out from her. She told them everything, from how she and James had met to how she had given him her virginity.

"I'm so sorry that I've lied and sneaked around behind your backs, but James is my soul mate, and I knew you wouldn't understand."

There was a moment of silence in the cottage. Althea opened her mouth but then closed it again and sat down.

Rose on the other hand went to stand in front of Maeve. "My beautiful girl," she said and cupped Maeve's cheeks. "How can you be so naïve? Have you forgotten what humans do to Earthens? They have no understanding or mercy for anything different from themselves. You told me how you witnessed Ellen's execution and how you learned that even the kindest humans with the warmest smiles can turn bitter and cruel when a witch trial takes place."

"James is different, Rose. He loves me, and we are going to be wed."

Rose swayed a little and then she reached for the table and sank to a chair.

"Don't be upset. It will all be alright," Maeve insisted when Rose hid her wet eyes in the palms of her hands.

It takes immense strength to stand by the fact that your actions have hurt others because that knowledge comes with a heavy amount of guilt. There was nothing Maeve hated more than seeing her aunt in pain, so as Althea moved to kneel in front of Rose and comforted her, Maeve did what she could to protect herself from that guilt – she blamed everyone else.

"This life may be enough for you. But it's not enough for me. I don't want to live isolated and poor anymore. James has promised me gold, jewelry, and experiences." Her finger flew through the air as she spoke. "I want to live a happy life with a man who loves me. James *wants* me to be happy! He *wants* to give me everything and he says I deserve the best that the world has to offer. You just want to keep me trapped here, with dirt under my nails and old clothes."

Rose and Althea both stared at Maeve with large and sad eyes. It was extremely rare that voices were raised in their small and humble home.

With her tone incredulous, Rose asked Maeve, "You think happiness is defined by the amount of gold and jewelry you have?"

"James says it is," Maeve defended herself.

Rose dried her eyes and sighed. "He's wrong. I know that I am happiest when I see you and your sister smiling or when I've healed an animal or made a difference in another's life. My happiness is not about exterior possessions or power, it's about inner peace and being around those I love."

"Inner peace? You've been terrorized by nightmares all the time I've known you, Rose. How can I trust anything you say?"

"Because I love you..." Rose said before she was cut off.

"You say you keep us away from humans because they're dangerous and you want to protect us. But you've filled our heads with lies." Maeve wrinkled her face in disgust. "You don't want to keep us safe. You want to keep us isolated so that we never leave you."

Standing from her chair, Rose remained calm and hid how deeply Maeve's words hurt her. "I love you. And I know that you are hurting right now because you're torn. But I have always and will *always* want what's best for you. I can't see how a human is anything other than dangerous. But..." A ball formed in her throat and made it difficult for Rose to speak. "If you choose to be with him... promise me one thing."

"What?"

"He must *never* know that you are an Earthen."

Maeve gave a small nod before she walked toward the door. "You're wrong." She stopped in the doorway and looked back at her sister, whose eyes were red and puffy, and her aunt, who stood with a pale face and a sad heart. "I never meant to hurt either of you, but I've never been surer of anything than I am now. James and I belong together."

Closing the door behind her, Maeve left her sister and aunt heartbroken inside, and then she began walking, determined to find James and be with him.

James had never taken her to his estate, but he'd talked about it enough times that she had a clear picture of it in her mind. It took him no more than half an hour on the back of a fast horse to get to town, but it took Maeve almost three hours to reach his castle. Once she arrived, she had no doubt that she'd found the right place. The long line of roses in the garden and the extravagant lavender plants were exactly where James had described them.

Even though he had described the home as a small castle, Maeve couldn't comprehend how massive the buildings were. She had never seen a house so grand or tall. Her eyes were wide open with wonder and her mouth dry from walking so far, as she made her way up the long gravel road toward her new home. It was three stories tall and had eight chimneys. Every plant in the surrounding park was cut like a square or circle, and an impressive carriage with six horses waited outside the large front door.

Though she was nervous, her heart fluttered with excitement at the thought of James' joy and surprise that she was here. She envisioned him picking her up and twirling her around with delight. For so long they had fantasized about their future, and now that they had consummated their relationship there was no need to wait for them to get married. This was where she and James would raise their many children and grow old together. She imagined them having a picnic in the garden while their children ran around and played. Rose and Althea would die of jealousy when they saw her new way of life. Despite her heated argument with Rose before she left, she intended to invite them to live with her. As she looked up at the castle with an endless number of windows, she wondered which one would be her bedroom.

The grand staircase felt like the last mountain to conquer before Maeve would reach her happy ending. Climbing the twelve steps, Maeve lifted her hand to knock on the arched door that had such impressive carvings. Just then the large double doors opened from the inside and a man gave Maeve a startled look.

Staring back at him, Maeve thought he looked strange with his knee-high socks, red pants, and stiff upper lip. Opening her mouth, she was just about to ask to see James but was distracted when a young woman came into view behind the man.

Elizabeth Dale was soon to be eighteen years old. She had been raised in a family of nobility with expectations of marrying a rich suitor. Though James was twice her age, her family found him very agreeable. Elizabeth was not a particularly pretty or nice girl, and she did little to hide her disgust when she saw Maeve standing outside the front door. Though only a fool could miss Maeve's natural beauty, Elizabeth was blinded by the simple fabric and design of her dress and the smudges of dirt on her shoes. No fine lady would be as tanned as Maeve and in Elizabeth's eyes, it was almost indecent the way Maeve's long red hair hung loosely around her shoulders.

Young Elizabeth scrunched up her nose at Maeve and turned her head toward someone on the other side of the door that Maeve couldn't see.

"When we are wed, I will have to teach your servants not to use the front door and to care about their hygiene. This one doesn't seem to know what a bath is."

The person Elizabeth spoke to came to her side to see to whom she was referring. The moment James appeared, Maeve's lips parted in a silent gasp. She chose to believe that the girl had been speaking to the old man beside her, but the quiet voice in the back of her head knew that she'd been addressing James. James was in shock to see Maeve outside his door and stood with a baffled expression beside Elizabeth.

As the rude woman walked out the door, Maeve was forced to step aside since Elizabeth acted as if she didn't exist and almost bumped into her.

Silently, Maeve watched as James walked right past her as well, following Elizabeth and her father to their carriage.

Once they had said their goodbyes and the posh carriage had taken off, James kept waving.

"James?" Maeve called out to him, feeling confused by what she had just witnessed.

Not until the carriage was far down the gravel road did James turn and hurry up the stairs to confront her. "What are you doing here?"

It confused Maeve that he showed no sign of joy. "I've come to be with you." She took a step toward him feeling exhausted from her long walk and the heated argument with her aunt. It took her last grain of strength to fight the urge to fall into his arms. "I had an awful fight with my aunt. I can never go back."

James remained quiet as his face was stern. "I think it's best we go to our spot in the woods. Come." He took her wrist and tried to pull her along. But Maeve's feet stood planted.

"Don't you understand, James, we don't have to hide our feelings anymore. We can be wed and live here, *together.* Just like you said you wanted."

Unable to meet her eyes, James's gaze rested on her sharp collarbone.

"Unless..." Maeve looked after the carriage, which was now far away. A part of her had dismissed the situation, hoping it was a misunderstanding. But the more she saw how James avoided her eyes, the more she knew she was wrong. "Who was she?"

"That was Miss Dale."

Maeve tried to read his face, but it remained impassive, and the warm charming man she was used to seemed cold and distant. "Was it true what she said? Are you engaged?"

"Yes. It's always been in the plans between our families," he answered.

"I don't understand. But you said we would get married." Maeve's voice broke a little as she reached for the railing of the staircase to steady her tired body. Her legs felt like they might give in.

"Whoa." James saw the distress on her face and with a firm grip on her upper arms, he moved her to sit on the wide railing. With a deep sigh, James looked around to see if anyone was watching them. "These things are complicated, Maeve. My heart belongs to you, but marriage isn't about love. I wish you came from a family of wealth and status." He gave another long and deep sigh. "but even if you did, I already proposed to Elizabeth. My situation in life comes with certain responsibilities that I must prioritize."

"Do you love her?"

The pain in Maeve's tone didn't escape him and so he assured her, "No, of course not." In truth, he barely knew Elizabeth Dale, but he respected her more than he loved Maeve. Elizabeth had money and power, and that was something that meant more to him than Maeve ever could.

"How long have you been engaged?"

"I proposed to her recently." He scratched the back of his head. "If only I had met you before her, Maeve, then maybe we would have had a chance. But I've already given my word to Elizabeth and her family."

Narrowing her eyes, Maeve finally saw through one of his many lies. "If it was in the cards before you even met me then why would you play with my heart and plant those ideas in my head of us getting married?" she asked, fighting back tears.

James took Maeve's hands and looked deep into her eyes. "Because I wish it could be so." Bowing his head he whispered, "I don't want to lose you, Maeve, but we can never be more than what we are now. Our love has to be secret. I hope that can be enough for you because I know that a mere second in your company makes life worth living. I'll gladly meet with you in the forest for the rest of our lives." From the time James had been a boy, he'd been talented with words and often used them to manipulate others into getting what he wanted. Maeve wasn't the first girl he had flattered and promised the world to, only with a plan of using her as he pleased.

"In secret?" she asked with her gaze dropped low.

Seeing a servant pass by a window inside the castle, James dropped Maeve's hands, not wanting anyone to see him showing her affection. "Our relationship is between you and me and no one else. I will meet you tomorrow at our spot, but I must ask you never to come back here again."

His demand hung in the air as he turned his back on her and walked away. The sound of the heavy wooden doors closing made Maeve blink her eyes as if that would wake her from the nightmare she was in.

Heartbroken with disappointment, she felt like a fraud and an idiot for believing James' lies. She had felt so sure of him and his promises when she claimed to her aunt and sister that this would be her new home and way of life. The deep embarrassment that she felt made her certain that she could never return home again. And so for the rest of the day, Maeve wandered through the forest feeling lost, hungry, and miserable. She had lost everything. Her family, the bright future she envisioned with James, and most of all, she'd lost her self-respect. Not only was she embarrassed for boasting about the life

James had promised her, but she was embarrassed for the way she'd spoken to her aunt, whom she loved dearly.

As if nature wanted to punish her further, a storm hit and forced Maeve to take cover under a tree. It helped little against the rain that still drenched her. Sitting on the cold and muddy ground, she wrapped her arms around her knees and thought about how much she hated young Elizabeth Dale. It seemed that her problems all pointed back to her. The girl had stolen the life that James had promised Maeve and never had she hated anyone so much. Her jaws locked tight as she thought about Elizabeth living in the castle that was supposed to be hers and sleeping in her bed, next to *her* James.

As her anger and hatred grew, she thought of a thousand ways to get what she wanted, and in the end, she concocted a plan fueled by envy and misery.

CHAPTER 8
A STAB TO THE GUT

Lying curled up against a tall root of a tree that had grown above ground, Maeve felt like the storm would never end. The howling wind and the thunder and lightning mirrored the chaos she was going through internally. Her hair had turned a darker shade of orange from the heavy downpour and clung to her skin. If Maeve had been human, she would have been freezing and possibly suffering from falling body temperature. At least as an Earthen, she could regulate her temperature, but that was about her only comfort in her bleak situation where each minute felt like a year.

While the aggressive winds and heavy rain eventually died down, it was another matter with the storm that raged inside of her. All night she had obsessed about the unfairness of her situation and was left with her emotional chaos spinning out of control. The more Maeve thought about how her life had drastically changed within a day, the more pain accumulated in her chest. She should have spent her night pampered by servants and sleeping like a princess in a warm and comfortable bed in James' castle. But instead, she was sleepless on the hard and dirty ground. Sadness, shame, and anger consumed Maeve and when the time came to meet with James at their usual spot, Maeve was no longer the same girl she had been the day before.

She came early and as she waited for him, she looked at the spot where less than twenty-four hours ago, she had naively believed all his lies. Yesterday, she arrived at this place feeling happy and optimistic about life. Today, there was a darkness inside her that cursed the mossy ground where she'd lain the day before, and what it represented.

Maeve heard the sound of James' horse approaching before she saw him. She had always seen him as her prince in shining armor, but as he rode toward her, she was the one wearing armor around her heart. No longer blinded by his handsome face, flattery, and empty lies, she would hold him to his promises and make him see that Elizabeth Dale would never be able to make him happy. James had said it himself; he loved Maeve.

The word "love" had lost its appeal to Maeve, but she wasn't ready to go back to living in poverty and isolation. James had painted too many images of them living in luxury and now that she had seen his beautiful home, she wanted all of it.

As if nothing had happened the day before, James got off his horse and walked over to pull her in for a kiss.

"I have to ask you something," Maeve said, pushing her upper body away from his embrace.

"What is it?" There was slight irritation in his tone as if he was warning her not to bring up what happened the day before.

"I know you said you weren't. But I have to ask you again. Are you in love with her?"

"No," he said sternly. "My heart belongs to you, Maeve. But Miss Dale and I are already engaged, and I am a man of my word."

Anger and ambition stirred in Maeve's stomach. How dare James say that he was a man of his word when he had filled her head with dreams that he had never intended to fulfill? A coldness spread in her veins as she said, "What if there was a way where you could keep your honor and be with me instead of her; would you do it?"

James picked up Maeve's hands and placed a kiss on each. "You know I would," he lied, "but there isn't a way. Miss Dale comes from a good family with money and influence, and I've already proposed to her."

Watching his face closely, she read his expression as she spoke. "What if I told you there is a way where you could get both? If you marry her, you'll get the money, the status, and the respect. But if Elizabeth were to die shortly after the wedding, that would leave you in need of a new wife."

At first, James dismissed Maeve's absurd words as humor and gave a small chuckle, but when Maeve's face didn't split into a grin, he frowned and asked, "You're jesting, right?"

Maeve's eyes narrowed a tiny bit, and she raised her chin with an expression of resolve that scared him. She had been innocent and pure when he met her but now there was a shift in her that made him uneasy. Widening his eyes in shock, he dropped her hands and pulled back a little. "Are you asking me to kill Miss Dale?"

Consumed with ambition and hatred for the woman who'd stolen her place, Maeve involved James in her plan. "I can make a remedy that would give her a peaceful death in her sleep. All you would have to do is slip it into her tea."

Scrunching his face up, James exclaimed, "That's madness. How could you ever suggest such a thing?"

Maeve's pretty features were distorted by her anger. "Because she's in our way. You said it yourself. I'm the one you love, and you're only marrying her out of a sense of obligation."

James stood stunned when Maeve took his hands and added, "I would do anything to be with you, James."

Backing away, he no longer found Maeve as delightful and beautiful as he once had. A bloodthirsty wolf goes after easy prey, and Maeve had been an innocent and trusting little bunny in his eyes that he could manipulate into doing what he wanted. Never had he imagined that she could turn out to be as predatory as him. Looking into her eyes, his instinct told him that Maeve's bloodthirstiness far surpassed his own.

Eager to get away, he quickly backed to his horse.

"Where are you going?" Maeve called out as he stepped into the stirrup and pulled himself onto the tall stallion.

"You're mad," he hissed.

"But James..." Maeve's eyes were pleading.

"Stay away from me," he demanded and kicked his horse hard. Not looking back to see how Maeve's eyes darkened he set the horse into motion and galloped away.

James' harsh rejection on top of her nightmarish past twenty-four hours made Maeve see red. She had given her virginity to him, bought into his lies, and left Rose and Althea to be with him. For James to call her mad and take off as if she wasn't worth his time made her so angry that she used her abilities to stop him.

Raising her hands in the air, she sent a gush of strong wind his way. The amount of emotion Maeve felt in that moment and channeled into her wind made it the strongest elemental spell she'd ever created. Attacking him from the back, the wind knocked him off his tall horse and threw him to the ground. His stallion was spooked and trampled his leg, which made James howl with pain.

Maeve calmed the horse from a distance. Using her powers, she brought the stallion from being scared and confused to standing close to James and nibbling at leaves from a tree.

When Maeve approached them, James yelled, "Get away from me" and crawled backward with one arm while the other was trying to stop the bleeding from his leg.

"I didn't mean for you to get hurt, James, but you have to hear me out."

"What happened?" he cried out and looked around with a perplexed expression on his face. "Where did that storm come from?"

"That was me. I couldn't let you leave."

He stared at her. "What are you talking about?"

"I created that gust of wind. Here, let me help you." When she squatted down and tried to touch him, he moved back again.

"I can heal you." Once again, Maeve stretched her hands out toward his wound, but the way James flinched made her stop.

He's scared of me. At first, the thought was absurd to Maeve. James was much bigger and stronger than she was, but it was right there in his eyes and actions. He had called her insane and now he was trying to get away from her. The desperation she had gone through all night intensified and, in an attempt to win him back over, she panicked and did the one thing she'd sworn never to do – she told him the truth.

"I'm not human like you, James, I'm an Earthen. We are healers by nature, and I use my abilities to help animals. I can tend to your wound if you let me."

"You're lying! Get away from me," he sneered.

"No, look. I'll prove it to you." Maeve held up her palm, where she made a small flame appear.

James's eyes grew to double size, and he stammered something unintelligible.

"I just want to help," she said, leaning forward to tend his wound once again.

Maeve saw it when James drew his dagger. A second ago he had been trying to get away from her, but now he drew closer. It all happened so fast and left her no time to react before he stabbed the blade into her stomach. Yesterday, he had loved every inch of her soft skin that he had kissed so tenderly. Now, she blinked her eyes in confusion and looked down at the shaft of the dagger planted right in her gut. Her throat began to shake as pained sounds tried to escape. The depth of his betrayal made her mouth fall open and tears stream down her cheeks. She stared at the trail of blood running from her wound to the man she had once loved more than life itself.

Maeve's large expressive eyes had been the thing that drew James to her in the beginning, but now he looked into them as if she disgusted him.

The emotional and physical pain was excruciating, but Maeve managed to speak one word in a brittle voice. "Why?"

"You hexed me! But now I know the truth. You're nothing but an old hag who used magic to appear young and beautiful so you could lure me in."

"N-no," she sobbed in protest.

James moved closer to Maeve, who lay on her back looking at him through her wet eyes. When he pulled his dagger out of her stomach, she groaned and pressed her hands to the wound, pleading with him. "Help me."

James blatantly ignored her and dried the bloody knife off on the mossy ground. As he stood up, he towered over her for a moment, and then he bent down and ripped off the silver necklace he had given her months ago.

Maeve's pained groans echoed through the forest but didn't soften James. He too was injured from his fall. But a cut in the leg wasn't as immobilizing as a knife in the gut. With a limp, he dragged himself toward his horse.

"Your witchcraft would never have worked. Even if I weren't engaged to Elizabeth and you came from a wealthy family, I would've never married you because I don't respect you and I certainly never loved you."

Unable to do anything other than keep pressure on her stab wound, Maeve remained quiet. She didn't understand his cruel words because she had been so convinced that they were in love.

James groaned as he used his strength to get up on his tall horse. Before riding off he looked down at Maeve, who lay on the ground in a pool of her blood. Her eyes were large and her gaze begged for an answer that would make sense to her, so without the slightest feeling of guilt he said, "A woman who lies with a man outside of marriage is nothing but a whore." James lifted his gaze from Maeve, turned his horse around, and left her to die.

Maeve wanted to scream, sob, or grab a rock and throw it after James. She would have even smashed it against her head to make the pain stop. But with the amount of blood she had already lost, there was nothing she could do but lie on the ground and watch the man she'd once been ready to kill for, ride away.

In that moment, she moved her hands from the stab wound. No one would save her, and she had nothing to live for anyway. Maeve's life had crumbled into nothing. She had lost her parents at a young age and been foolish enough to push away the two people who loved her to be with a man who only used her for his entertainment. More than anything, Maeve just wanted to die in that moment, and when her vision became blurry and the world went dark she thought her prayer had been answered.

CHAPTER 9
APOLOGIES FROM A BROKEN HEART

Despite Maeve's harsh words, Rose loved her more than she loved her own life. Her eyes were red with large bags underneath from the sleepless night she'd spent worrying about Maeve. She'd been sitting in the garden all morning hoping her niece would come back home.

"She'll come back," Althea assured her aunt as she sat down beside her in the tall grass.

"I hope so," Rose whispered.

Althea and Maeve had been best friends all of their life, so being apart felt like a nightmare to Althea who missed her sister. She was deeply hurt that Maeve hadn't told her about James, and she was even more hurt by the way Maeve had stormed out and abandoned them for a man she'd never told them about.

Although Althea was in deep pain, she didn't dwell on it, because she recognized how her aunt was hurting and needed her to be strong. All morning, they searched for Maeve and even went as far as walking through the town looking for her.

There was no trace of her anywhere and once they were back in the forest, Rose had fallen to her knees and cried.

The moment a group of sparrows flew by, Rose and Althea both looked up and listened to the shrieking birds. When they picked up on their message about Maeve's need for help, Rose and Althea sprung to their feet and set off in a run. Althea was fastest and followed the direction that the sparrows led her in. Her heart was pounding from fear that the birds were right about Maeve dying.

Never had Althea sprinted as fast in her life. Her lungs hurt and her mouth was completely dry when she saw the birds land next to a body on the ground.

"Maeve." Althea threw herself to her sister's side and felt cold to the bone when she saw Maeve's pale complexion and blue lips. Calling Maeve's name, Althea received no reply. The size of the blood stain on her twin's dress made Althea sick to her stomach. Maeve's eyes were shut, her body was limp, and Althea felt certain it was too late to save her.

Since yesterday when Maeve left, Althea had tried to remain strong for her aunt, but now she shattered inside and burst into tears as she leaned over her sister and buried her head against her hair. Her cries were so loud that all animals near them fled in a hurry. With shaking hands, Althea cupped Maeve's face trying to wake her, not caring that their closeness stained her dress in Maeve's blood. Althea's screams and cries burned into Rose's heart when she arrived to see the two sisters. Instead of throwing herself on top of Maeve as Althea had, Rose worked fast, doing everything she could to save her niece's life.

Althea heard her aunt's orders but was frozen in grief. It wasn't until Rose shook her arm and yelled at her. "Maeve is still alive, and we need to heal her" that she began helping.

They worked on Maeve for hours to stabilize her with their healing powers. Althea ran home to get Tobias and at a slow pace, they brought Maeve back to the small cottage.

It was past supper time when Maeve opened her eyes again. Seeing the branches of a familiar tree with the clear sky above brought her comfort, but she quickly drifted back to sleep. Over the next thirty hours, she kept drifting in and out of consciousness. Not just because her body felt weak, but also because the part of her that had wanted to die, didn't want to wake up and face reality or the stabbing pain in her stomach and her broken heart.

Maeve felt the gentle hands of her sister helping her to eat and drink. Althea and Rose tended Maeve's wound and kept a close eye on her. But for the most part, she was in deep sleep and the house was quiet during the days while Maeve slept.

Rarely did Althea leave Maeve's side. Lovingly she stroked her arm and tucked her sister in with blankets while singing their special song in a soft voice.

A scared and fearful heart can see no light.
But I see you, lying in the ground.
Take my hand, I'll help you out.
The shadows are near, but I have no fear.
Hmm-hmm-mm-hmm

The world is dark, and evil lies near.
Your angry heart carries that fear.
You don't see how the sun shines down.
Your back is turned, with your gaze on the ground.
Hmm-hmm-mm-hmm

Finally, Maeve gently opened her eyes to the sound of her sister singing. For a moment she wished she could be a young child once again, without worries. But soon the memories of what had happened came rushing back reminding her that the innocence of her childhood had died the day Ellen was hung. "I'm sorry," Maeve whispered to her sister who hadn't seen her eyes open.

Althea stopped singing and stroked Maeve's hair. "How are you feeling?"

It hurt to breathe because of her injured stomach and her heart felt heavy and miserable. "Better than I deserve," she answered, "I'm so sorry, Althea. I feel so ashamed of how I've acted. I thought James loved me, but I was wrong. And I let him ruin my relationship with you and Rose."

"Few things are so broken that they can't be fixed," Althea said as she leaned her head against Maeve's. "But don't ever leave me again. You're my other half, Maeve, and I need you."

"I won't," Maeve promised with tears running down her cheeks.

They both lifted their gazes when they heard the sound of Rose climbing up the tree. Maeve wanted to crawl under the blankets and hide from the guilt she felt.

"It's good to see you awake," Rose said as she sat down on the small terrace that Althea and Maeve had slept on together.

Maeve nodded and spoke with a brittle voice. "I'm so sorry Rose. I didn't mean any of the things I said. You were right, humans are nothing but evil. I don't deserve your forgiveness, but I want you to know how truly sorry I am."

Stroking Maeve's cheek, Rose placed a kiss on her forehead and smiled with teary eyes. "My love for you is unconditional. I want you to be happy even if it's not with me. But above your happiness, I value your safety, that's why I may seem controlling at times. I'm sorry if I've made you feel trapped." A tear ran down Rose's cheek that Maeve was quick to wipe away with the back of her hand. "Do you remember what your name means?" Rose asked.

Maeve thought for a moment while searching her mind. "Althea means healer, but I can't remember what my name means," she answered honestly.

"Maeve means 'she who intoxicates' and I've always thought that name suited you well. Your beauty and personality draw people in, but intoxication is not love, so choose carefully who you trust in this world."

"What happened?" Althea asked, "Who hurt you? Was it *him?*"

Maeve's head hung low as she nodded. "James wasn't the man I thought he was. He promised the world, but it turns out that he used me and played with my heart. When I found out that he was engaged to another woman, he... he..." Maeve didn't want to admit to Rose and Althea that she had revealed to James that she was an Earthen and shown him that she had abilities. "We got into an argument and then he stabbed me and left me to die." To Maeve, thinking about what had happened, made her feel like getting stabbed in the gut for the second time. Though Rose and Althea tried to ask questions, Maeve changed the subject, and so, Rose and Althea never knew what danger they were really in.

Some weeks passed, and Maeve's wound which had been deep and large healed nicely due to their abilities and healing herbs.

"I hate that scar," Maeve said while applying the homemade cream on her stomach while Rose cooked up supper. "It will be a constant reminder of what happened for the rest of my life."

Rose arched an eyebrow. "At least you're still alive. That's the part that matters."

"I want my necklace back," Maeve said and touched her collarbone.

"The one you found in the forest?" The moment Rose asked, she saw the expression on Maeve's face. "Oh, I see. He gave that necklace to you, didn't he?"

"Yes. But I couldn't tell you. It was the only thing I had of value, and he stole it from me. When I'm strong enough and my wound is fully healed, I intend to go get it back."

"Absolutely not!" Rose protested in a stern tone.

Althea who was stirring a pot was quick to support their aunt and put the large spoon down. "It's too dangerous, Maeve. What if he tries to hurt you again?"

Maeve's tone turned icy. "Then I'll hurt him back."

Rose blinked her eyes twice and stared at Maeve in shock. "I did not raise you to use violence. We never attack, it's not in our nature. We are healers and caretakers who only take from nature what we need. It's against our nature to harm others."

"I just don't think it's fair he gets away with it. James doesn't deserve that locket," Maeve insisted.

Althea spoke in a soft voice as she placed her hand on top of Maeve's. "A necklace isn't worth dying for. That awful man already took enough. Don't let him take your life too."

Maeve tightened her jaw and looked away and it made Althea and Rose exchange a glance of concern. With a sigh, Rose tried to cheer Maeve up.

"Besides, your twenty-fourth birthday is coming up, maybe I'll head into town and get you a pretty new locket." Rose took a sip of the soup she and Althea were making with smiling lines wrinkling the edges of her eyes.

Althea on the other hand lowered her brow with concern. "I thought we would avoid that place after what happened to Maeve. Don't you think going to town is dangerous?"

"I think it's a lot safer than Maeve going to get her locket back from James. And you know I'm always careful." Rose walked over and cupped Maeve's chin tilting her head upwards. "He only saw me for a mere second that day I found you together. Even if I met him, you don't think there's much of a chance he'd recognize me, do you?"

Maeve shook her head. "I doubt it. James is too self-absorbed to pay attention to people other than himself."

Soon, she would come to wish she had been right.

CHAPTER 10
WHISPERS IN THE WIND

Just as all Earthens did on birthdays, Althea, Maeve, and Rose woke before the sun and sat in a circle on the damp grass outside their small cottage reflecting upon their decisions and accomplishments of the year.

"What have you contributed to this earth since your last birthday?" Rose asked the girls, just as she did every year.

Most would have struggled to see anything in the dark night, but with their superior eyesight, Rose saw how Maeve's gaze fell and her body shrunk.

"I have helped many injured animals, and I've tended to the rough soil by the creek, which is now blossoming with wildflowers," Althea answered with her hands in her lap as she looked over at her sister.

"I've contributed with a lot of pain," Maeve added, "and I'm truly sorry for that, but in my twenty-fifth year of life, I hope to make some better choices for myself and to help those around me."

Althea leaned closer to her sister and placed a hand on her knee. "Don't let the pain and few mistakes drown out all the good you've done this year, Maeve."

Rose nodded and was quick to add, "I have always been a fast learner and a gifted Earthen, but never in my forty-six years of life have I created a new potion as you have. Nor have I ever met anyone as gifted at making remedies and potions as you."

"Thank you," Maeve said as she looked down at the seed in her hand.

"And your favorite part of the year?" Rose asked, coming to the last of her questions. Earthens had many traditions, and birthdays were a time of reflecting and setting intentions.

Althea smiled. "Probably, nursing the wolf cub back to health."

"Yes, he was adorable, I think having him live with us for two weeks was my favorite part of the year as well," Maeve added.

"Are you ready to plant the seeds of your twenty-fourth birthday?" Rose asked when she saw the sun beginning to rise.

The girls smiled and looked down at the small seeds in their hands.

As an Earthen Rose had grown up planting a seed for each of her birthdays. It was tradition to tend the seed and watch it grow; if the plant died the year it was planted, Earthens took it as a sign of lacking inner peace because the plant was a representation of them until their next birthday.

This was a tradition Althea and Maeve had first been introduced to when they came to live with their aunt because their father had never shown it to them. He had however planted a tree for each girl on the day of their birth following the custom of Earthens.

As the sunlight got closer to where they sat in a circle on the ground, the three women each placed their seed in the small hole they had dug and covered it with dirt just as the light of the sun reached them and warmed the ground. This year, Maeve had planted a pulsatilla vulgaris flower and Althea had planted a Fool's Parsley. Though birthdays landed during all times of the year, a good Earthen could make a small flower blossom, even in the hardest of winters, if they used their abilities in the right ways. Placing their hands where they had planted the seeds the girls closed their eyes and whispered affirmations of love.

Soon after they finished, Rose took off with her horse Tobias to the village. Her goal was to sell enough vegetables and fruits to buy each of the girls a little gift.

By mid-morning, the girls were foraging the woods. In their baskets, they carried the flowers and sticks they would use for their celebration in the evening where they would make a large fire and dance under the moon and stars until the day turned into night.

Walking side by side Maeve gave her sister a sideways glance and said, "Thank you."

"For what?" Althea looked at her sister with a curious smile.

"For forgiving me and loving me; it's more than I deserve." It was late summer and with each step they took, the leaves under their feet made crunching noises. "I realize now that I never needed James to make me happy. I don't need any human. As long as I have you, Althea, I know I will be happy."

"You're my best friend, Maeve, and I can't imagine how today would have been if we hadn't found you just in time. You'd better not ever do something as dangerous again," Althea lectured, playfully bumping into Maeve's shoulder.

Maeve turned serious. "I used to resent this lifestyle of isolation. But after what happened with James, I'll happily live in the cottage foraging the woods till the day we're seventy. I'll die happy if I never see another human being again."

Althea smiled and looked down at her full basket. "I think we have enough now, shall we head back?"

"I was thinking of going to get some of the red flowers for Rose's flower crown that she loves."

Althea sighed and used the back of her hand to push away strands of orange hair from her forehead. "Are you sure? That's a long walk."

"Yes, but I want to do something nice for her."

"Alright, I'll head back inside and start baking the pie." Althea kissed her sister on the cheek before they parted ways.

The leaves on the trees were beginning to change color, and some fell to the ground as Maeve walked through the beautiful forest that was untouched by civilization. She walked with her head down, watching as her hard bare feet stepped on the crunchy leaves and sticks. Her thoughts were focused on finding the field of red flowers that her aunt loved so much that she didn't notice the energy shift around her.

A wind seemed to follow close behind her making the leaves rattle on the ground and some fly through the air.

When Maeve felt the breeze around her, she stopped to see that something peculiar was going on. The leaves on the trees didn't move, but the leaves around her were lifting from the ground and flying in circles like a small dust devil created by the wind.

Maeve was so surprised by the unusual phenomena that she took a step backward and tripped over a root on the ground.

Lying on the ground she watched how the leaves flew in circles until they began to take shape.

Squinting her eyes, Maeve took in the incredible sight in front of her. It was as if the leaves created a shape of a human. At first, it was hard to see, but then a female figure appeared that moved closer to Maeve.

A voice with a soft, ethereal quality to it made Maeve turn her head in all directions to find the source.

"Hello, Maeve, I'm Zosia," the wind whispered, and it seemed as though her pleasant voice was a hundred yards away yet also right next to Maeve's ears.

"Zosia," Maeve breathed as she got to her feet.

"I've been watching you. You are a woman with great strength and ambition that is uncommon for an Earthen."

"Thank... thank you," Maeve stuttered.

Zosia moved closer in her feminine body made of leaves. "I've come to ask for your help," she said, each of her words echoing through the soft wind.

"My help?" Maeve asked with large eyes and her mouth gaping a bit.

"Earthens are the most peaceful species alive, yet you possess something inside you that made you willing to kill out of hatred. It's something I have never seen before in an Earthen."

Maeve was mortified that someone as wise and godlike as Zosia knew of her suggestion to James about killing Elizabeth Dale. With remorse in her voice, she looked down. "I'm so sorry, Zosia. It was a mistake and I beg for your forgiveness; I will never stoop so low again."

"Do not beg, Maeve. It's not my place to forgive you. I myself kill often," Zosia answered and although she had no eyes, it felt as though she saw right through Maeve, and accepted every part of her.

"You do?" Maeve asked.

"I am nature," she answered, "Death is a normal and healthy part of the life cycle that creates balance." The leaves seemed to move around within Zosia's body, but her figure never shifted. "I created Earthens as peaceful healers to serve the balance of life. Sadly, that balance is no more. Evil lives in this world and the darkness it represents is growing with alarming speed. We need powerful beacons of light to bring together the people with kindness in their hearts to overpower the darkness. That's why I need your help, Maeve. You must put an end to the Cobra."

Overwhelmed, Maeve gaped at Zosia. "You want me to kill a snake?"

"The Cobra is a Fader who shifts into many shapes. He walks the Earth looking like a human, but he also flies over the sky like a bird. It is in his shape as the black cobra that he kills with his venom."

"Why me?" Maeve asked.

"Because you are not just your father's daughter but your mother's too. Your thoughts went to a dark place the night you planned to kill that girl. Something I've never seen in another Earthen. Therefore you may be my only hope."

Maeve's gaze fell to the ground. Being chosen by Zosia because evil lay inside her didn't make Maeve feel any better about herself. But maybe it wasn't her fault; maybe she had inherited it from her mother. "Rose says I look like my mother, whereas Althea takes after our father."

"You've taken from your mother in more ways than looks. She too was willing to kill."

"She was?" Maeve asked with curiosity and surprise. Rose rarely spoke about John and hardly ever about Anne, and it had left Maeve curious about her parents.

"Your mother was the reason Rose was nearly killed and had to flee for her life. But I see your father in you too; you have his heart to balance out your mother's opportunistic character."

"She did what?" Maeve shook her head not wanting to believe the words she heard. It explained why Rose hadn't liked talking about her mother. At the same time that she wondered why Rose had never shared the truth, she knew the answer in her heart. Rose had only ever talked kindly about Anne and said that Maeve got her good looks from her because she didn't want to ruin the idea Althea and Maeve had of their mother. Now that Maeve knew the truth, however, she was left with even greater anger and resentment towards humans. It also made her feel like she had to make up for what her mother had done and clear herself of being anything like Anne.

"Anything I do will come from a place of love and protection. I don't want to be associated with evil and I don't want to be associated with my mother; I'm not human."

Zosia bowed her head. "Your intentions are pure."

"What is the evil cobra that you speak of and how do I kill it?"

"He is older than any human alive and more powerful than any Earthen. The Cobra is the force behind all Faders."

"Faders? But I thought they were nothing but a myth," Maeve whispered, partly to herself.

"I wish it was so. You Earthens are not the only species that humans don't know about. Faders live amongst them as well, and they take everything they can get their hands on. They are thirsty for power and will do whatever it takes to get it. Thousands of years ago I thought of them as a nuisance much like when you discover a new type of weed in your garden. I've kept an eye on them but sadly, they are an intrusive species and have been attacking my Earthens. I now consider them dangerous to everything we serve to protect."

"What are Faders exactly?"

"They are altered humans. The Cobra is their leader and father. It is he who gives them immortality at the price of being his slaves. He's the oldest living creature on this Earth and I'm ashamed to say that I've underestimated him."

Maeve's eyes were large as she absorbed every word.

"The Cobra grew stronger so gradually that he managed to keep it hidden from me. While my attention was elsewhere, he has become the most dangerous man in the world and so powerful that even I can't kill him. That's why I need your help, Maeve."

Maeve was both terrified and honored to be tasked with such an important mission. Her thoughts were running in all directions with questions. Before she had a chance to ask any of them, Zosia answered them.

"In order to stop the menace that he causes, you must kill him, Maeve, and you won't be the first to try. It's taken me centuries to understand how the Cobra came to be and what gruesome acts he did to gain immortality. His actions were so evil, vile, and disturbing that they're best not spoken of."

"I want to help if I can," Maeve bravely said because being in Zosia's presence filled her with awe.

"Good. To destroy the Cobra, you will need the objects he used to become immortal. He knows this and guards them well."

"What are those objects and why didn't he just destroy them so they couldn't be used against him?" Maeve asked.

The leaves forming Zosia moved so fluidly that she looked lifelike. "The Cobra's immortality is linked to these artifacts. Interestingly enough, he can't be close to them either as they drain him. That's why he has hidden them in places few can reach. Hidden deep within the largest of mountains is the spear he stabbed himself with to become immortal, but it's cursed and anyone who touches it will meet a fate much worse than death. So first you must search out the powder of blood, and throw it onto the handle; only then may you touch the spear."

"The powder of blood?"

"It's the blood of his sacrifice which has been preserved and turned into a powder.

"Lastly you need his blood dripping from the blade before you stab him with it. Only then will he die."

"If he's so powerful, and many have tried to kill him before, what makes you think I would stand a chance, even if I had the spear?"

"If he saw you with his spear, he would kill you within seconds," Zosia agreed. "But I've been waiting for the right person to send on this quest, and in that time, I've channeled my energy into creating the one thing that will give you the strength to face him." Bowing her head, it felt as though the earth shook a bit, and then a flower grew between them.

Maeve widened her eyes and stared, as she had never seen anything as strange and marvelous. The white flower stood with its head reaching out towards Zosia and spreading the most angelic melody Maeve had ever heard.

"You will find my gift to you in its roots." Zosia nodded toward the flower.

Maeve approached it and got to her knees. The ground that the flower stood on seemed to split apart, giving her direct access to the roots. Digging her hand in, Maeve expected to find a rootling, but instead, she pulled out the most beautiful crystal she'd seen in her twenty-four years of life. It was soft and smooth. Like the reflection of a rainbow, the crystal was shiny and seemed to glow in every color.

"This gem will prolong your life indefinitely and give you immense strength. With it, you will never experience physical pain again. You don't need to crush it to consume it."

Maeve looked up at Zosia with a confused expression, but Zosia was quick to elaborate:

"Put the crystal on your tongue and let it dissolve into your body."

Maeve hesitated and thought about how she'd promised never to leave Althea. "Could my sister have one too? I don't think I can go on this journey alone."

"I'm afraid Althea has a heart much too pure to ever kill someone. It's best if you keep this information to yourself and go on the journey alone."

"But even if I succeed in killing him, I don't want to live forever without my sister."

"My child. You must understand that creating this treasure has taken time and isn't easily done. Cutting it in half and sharing it between you may work but it may also drain all the magic out of it and that's not a chance I'm willing to take. You'll have to do this alone, Maeve."

Maeve's shoulder sunk as she looked at the shining rootling in her hands.

"I won't force you to accept this quest. Nor will I hide from you how dangerous it is. You're not the first I've sent on this assignment, but I hope you make some smarter choices than the last Earthen..."

"Is murder the only choice? Can't we try reasoning with him?" Maeve suggested.

"That's what the last girl said too; she didn't want immortality, so she went to talk to him."

"What happened?" Maeve asked.

"He turned into a cobra and bit her."

"Did she die?"

"No, it's something much worse." Zosia looked to the ground. "It's a fate I wouldn't wish on anyone, and I hope you will make better choices. The quest won't be easy. Maeve, take some time to think about it before you accept," Zosia said before all the leaves fell to the ground like snowflakes.

Maeve was left in silence but with a thousand questions.

108

Her mind was running fast while she slowly walked back to the cottage. Zosia had given her a chance to prove to herself that she was a good person, and a good person wouldn't think twice about helping others. She felt that she had no choice but to accept Zosia's plea for help. Yet her heart ached at the thought of leaving her sister and aunt and she was afraid that she might fail like the Earthen before her.

Althea was cutting up bread when she saw Maeve walking through the meadow around their cottage. Walking over to the window, she put down her knife and leaned down on the windowsill. "Where are the flowers?"

Maeve looked up at her sister and felt further conflicted. She had forgotten about the red flowers she had gone out to pick for Rose. "I didn't make it that far," she answered in a serious tone.

Sensing something was troubling her sister, Althea hurried outside, bringing with her a scent of baked bread. "What happened? Did you see James again?" Althea asked as she searched for answers on Maeve's face.

Blinking a few times, Maeve stared at her sister. "No. I saw Zosia."

Althea's eyes grew to a size Maeve had never seen them before. "You saw Zosia? How is that possible? She is the earth we walk on and the air we breathe. Zosia isn't a person, Maeve."

"I know. But..." Maeve frowned and explained. "I was searching for the flowers, but then all these leaves from the ground rose and formed the shape of a woman. She spoke to me, Althea."

"What did she say?"

"She gave me this." Maeve lifted her hand and opened it to reveal the beautiful crystal that lay inside. "Zosia wants me... she wants us... to go on a quest,"

109

Maeve spoke slowly. "To do that we'll need the strength this will give us." She looked down at the crystal again and knew that she was lying and going behind Zosia's back. But unlike Zosia, Maeve didn't fully comprehend that it had taken centuries for the crystal to form. She couldn't bear the thought of leaving her sister again and that made her willing to take the chance of sharing the crystal with Althea. On her walk back to the cottage, Maeve had rationalized that she would be doing the world a huge favor, and so she was allowed one selfish decision and that was to go on this quest with Althea by her side.

Walking to the open window she picked up the knife and used it to break the crystal into two halves before giving a part to her sister. "Put it in your mouth and it will dissolve."

"Are you sure this is safe?" Althea asked hesitantly.

"I trust Zosia, don't you?"

"Yes, but I don't understand why she wants us to go on a quest and I don't understand what she wants us to do."

"It's a long story and I'll explain it later." Maeve was hesitant to tell her sister the truth because she knew in her heart that Althea was too much of a pacifist to ever take part in ending another's life. She would tell her the gritty details later.

Nodding her head, Althea lifted her hand with the crystal inside and placed it on her tongue. Maeve did the same and for a moment they stood without speaking.

As the crystals dissolved in their mouths a strange sensation spread in their bodies. The magic seeped into their bloodstreams and gave them a hallucinogenic experience of being sucked down into the earth. Maeve reached out and clung to the windowsill, trying to steady herself as all her senses felt overstimulated and intensified. It was as if the reality around her transformed into a different version, much more vibrant. The thought that she could smell the colors around her was laughable, but Althea experienced the same symptoms and had sunk to sit on the ground, touching the grass with fascination.

For a while, they were consumed by their experience of being one with nature, but eventually, their heartbeats slowed down to normal speed.

"How do you feel?" Maeve asked her sister once she found her voice.

"Incredible. Does everything seem lusher and more colorful to you as well?" Althea asked, shaking her head with a smile and looking down at her body. "That's strange. My scar is gone. How can that be?" Althea examined her hand where a thin scar had been since the age of sixteen.

Maeve was quick to pull up her shirt and see that the massive scar she'd had from being stabbed was healed and there was no trace left to show it was ever there.

"Zosia did say the crystal contained powerful magic, but I didn't know it would heal our scars." Maeve studied her fingers. "I feel strong and have this strange sensation that anything is possible." The sisters beamed at each other with massive smiles, but those smiles quickly disappeared when Tobias the horse came running out of the forest towards them with frantic eyes.

"No!" Maeve breathed in horror as she picked up his message of Rose being in danger.

CHAPTER 11
GOODBYE OLD FRIEND

Throughout the morning Rose had kept to the town square, selling her fruits and vegetables. As always, she kept a low profile and only conversed with those that approached her.

James Lanchester didn't arrive in town to buy anything. Being the biggest landowner in the area, he was the landlord of more than half of the houses in Lerwick. For the most part, he had employees who dealt with collecting rent and taking care of improvements on the houses. But his father had taught him to keep an eye on things and never let his people think they could get away with anything behind his back.

Ever since he was a boy, James had visited Lerwick with his father and learned to always stay on his horse as he rode through the streets of the town. Looking down at the tenants and townspeople reminded them that he was above them in both rank and fortune.

Normally, he would greet people, but today he ignored everyone who stepped aside for him to let his horse pass. He was in a bad mood because he couldn't stop thinking about what had happened in the forest. As far as he was concerned, he had killed Maeve, but when he went back to make sure she was dead, her body had been gone. James was used to confrontations and drama in his life. People often accused him of being heartless when he put out families with young children who couldn't pay their rent. That part didn't concern him much, but his fight with Maeve was troubling because if

112

she was truly a witch, she could be conspiring with the devil himself.

James didn't like the idea that Lucifer might be targeting him to get revenge for his killing Maeve. As his horse reached the market square, he shot a glance around to see the tradesmen selling their products. A woman with curly brown hair pulled back in a braid caught his eye and made him bring his horse to a stop.

It took a mere moment for him to remember where he had seen her before and then he narrowed his eyes. Rose's facial expression was soft and her tone kind as she spoke to a young woman. She looked very different from when she'd caught Maeve and James together, but even without her pale and shocked face, James recognized Rose. He didn't have a talent for remembering names or faces, but he remembered thinking Rose was quite ugly and looked nothing like Maeve. He was angry and embarrassed to think that he'd been fooled by Maeve, who was most likely a hideous hag in real life.

James didn't know that Althea and Rose had saved Maeve after he'd stabbed her, but Maeve had talked about having a sister and an aunt and he suspected that they were witches too. He always took pleasure in squashing his opponents and in this case, it was his civic duty and responsibility to protect people from the devil's servants. Kicking his horse, he got it to move again and steered straight to the church. The local pastor, Mr. Bancroft, had long suspected that the devil had local allies and when James, the most powerful man in the area, came to ask for his help in the matter, he saw it as an opportunity to show everyone that he was a man of bravery and action.

Within an hour, Rose had been detained and confronted with a list of accusations. She denied having anything to do with the death of the hatter's daughter or

113

the sinking of the boat that went missing with two local fishermen. Rose denied being a witch, but James' accusation weighed heavily and quickly convinced the townspeople.

Despite how kind Rose had been to her customers or how hard she'd tried to keep a low profile, she was doomed the moment the first bloodthirsty townsman shouted, "Burn the witch."

Sending a message to Tobias, Rose let the horse know that he needed to run home and warn Althea and Maeve to leave immediately. She was smart enough to understand that they weren't safe in these parts of the country anymore.

By the time Tobias got back to the cottage, he nearly collapsed to the ground in exhaustion.

When Maeve looked into Tobias's tired and fearful eyes, she recognized the faces he'd seen, and her heart felt like someone was squeezing it too tight when she saw James pointing towards Rose in Tobias's memory.

Althea and Maeve didn't follow Rose's warnings to run away. With the new feeling of power running through them from the crystal, they were determined to free Rose from the awful humans detaining her. They ran toward the town as fast as their bare feet could carry them. And yet, it wasn't fast enough.

The smell of smoke assaulted their nostrils as they got close to town and ran through the streets to the square. There, right in the middle, the last of a pyre was still burning, but few people were still around to see it. "You missed it all," a teenage boy told Maeve with a grin that quickly disappeared when he saw the pain on her face.

"What happened?" Althea asked and stopped to stare. Her mind was searching for proof that Rose hadn't been the victim of a witch-burning.

"They caught an ugly witch. Had you come half an hour ago you would have heard her scream and beg for her life."

Althea's hand went to her mouth and her eyes teared up as she stumbled closer to the stake. Her mind couldn't comprehend that the charred pile was what was left of her beloved aunt.

Maeve's shock quickly turned to anger. Spinning around she searched for James, but now that the execution was over, and Rose was dead, he and most of the people had already left.

While Althea fell to her knees and buried her head in her hands, sobbing with grief, Maeve stayed on her feet with a jaw so clenched it might've broken her teeth if she hadn't taken the crystal. She couldn't rip her gaze away from what was left of Rose's dead body and her imagination kept showing her what agony her aunt had gone through. Like boiling water, the fuming bubbles intensified inside of Maeve. Rose wouldn't have gone into the village today if Maeve hadn't wanted to get her locket back from James. He wouldn't have attacked Rose if he hadn't recognized her from the run-in. Silent tears ran down Maeve's cheeks as her inner voice screamed that this was *her fault*. She was the cause of her aunt's death. Rose, the woman she loved like a mother and who loved her back unconditionally.

Maeve's eyes narrowed when she spotted four young men kicking at some of the embers and laughing. Even though Maeve was the reason Rose had insisted on going to town, she wasn't the one who had tied her aunt to a pole and set her on fire. Humans were the essence of evil, and Maeve had reached her limit. They betrayed, they lied, and they murdered for the fun of it. It wasn't fair that Earthens had to flee into the woods for safety, while humans paraded around ruling the world. Fueled with anger Maeve decided that she was done bowing her neck and keeping a low profile. Zosia had chosen her because she had what it took to fight back. Her mother had been cold-hearted, and she would use that part of her to get back at every human who had hurt Rose.

Just like water boiling in a kettle, a loud howl escaped Maeve as she turned toward the teenagers, cursing all humans.

"Get away from her," she ordered them, but they just stared in confusion.

Raising her hands, Maeve instinctively let her fury form balls of fire that she shot from her hands in their direction.

The boys jumped back with a loud outburst of surprise and even Maeve quivered in shock when she saw the size of the fire she had produced with her bare hands.

While some people screamed, others grabbed weapons and pointed fingers. "Another witch!"

Althea, who had been sobbing on the ground, managed to pull herself together. "Maeve, we have to go." She got to her feet and pulled at Maeve's hand. The square that had been sparse with people before suddenly filled up again as screams and sobbing alerted them that something was happening.

"There are two more witches," a woman yelled as she marched in a group towards Maeve, who stood still and ignored Althea trying to pull her away.

"Maeve, come on," Althea sobbed. She had been close to losing her sister once before and now she had lost her beloved aunt.

No matter how much Althea pulled at Maeve, her twin didn't move.

The enormous pressure Maeve had undergone from James' betrayal, her night alone in the forest, and now Rose's execution took away her last shred of empathy for humans. In that moment, as she stood stiff in the marketplace with her nostrils flaring and her sister pulling at her, Maeve became someone else. The naïve and pure part of her that James had once loved withered and died, and so did her hope and faith in the good of life. Everything inside of Maeve's heart turned dark and angry and in a booming voice full of hatred, she shouted, "If you want fire, *that's what I'll give you!*"

Raising both her hands, Maeve sent fireballs flying toward the townspeople. Panicked screams were heard as houses and people caught on fire. Everything was chaos with people running around like headless chickens trying to escape while their homes blazed into flames.

"No, Maeve. Stop!" Althea yelled through her tears. "You're not a murderer."

Maeve turned to her sister and let the screams of the townspeople turn into meaningless noise. "But they are, Althea. Don't you see that we have to stand up for ourselves?"

Wiping her tears from her face, Althea grabbed her sister's hands and looked deep into her eyes. "Not like this. What would Rose say? She taught us to love all and rise above the ignorant."

Maeve pulled her hands back. "That was before they killed her. I'm not letting these evil humans take any more from me."

"Killing them isn't the answer. Can't you see that you are doing the same thing to them as they've done to us? We're better than this," Althea pleaded, and it made Maeve bark out in anger.

"It has to be done."

"We Earthens don't harm humans. We heal and protect," Althea insisted with tears running down her face.

"And who is going to protect *you*, *me*, and all other Earthens if I don't do it!" Maeve exclaimed and looked around at the burning houses.

"That's not how it works, Maeve. Please can we just leave?"

Maeve looked at her sister and a large part of her wanted to flee back to their cottage and never leave the woods again, but too much had been taken from her and she couldn't rest with her broken heart.

"I can't live in the same world as humans. I can't find peace while they rule the world. Help me, Althea. Together we can avenge Rose and make this a world where we don't have to hide."

The light from the flames lit up Althea's face and made the tears in her eyes glisten. "I won't harm them. I can't..."

Maeve found it unfair that Althea was making her feel like a villain when really Maeve was the only one with common sense. Her tone hardened. "Your softness and kindness are your biggest weaknesses, Althea. I should have listened when Zosia warned me that you aren't strong like me. If you won't help me, I'll do it alone."

Turning her back to her sister Maeve looked at the people screaming and crying all around her. All their pain and misery were justified in her mind. They did this to themselves and only got what they deserved. With Maeve continuing to send small balls of fire through the air, the entire town soon stood aflame.

By then Althea had long realized that the crystal had done more than give them strength. It had advanced their abilities to a level she hadn't thought possible. And though Althea loved her twin sister dearly and would've done nearly anything for her, she wouldn't tolerate murdering a town full of people. Using her hands, she killed the fires, strangling the flames until most had disappeared.

With annoyance, Maeve accused her, "You would rather protect the people who killed our aunt than stand by my side?"

"I wouldn't be standing by your side if I let you do something I know you'll regret. This isn't you, Maeve, and I won't let you make this mistake."

Maeve's eyes were crazed when she raised her chin and sneered, "My only mistake was pretending to be someone who I'm not. I was never soft and quiet like you, Althea. I am angry and I am hurt, and I'm done playing nice."

Althea ran after Maeve when she began walking. "So, then what?" Althea shouted over the screams around them. "You'll kill all humans? Is that it?"

Narrowing her eyes, Maeve repeated her words, "I told you that I can't live in the same world as humans."

Althea had put out most of the fires, but the humans still ran around in confusion and panic, with most of them trying to flee.

A small boy who couldn't be more than five was crying and calling out for his mother as he ran past Althea and Maeve. Both twin sisters looked at him but saw something very different. Althea saw a young boy with fright-filled eyes, who was lost and scared in a flock of taller and stronger adults. They pushed him around as they ran through the streets trying to get away. In frightened sobs, he yelled, "Mummy, mummy, mummy."

But Maeve didn't see a small, scared boy, she saw a young version of James. A human that would grow up to lie, betray, and kill harmless women like Rose.

When she set the boy on fire, in her mind Maeve set a part of James on fire, and that felt satisfying to her.

"*Nooo!*" Althea shouted in shock that her sister would do something so cruel. The small boy, who had flames running down his arm, clothes, and legs, screamed at the top of his high-pitched lungs. He wasn't on fire for long before Althea absorbed the flames, but they had already left burn marks that would likely scar his skin for the rest of his life. Running to his side, Althea tried to ease his pain, but she had never tended a burn mark on a human before, and she didn't know where to start, so instead, she shouted out to the crowd trying to find his mother.

The small boy's face was wet from sobbing, and he had snot running from his nose down into his mouth when a man came running with a baby in his arms and picked up the small boy.

"Maeve, stop this insanity." Althea turned to her sister, who was starting fires all around them. When Maeve ignored her, Althea put out the fires once again, only this time Maeve didn't feel like arguing with her sister. She felt utterly betrayed by Althea, and to her, that moment was a breaking point. James had chosen Elizabeth over her and now Althea choosing the townspeople over her felt like the ultimate betrayal. Broken-hearted, Maeve turned cynical with a taste for destruction. She had lost her parents, her aunt, her future with James, and now her twin sister as well. Ignoring the rejection that she felt, Maeve convinced herself she was stronger than any Earthen before her, and she didn't need anyone.

"Stop!" Althea ordered before Maeve reacted in fury by sending a gush of strong wind at Althea, so powerful that it hurled her from one end of the square to the other. Colliding with a wall headfirst, Althea fell to the ground with her skull cracked open and passed out.

Maeve saw how close Althea was to the flames of the burning building but in her deranged state of grief and anger, she no longer felt a bond with her twin. All she saw was yet another person who had rejected and disappointed her. Raising her chin, she shouted, "If you want to protect the people who burned Rose, then you are no better than them. They would burn you as well."

Not even when Althea's dress caught on fire did Maeve try to help. Tears ran down her cheeks as she turned and continued her rampage.

CHAPTER 12
IN THE ASHES

Once Althea opened her eyes again, it took her a moment to catch up to where she was. The smell of smoke, burned wood, and flesh hung in the air but there were no more screams. With a head pounding in pain, she moved slowly as she sat up and looked down at her body. She was naked and covered in the same ashes that lay all around the ground along with large amounts of something sticky that had to be dried blood.

Her lips parted as she remembered how Maeve had thrown her through the air. Above her, the wall she had collided with was gone. Smashing against a wall with that much speed should have killed her instantly, and Althea struggled to understand how she was still alive and where her clothes were.

Carefully, she tried to get up, and that's when she saw a bit of fabric on the ground in the ashes. The pattern was from her dress. Blinking her eyes, she tried to put the pieces of the puzzle together. Her dress had burned, and she had been smashed against a wall. But if her dress had burned, then why didn't she have any burn wounds?

With her hands, she felt her neck and face and it wasn't until her fingers touched her eyebrows that she stopped. There was no hair. It was the same with her eyelashes. Quickly, her hands rose to her scalp and her eyes widened when she realized she was bald.

Pivoting, she stared at the ruins around her. This was the town square, but now that all buildings were burned down, she could see the forest.

No one moved. No birds sang. Everything was black and incinerated.

Althea's logic told her she had burned as well, but except for a headache, she felt no pain. Searching for an explanation, her thoughts brought up the crystal Maeve had given her that was supposed to bring them strength.

Maeve.

Opening her mouth, Althea tried to call for her sister, but it was as if her throat was rusty and dry, and only a croak came out. Moving her legs, she walked stiffly across debris but quickly had to stop when she realized that among the burned buildings were dead people.

Lifting her hands to cover her mouth, she took in the devastation around her. Althea didn't know how long she had been unconscious, but there was nothing left of the small town other than the black ash on the ground and the corpses of the people who had once lived there. With tears of shock and horror, she looked at the hundreds of bodies lying dead on the ground covered by the black ash from their homes.

Althea mourned for the people as she walked through the town, careful not to step on any of the burned corpses. What had become of Maeve? She searched for her among the dead but most of the bodies were burned beyond recognition.

Memories of seeing Maeve burn down the town played in Althea's mind. Never had she imagined that such darkness could lie within her sister.

When she saw the small boy who Maeve had set on fire lying on the ground with dead eyes and his face black from ash, Althea stopped walking and collapsed to her knees in pained sobs. Rose's life had been stolen, and that was something Althea would mourn for the rest of her life, but this boy's life had been stolen too, and so had everyone else's in the town that Maeve had killed.

For twenty-four years, Maeve had been Althea's closest confidante and they had shared the tightest of bonds. Now, that bond had been ripped apart in the most brutal of ways for just like Maeve, Althea had lost everyone she cared about and was all alone in the world. Maeve thought Althea was dead and Althea didn't know if Maeve was alive either.

Rose's death had spiraled the sisters onto different paths. While Maeve wanted to destroy all humans, Althea in return became determined to avoid any more unnecessary suffering and death.

It was a tragic day, one where far too many lives were lost. But it was far from over because Maeve had one more person to add to the list.

CHAPTER 13

CAT GOT YOUR TONGUE?

The contrast between the first time Maeve had approached the Felton Hill Estate and now was like night and day. The first time, she'd been so full of hope for the future and her heart had been full of love for James. Like a young seed, ready to burst through the soil, she had longed to see the sun and grow into a beautiful flower.

Now that her heart was filled with hatred, she was like a withered rose with a stem full of thorns that would hurt anyone who came close.

It had only been a month since she'd last walked up the entranceway of the manor, but it might as well have been years. Back then Maeve had been a curious and loving girl who was light on her feet. Now her steps were full of purpose, and she walked like a predator with her head high and her gaze steady.

Her large, pretty eyes had turned cold, leaving Maeve to appear older, bitter, and cynical.

James didn't see Maeve walking up the long entranceway because he had his back turned, but Maeve saw him through the window. She didn't announce her entrance by knocking on the door. Instead, she let herself in and stood for a moment looking around the quiet home. Everything was stylish and expensive from the grand chandeliers to the portraits on the walls and the murals on the ceiling. The wallpaper had golden hues and every piece of furniture looked like it was a piece of art.

Although Maeve had loved her childhood, she found it utterly unfair that swine like James were lavished with such luxury while innocent Earthens like Rose were driven out of society to live in isolation and poverty. Spending so much time with James had left Maeve with the mindset that materialistic wealth meant success and happiness. She didn't understand that Rose *had* been happy and wasn't hung up on wealth the same way Maeve was.

The sound of a small bell made Maeve look to her left and listen as James yelled in his obnoxious entitled way, "Oh, hurry up with the tea, will you?"

"Yes, sir," a female who was out of sight answered. Maeve didn't pay attention to any of that. She walked to James' study where he sat by the window unaware of how his life would drastically change in mere moments. Maeve had bought into all his lies about them living a privileged life together with fine gowns and jewelry. She had dreamed of attending wonderful balls and living in the finest castle in town. Now those dreams seemed foolish and naïve, making her feel repulsed by the house she stood in. The thought of how living here with James had once been her dream made her taste vomit in her mouth.

Slowly walking past the grand stairs in the entrance area to the door leading to his study, each step creaked under her dirty feet.

Maeve kept her head high and her face emotionless. The hatred in her heart made everything numb inside her. Her facial features had turned cold and distant.

James sat in a chair reading. Next to him stood an empty cup and a plate. Maeve instantly spotted the silver knife on the plate. She was in no hurry to end his life and enjoyed the power she held in that moment as James sat unaware of her watching him.

"About time." James huffed when he sensed Maeve slowly walking toward him, only he thought it was one of his servants bringing him tea and didn't stop reading.

When a cup wasn't placed on his side table, he turned his head to see what incompetent servant he had to lecture and scold. Seeing Maeve behind him, James reacted as if he'd seen a ghost. With his heart skipping a beat and his face turning instantly pale, he jumped out of his chair and took a step back to create distance between himself and the woman he thought he'd murdered.

James stared at her with large eyes and although he tried to speak, he was so puzzled to see her that his sounds were incoherent.

"Cat got your tongue?" Maeve asked, taunting his inability to form a sentence.

"I told you to stay away from me," he finally managed to say. "Your obsession with me isn't charming. Haven't I made it clear that I don't love you?"

"Why did you have Rose killed?" Maeve asked with a steady voice as she imagined all the different ways she wanted to hurt him.

James' eyes darted around the room, and he moved to the left to have the table between them. "She was a witch, just like you. I would have never been enchanted by you if I'd known what you really are," he spat out.

Maeve had intended to tell James how much she hated him and thought he was the worst human of his kind. But the moment he insulted her aunt, she lost all patience and saw red. Slashing her hand through the air, Maeve used her powerful new abilities to make James fly through the room and hit the wall before falling to the floor with pained groans. The old floorboards creaked under Maeve's feet as she slowly walked toward James, who lay on the ground holding onto his ribs and cursing her name.

"Get away from me, you witch, or I'll fucking kill you," he threatened, but Maeve wasn't afraid.

Standing in front of James, she looked down at him and felt like a cat with a mouse under its claws. The moment seemed symbolic compared to the first time they'd met when James had sat high on his horse and looked down at Maeve. Back then he had seen her as easy prey he could devour and use for his gratification. Now the roles were reversed.

Raising her hand, Maeve used the element of air to force his body up against the wall until he was dangling with his feet under him. James didn't understand how she was pressing him against the wall without touching him. To him, it was proof of her dark magic and in a way he was right. Maeve's strength was magical. No Earthen would have ever been able to hold a human up simply by using the element of air. But Maeve had taken the most powerful crystal in the world, and it had left her with a strength beyond that of any Earthen before her.

Now her face was stern and seemed otherwise emotionless, but the pure hatred in her eyes revealed the fire burning in her heart. Locking her jaw, she raised her hand and forcefully struck James across the face. The slap was loud and cathartic. It wasn't merely that this weasel of a man filled her head with lies, stabbed her in her gut, and left her for dead. He had also been the reason Rose had died a horrendous and unjust death. His pathetic whimper didn't soften Maeve. He had shown no mercy toward her and Rose and she would show him none in return. His head swung down to the side and Maeve saw that like a cat with sharp claws, she had left a large red mark across his cheek. Again, Maeve tightened her hand and tossed James across his large study. She took pleasure in every expensive vase and figurine he broke as his body knocked them over and they shattered against the floor. His body slammed against the wall and this time he coughed up blood as he lay on the floor.

With fear in his eyes, he begged, "Please, Maeve. Don't hurt me. I'll do anything!" The usual arrogance in his voice was gone and replaced by a brittle and high-pitched begging for her mercy. Maeve relished the sight of James' humiliation and took her sweet time walking toward him again.

"This can all be yours. We can live here together as we've always dreamed of. You can't kill me! You need me to have this privileged life!"

Maeve didn't answer him, which frightened James all the more. He felt like a small fragile animal that stood no chance against this bloodthirsty predator.

Her face still showed no emotions as Maeve asked, "How does it feel?"

James shook his head signaling that he didn't understand her question.

"How does it feel to be an arrogant and entitled excuse for a man who has never been scared of a woman in his life, to be at my mercy? You've always viewed us, women, as toys to be used for your pleasure, haven't you? How ironic that one of your toys turned out to be more powerful than you."

Like a small, frightened boy, James pleaded with Maeve, "I don't deserve this! Please spare my life, I'll give you *anything*."

Maeve considered his words for a moment and said, "Can you give me my aunt back? Can you give me back the loving, sweet girl I used to be? You took that all away from me, James. But you're right. You don't deserve to die." Her voice was steady, and her eyebrows were arched.

James breathed out in relief and lowered his head. "Thank you."

"You don't deserve the mercy of death. Instead, I want you to live with the knowledge that you will never escape me. You promised me this life, and I will take it, but not today. I'll wait patiently until you have built a life for yourself with a wife and children. Every day, you'll live with the fear that tomorrow could be the day where

I'll show up and kill everyone you love just like you killed my aunt."

James shook his head with moist eyes. "Please don't! I'll give you money to stay away, Maeve. I'll do anything."

Maeve stared down at the broken man lying on the floor and couldn't remember why she had once loved him. "*Anything?*"

He nodded eagerly before spitting out more blood and touching his mouth, revealing that he lost one of his front teeth.

Maeve's slowly spoken words came like whiplashes from her tongue. "*Kiss. My. Dirty. Feet.*"

James swallowed hard but seeing the hardness in her stare, he leaned forward and placed kisses on her bare feet, which were gray from walking on ashes.

"You felt you were too good for me and that I was below your station in life. But when you lie in bed at night, remember this moment with you on the ground kissing *my* feet." Lifting her right foot, she kicked him away, leaving him to violently cough from the taste of ashes in his mouth.

Though James was in severe pain and had several broken ribs from being thrown around, he tried to crawl away to escape Maeve.

He didn't get far before she once again continued to brutally destroy all his fine objects by throwing his body around the room and knocking over his expensive art and artifacts.

Deep inside Maeve, there was a voice that scolded her for inflicting harm upon another, but James had made her feel powerless and with each time she beat him using her abilities, it felt as though that power returned to her.

As Maeve approached James for the last time, he looked up at her with fear shining from his eyes.

"You've taken everything from me," she said without blinking. "My innocence and virginity, my sister, and my aunt." Her fingers dug into her palm at the mention of her aunt whose death she felt guilty for. "You took the happy girl I once was ... and you killed her. In return, I will take something precious from you as well."

James flinched at her words and though he tried to crawl backward, his body was far too weak and damaged.

"You took my bright future and now I'm taking yours. Never will you feel safe in your own house again. I can reach you anywhere and I promise you that I will. One day when you least expect it, I will show up and kill everyone you love."

This was a promise Maeve didn't intend to keep because she didn't plan to live for much longer herself. But she had witnessed Rose living with constant fear and nightmares and knew it was a fate crueler than death.

James was crying now, but Maeve wasn't done.

"And secondly, you have a problem with lying, don't you, James?" She crouched down and leaned close to him looking into his frightened eyes. "I will give you the gift of eliminating that problem."

Reaching for the silver knife that had been on the plate when she first walked in and now lay on the floor, Maeve held it to his face. "I'll help you to never tell a lie again."

It was a brutal moment when Maeve held James down and cut out his tongue.

Two maids had finally gathered the courage to come and investigate their master's screams, but Maeve saw them and slammed the door to the study shut. They were too stunned and scared to run for help, and instead hid in the linen closet.

The excruciating pain of having his tongue cut out with a dull knife would haunt James for the rest of his life, but to Maeve, it seemed like justice well served.

Just as he had done to her in the forest, she left him sprawled on the floor in his blood. When the house was quiet, the maids came out from the closets where they hid to find their master lying unconscious with his tongue on the floor beside him. Despite losing a lot of blood and breaking a shoulder and three ribs that day, James survived. As Maeve had promised him, he never told another lie. Without his tongue, there wasn't much left to say. Her second promise, however, was something that even if she had returned, she wouldn't have been able to live up to. The morbid fear that Maeve would return just as she had promised him drove James mad. Elizabeth's family called off the wedding and with his silver tongue gone and several of his teeth missing, no other young women were eager to take her place. Not even two years after Maeve's attack, James took his own life leaving behind no wife or children.

When Maeve walked away from the beautiful estate that she had once dreamed would be her home, she went straight for the cliffs behind the manor that overlooked the sea.

A gust of wind pulled her hair back as she reached the end of the cliff where few were brave enough to stand. Calling out, she yelled for Zosia to come and talk to her again.

"Why did you let the humans kill Rose? You could have extinguished the fire with rain or sent lightning to strike down all the humans hurting my aunt. Why do you let innocent Earthens get murdered? Why do you tolerate humans treating us this way?"

When nothing happened, Maeve turned to the nearby tree that had grown diagonally to hang out over the cliff side. Most of its orange leaves had been blown

132

away and some lay by its roots on the ground, leaving the tree's gray branches naked. In aggressive movements, Maeve kicked at the leaves on the ground as if she could get them to rise from the ground to form a female shape like they had the last time.

"Zosia, come and talk to me," she demanded with frustration and kept looking around.

The silence felt like yet another rejection and added to Maeve's feeling of loss and despair.

"You chose me because I'm strong enough to kill." Throwing her hands up, Maeve shouted. "Did you see me kill all those people in town? It wouldn't have happened if you had protected Rose. Why do you look on when humans persecute us Earthens? You called us *yours* and yet you do *nothing* to help us." She shouted into the wind with a voice hoarse from yelling.

When Maeve stopped shouting it left only the sound of a few birds chirping in the distance and the sound of waves crashing against the rocks at the bottom of the cliff.

"Zosia!" she screamed from the bottom of her lungs, but still received nothing back.

Ever since Maeve came to live with Rose, she had learned about the greatness and goodness of Zosia, but now all those stories felt rotten and untrue.

"You should have protected Rose!" she accused and spun around searching for any type of sign that Zosia was listening. "You want me to go and kill for you, but I won't," Maeve yelled into the wind.

Refusing to do Zosia's bidding was the only leverage Maeve could think of to get her to come and talk to her, but it still had no effect. Drying away tears with the back of her hands, Maeve felt Zosia's rejection as yet another major betrayal and raged, "You're no better than James. You both just wanted to use me to your advantage. He pushed me to do unspeakable things. I would have never

133

killed all those people if not for him trying to kill me and then executing Rose... and you... you could have stopped it all, but you didn't." A sob burst from Maeve's lungs as she stumbled a few steps to support herself against the tree.

There was too much noise and chaos in her mind. So much had happened in such a short time, and it wasn't until now when she stood still that the pain finally caught up to her. Collapsing against the crooked tree, Maeve closed her eyes and tried to tune out the screams of the people she had burned that echoed in her mind. Falling to her knees, she pressed her forehead against the tree and sobbed. The memories came flashing back showing her the look of disappointment in Althea's eyes. She remembered how scared the townspeople had been in their last moments of life, and no matter how hard Maeve tried to forget it, her mind kept showing her the faces of the children she had killed. There hadn't been much thought behind it when she'd burned a young girl and her mother, other than the fact she wanted everyone else to feel the pain she felt. But now, the young child's fearful eyes burned into Maeve's mind, and she couldn't help but recognize the same fear in the girl's eyes that she herself had felt when she'd seen Ellen be executed. Only this time, Maeve had been the executioner who had taken everything from the little girl. A loud sob of regret escaped Maeve as she remembered seeing the young girl in the arms of her mother attempting to escape the town. They had been running to the forest to escape Maeve, but they never made it very far. Shaking her head, Maeve cried and wished she hadn't followed the mother into the forest and hunted them down to burn them both alive. At that moment, it had seemed righteous, but now all she could hear were the screams of the little girl and her mother, and it burned into Maeve's agony and made her hate herself all the more.

She didn't want to be evil but the more she thought about it, she remembered how the same humans she'd killed had burned her aunt and celebrated her death. Even the little girl who was the essence of innocence and who reminded her of herself when Ellen died, would have one day grown up to be a woman that hurt others just as all humans did.

It was the fault of humans that Maeve was left with no parents, aunt, or sister and no hope for a future either. As an Earthen she was unwanted and unloved. James had made that very clear. Maeve's hands were shaking against the tree as she rose from the ground wanting desperately to leave everything behind and escape the horrible nightmare that she was caught in.

Walking back toward the edge of the tall cliff felt like she had reached the edge of the world. She stood close enough to the edge that if the wind had blown in the opposite direction, she would have been pushed off. Her feet were shaking as she stood for a moment dwelling in her pain. The strong breeze from the ocean hit her high cheekbones and her nostrils expanded as she inhaled the salty air. Bowing her head, she looked down to where the waves crashed against the rocks. Calculating the height, she guessed it to be more than enough to kill a person. It should have frightened her, but in her state of grief, shame, and misery, death beckoned her with promises of peace and a welcome escape from all her pain. And yet, her feet were heavier than her broken heart and wouldn't take the step forward. A tear ran down Maeve's face as she remembered the girl she had been not so long ago. How she had loved to daydream and imagine her bright future. Never had she imagined that her life would end like this.

"Forgive me, Rose. For everything that happened and everything I've done," Maeve whispered in a broken voice.

Taking a last look at the beautiful horizon, she closed her eyes, fisted her hands, and took a deep breath. Maeve stood silent for a long moment in the salty air and thought of her aunt's face smiling down at her, just as she had done when she was a child. Rose had never been a conventional beauty like Maeve was, but Maeve had always found her to be the most beautiful woman, because of her kind eyes and charming smile. With that smile in her mind, Maeve took a step forward into thin air. The world felt quiet when her feet left the ground but as soon as she fell, the vicious noise of the wind attacked her ears and made her long orange hair and the fabric of her dress whip around her. She fell quickly, and a part of her felt sure it was all her pain that weighed her down like a heavy rock.

The thought of her loving, smiling aunt was ripped from her the moment her body broke through the surface of the water. All the air was pushed from her lungs as they collapsed from the speed upon impact. The skeletal damage to her body and internal bleeding from her broken ribs and bones should have killed her. She felt physical pain so excruciating that it numbed her emotional pain and left her unconscious. Maeve sank deep into the dark waters surrounded by rocks. Her eyes, which had once been so full of life, were now closed and her face, which James had once called the prettiest in the world, was marred with suffering. As she drifted further and further down into the dark blue sea she began to wake and became painfully aware that she was still alive. Unable to move a muscle, she lay in the cold water and remembered Zosia's words about the crystal giving her immortality.

As the salty water washed through her lungs, the powers of the crystal ran through her veins and repaired her broken body. When she regained control of her movements, it happened gradually. Her eyes painfully opened to see the quiet and dark ocean around her. But as her body healed itself, her lungs struggled for air and repeatedly made her feel like she was drowning, only for them to heal themselves and beg for air again. When her broken bones were healed and strength returned to her muscles, her hungry lungs begged for air and pushed her to swim toward the light that felt as if it was hundreds of yards away.

When her head burst above the surface, she coughed up water before her lungs gasped for air. Greedily, she inhaled the fresh salty air as she spoiled those organs with deep breaths, but the burden of her wet dress weighed her down making Maeve swallow some of the salty water.

Only now did Maeve realize that in the time she had been down in the dark ocean, her body had drifted out to sea. Looking toward shore, she saw the tall cliff that she had fallen from. Some may have seen such a survival as a miracle, but to Maeve, it was a tragedy. Was she truly imprisoned in a world she wanted no part of, for the rest of eternity?

CHAPTER 14
LEAVING BEHIND BROKEN DREAMS

Althea kept thinking about the version of Maeve that had set fire to a whole village, and she struggled to understand how the sweet Maeve she had known could have been so cruel and bloodthirsty.

They'd grown up the closest of friends and Althea felt she'd known her sister's heart inside and out. That's what made it difficult to encompass the fact that her sister had slaughtered a whole town of people.

Every time Althea closed her eyes, Maeve's twisted face and dark eyes were there to haunt her with the memory of being pushed backward and flying through the air again.

Althea knew that her miraculous survival had something to do with the crystal. It had to be connected because as soon as they let it dissolve on their tongues, they had felt stronger, and once they reached the town their powers had been like nothing they had experienced before. Althea sighed and thought for the hundredth time how everything would have been different if they had made it in time to save Rose.

The thought that Maeve had tried to kill her when she objected to her setting the town on fire still was hard for Althea to come to terms with. But the fact remained that if her body hadn't magically healed itself then her own sister would have been the cause of her death and that knowledge terrified her.

She empathized with Maeve's pain because she too had lost an aunt, but although Althea was a kind and empathetic Earthen who loved her sister, she wasn't sure she could ever forgive her for killing innocent people. For the same reason, Althea didn't go looking for Maeve.

The complete loneliness Althea experienced when she walked naked from the town made her wish over and over that she had Rose to comfort her. She went to the lake and watched the black ashes that had stuck to her body float on the surface around her. Washing her body, she discovered that the stubble of her hair was already back and by the time she returned to the cottage her eyebrows were back to normal.

Stepping inside the cottage that Althea had called home for almost nineteen years, she suddenly found the vibrant colors dull and gray. She found a clean dress and put it on while listening to the birds that lived in the trees outside. Today their chirping had a sadness to it like the melody of a melancholy song.

Unsure of what to do, Althea stayed in the cottage for weeks. Without her aunt and sister, the place no longer felt like home. All the memories that lived there couldn't fill the absence of laughter, hugs, and shared meals. It was a strange time in Althea's life where days and nights blurred together in moments of deep despair mixed with trivial chores that were required to keep herself and Tobias alive.

Sometimes, she would find herself lost in thoughts while digging up carrots or weeding the garden. Looking around, she still expected to see Maeve or Rose, but then she remembered everything, and a new wave of despair washed over her.

Rose would never return, and Maeve had lost her mind. The more Althea thought about what questions she would ask her sister if she returned, the more she realized she didn't care about the answers. No apology or remorseful look could change that Maeve had murdered hundreds of people in a fit of uncontrolled rage. And if not for the crystal, Althea would have met the same fate as them. Over the weeks of solitude, Althea's initial empathy for her sister's mental breakdown transformed into her blaming Maeve for their aunt's death. If Maeve hadn't lied and acted the way she did, Rose wouldn't have gone into town that day, and she wouldn't have died.

Unlike Maeve, Althea had been happy with their simple lifestyle. But due to Maeve's selfishness, she had lost everything. Eventually, Althea reached anger in her grief and concluded that she didn't want her sister to return home. It was clear to her now that all her pain pointed back to the person she'd once loved more than anything.

By the sixth week, it became too difficult for Althea to stay in the cottage. It was simply too painful to sleep alone in her and Maeve's bed, smelling the scent of her aunt around the house, and living one more meaningless day after the next, always hoping Rose would walk through the door and hug her and always being disappointed when she didn't.

She fantasized about finding other Earthens with whom she could start a new life, but she had no idea where to search.

It was with a hammering heart and shaking hands that Althea finally packed her few possessions and led Tobias away from her childhood home.

They walked in a random direction and after half a day, they reached a large village. Just standing close enough to see people walking by and riding horses reminded her painfully of Lerwick, the town where her life had changed so drastically six weeks ago. She was sure that once they spotted her standing next to Tobias with a pale face, they would bring out their torches and burn her like they did Rose. Suddenly moving a foot seemed as hard as moving a mountain.

She thought back to the time she and Maeve had convinced Rose to bring them with her to town. The twins had been fourteen years old, and more than excited and curious to see humans up close. Now seeing humans created a pressure in her chest that made it hard to breathe.

Despite Althea's desperation to flee, she stood paralyzed with wet eyes. Tobias sensed her beating heart and nuzzled his head against her chest trying to calm her panic attack. It helped her and after a few deep breaths of air, she stroked his head and whispered, "Come on." Together they hurried back toward the forest while Althea had tears running down her cheeks.

Tobias watched with his kind and gentle eyes as Althea walked over to a tree and placed her hands on it. Leaning her head back she looked up at the leaves that were starting to change color and fall to the ground now that it was October.

"Zosia, I beg for your help," Althea whispered to the old tree. "I need to know if there are other Earthens like me left. And if there are, please will you help me find them? I won't go close to humans... I can't... but I need some guidance to find where the healers are."

Althea stood in silence hoping that Zosia would show herself just like she'd done with Maeve and in the myths that Althea had heard about so many times before.

She gasped in wonder when the leaves began to lift from the ground and fly around Althea's body. Taking a step back from the tree she stared at the leaves. Just as Zosia had done with Maeve, she whispered through the wind. It was startling to Althea to hear a soft and melodic voice echoing in the air. As Zosia spoke it sounded like her voice was far away yet also just beside Althea's ear.

"Follow the leaves," she whispered.

Althea looked to the few leaves that were still dancing around her body. As if they took Zosia's words as a cue they blew through the air and guided Althea through the woods.

For hours, Althea and Tobias followed the leaves that danced elegantly in the wind. Only the last rays of the sun were left when the leaves finally fell to the ground. Standing on a dirt road in the middle of nowhere, Althea spun and turned but saw no one.

Tobias was as tired as she was, but he still kept going a little further and across a small hill they met a peculiar sight. A woman sat on the side of the road with the head of a horse in her lap. The large animal lay on its side with closed eyes, and nearby stood an old, rickety-looking enclosed wagon. Althea stared at the woman that the leaves had guided her towards. Her hair was blonde, and her long blue dress looked dusty and worn. With her head leaned down over the horse, the woman didn't see Althea and Tobias at first.

Although Althea had asked for Zosia's guidance to find an Earthen, she kept a safe distance from the woman as she carefully approached her. Based on first looks it was impossible to spot the difference between a human and an Earthen.

"Is your horse sick?" Althea asked softly, but it still startled the grieving woman, who looked to be in her thirties.

Looking up, she dried her eyes and answered, "I'm afraid old Brendan gave up. He died in my arms."

Not sure what to do, Althea watched the woman closely and prepared herself to run if she showed any sign of danger.

With wet eyes, the woman gently put the horse's head down to rest and rose to her feet.

"My name is Annabel, miss. Can I help ye?"

Althea stayed at a distance. "You speak..." She frowned but didn't finish her sentence. Annabel still understood and answered anyway.

"My accent is Scottish. It's not so common in these parts, but surely ye've heard it before."

Althea had never met a person from Scotland and shook her head. She tried to sense the woman's energy and picked up on a guardedness. It seemed they were both trying to determine if the other was a danger.

Dry-washing her hands with nervous energy, Althea opened her mouth to speak but closed it again before she pushed herself to take a chance. "Are you an Earthen?"

Annabel was quiet for a long moment, but then she admitted, "Yes, I am."

The relief in Althea's heart showed on her face. "Me too." Slowly Althea moved closer to the dead horse. Squatting down, she rested a hand on its still body. "What happened?"

"Brendan lived a long life. Longer than I thought possible, but we've known for a while that his time was coming. We've been best friends for more than ten years and I'll miss him every day." With warmth in her gaze, Annabel stroked the horse lovingly.

Althea sympathized. "I know what it feels like to lose someone you care about and I'm terribly sorry for your loss."

Looking up at her with furrowed eyebrows and sad eyes, Annabel sighed. "Brendan was more than my best friend. I also depended on him for traveling."

"Well, where do you need to go? I'm sure we can help you." Althea gestured toward Tobias, who was grazing on the side of the road.

"I'm always traveling. With the dangerous times we live in, I wouldn't dare settle down, but I don't want to hide either like so many other Earthens. Brendan and I have been traveling throughout England, Wales, and

Scotland for the last decade. That way I've been able to heal humans without staying long enough for them to grow suspicious." Annabel looked toward her small, enclosed wagon that Brendan had been pulling on the trail until his legs had given out and Annabel took him over to the soft moss where he'd closed his eyes for the last time.

"Maybe we can help each other then. I left my home after I lost my family and I asked Zosia to help me find other Earthens so that I wouldn't be alone. Tobias is strong and if we ask him nicely, he might not mind dragging the wagon."

Swinging her long blonde hair to one side, Annabel reached out with a warm, maternal expression on her face and placed a hand on top of Althea's. "I understand loneliness and I'm glad you and Tobias found me. I would gladly accept if you would like to tag along with me for a while."

For a long moment, the two women smiled at each other, exchanging a feeling of relief, and understanding that they had both suffered greatly in their lives.

"Come, let me show you my humble home," Annabel said and led Althea to the wagon. It was small and there was barely room for her bed let alone all the herbs and jars she had inside.

"It'll be cramped, but we'll make it work," Annabel said with optimism.

With the night already upon them, they agreed to camp for the night. "Aren't you scared they'll accuse you of witchcraft?" Althea asked as they sat admiring the stars in the sky.

"I wouldn't be living on the road if I weren't afraid," Annabel answered honestly in her Scottish accent.

"I sometimes wonder why Earthens help humans at all. They seem so evil, and they've taken everyone I love."

Annabel gently placed her hand on Althea's back. "I'm sorry for your loss and I empathize with your pain. They've taken much from me too. I left my home village in Scotland after the humans came for my brother."

Althea looked at Annabel, whose face was lit up by the bright moon and the flames of the fire in front of her. "Then why do you heal them? Don't you hate humans?"

"I think it's in our nature to heal and help those in need. And despite the pain they've caused me, I don't hate humans. They too are scared, and their heads are filled with lies and fear. They only do what they think is best, just like everyone else."

Althea sighed. "Sometimes I just wonder if my sister was right. Maybe our kindness is worth nothing when they can't even appreciate it."

Annabel thought about Althea's words for a long moment before she spoke in a compassionate tone, "Did you know that without bees, all of the beautiful nature around us would die?"

"My aunt, Rose, always had great respect for bees and told us we had them to thank for our flowers."

"She was right. Not only do they make flowers beautiful, but without bees, most plants couldn't grow or reproduce. And without plants, slowly animals would die too. Without a small bee, the big bears wouldn't survive, and neither would the rest of us."

Leaning her head back, Althea watched the star-filled sky with thoughtful eyes for a moment. She had known bees were important but not that nature was so dependent on them.

"Our work is not meaningless just because humans do not value it. Bees are often knocked away or stepped on by humans, but that doesn't stop the rest of them from pollinating flowers and bringing life to all. They don't let the ignorant bring destruction to the world. So why should we?" Annabel asked and it gave Althea a deep sense of peace inside.

"I don't have your wisdom and tolerance," Althea spoke in a soft tone and stared into the flames of the small fire they had built to make some oatcakes. "When I saw the humans walking around in town today, I panicked and all I wanted to do was run, yet I couldn't. I don't know how I will ever be able to go near humans again after what happened. And even if I do, my aunt only taught me how to heal animals and plants, not humans."

Annabel took Althea's hand and it instantly made Althea relax. "With me by your side, you'll meet many different humans and learn that some are kind and appreciative. I know it's scary after what you've been through, but we'll take it one day at a time."

"Have you met other Earthens?"

Annabel nodded. "I have. They are rare, but some manage to blend in among the humans and others travel like me."

It felt so wonderful to feel Annabel's warmth and friendship that Althea squeezed her hand and smiled. "You mean others travel like *us*."

CHAPTER 15
BEHEADED AND BURIED

Maeve's first attempt at ending her life had failed. Unwilling to give up and accept that her body would heal itself no matter how she died, she was forced to think of an alternative.

Rose had spoken of Abingdon where they grew up enough times that Maeve remembered the name of the village. Asking tradespeople on her way, they led her in the right direction until she arrived one early evening as the sun was about to set.

Memories from when she was five brought her down Bakers' Street where she had once lived. Both Rose and Zosia had pointed out how similar she was to her mother and seeking out her family might bring her answers. Maeve longed to understand why she was so different from her sister who never strayed far.

The smell of baked goods brought back early childhood memories, but once again it was as if every straw Maeve grabbed for disappeared before she could hold on. Her family had moved away more than seven years ago. From the hushed voices of the people she asked, she gathered that the circumstances hadn't been good.

"Ah, Anne was never herself after that awful fire. She blamed John for the death of their two young daughters. Never regained her joyful nature after that," an older woman told Maeve. For hours, she walked around remembering things from her past while trying to decide what to do with herself now that her hope of reuniting with her family had burst.

That's when she spotted a man she would never forget. He was aged, but she would have recognized Ellen's executioner anywhere.

His large back was a bit hunched now and his strong arms looked veined, but his crooked nose and close-set eyes remained the same. Maeve kept close enough to follow his steps and noticed that no one greeted him as he walked through the streets.

When he entered a house with a cracked window, Maeve considered the crazy idea that had entered her mind for about ten minutes before she knocked on the door. Swinging the door open, the man had an annoyed expression on his face as he looked down at Maeve. "What do you need?"

"You are the executioner, yes?" she asked.

He grunted and nodded.

"Good, then you can help me."

The large man looked over his shoulder. Peeking around his large frame, Maeve saw his family eating supper inside. "Sorry, ma'am, I'm off duty, can't help ya." He began to close the door when Maeve stopped it abruptly and dropped the small bag of money in his hands. She wasn't sure how much money the coins were worth, but she had stolen them and hoped it was enough.

The large man stepped out of his humble home and closed the door behind him. "What do you want?" he asked with impatience.

"I want you to murder me," Maeve informed him with a straight face.

"You?" he asked with a frown. "Why would ya want that?"

"That's my business," she replied dryly.

"Alright, but couldn't ya just do it yourself?" The large man looked down at Maeve, struggling to read her cold attitude.

"No, because I need you to dispose of my body."

Scratching his neck, he looked up and down the street before muttering, "What'd ya mean?"

"Cut my head off and bury it as far away from my body as you can."

The man's eyebrows rose, and his mouth fell open as he stared at her in utter shock. He liked to think of himself as a good man of God who served the law, by executing those that deserved to go to hell. If Maeve had come to him five years prior, he would have sent her away without a second thought, but times were tough, and his wife was now pregnant for the eleventh time. With a last look over his shoulder, the executioner accepted the job. "If you're serious, I'll do it. Can it wait until I had my dinner?"

"No. I want to have it over with now."

The executioner's shoulders rose and sank as he sighed. "Fine. Meet me by the old mill outside town. I don't want anyone seeing us together."

With Ellen having been the old miller's daughter, Maeve found it ironic that the executioner who had killed her asked to meet at the mill. But she did as he requested and once they were outside town, he led her deep into the woods.

"This will do," he concluded after a while and put down the lantern and the sack he carried with him.

For a moment, Maeve and the executioner stood watching each other until he pointed to a fallen log. Pulling out his ax, he instructed her, "It's easiest if you sit on your knees, place your hands behind your back, and put your head on that log. If you hold still, I promise to make it a clean cut."

Maeve sank to her knees and positioned her head on the log as he had instructed. Closing her eyes, she thought of how peaceful everything would be in just a moment.

She heard the large man positioning his feet on either side of the log and raising his arms. Once, she had seen this man as a monster when he hanged Ellen, but today she would take his help to end her misery. The quick and sharp cut of the ax startled the birds in the trees, making them take flight.

Some hours later, Maeve opened her eyes and found herself surrounded by darkness. Though the dirt she was buried in felt suffocating, she was far from dead. To Maeve, it felt like centuries before she managed to dig her way out of the ground. Her dirty brown hands clawed their way up for air. Maeve's hair and skin had turned brown from the dirt she'd been buried in, and the worst part was that the executioner had stolen her dress and shoes, leaving her stark naked. It was late into the night, and she was left confused and furious that her plan hadn't worked. Her body had healed itself and clearly that dimwit of a man hadn't followed her instructions of splitting her head from her body. It left her furious and thirsty for revenge.

With dirt covering her body, Maeve marched out from the deep woods. It was a dark and windy night as she passed the church and headed straight for the executioner's house. Other than the wind that gusted against the closed doors in the village, everything was quiet, as every human lay in their beds deep in sleep. That was a good thing because if a human *had* been awake to see Maeve marching through the village completely naked with something close to steam coming out of her ears and flames burning from her eyes, they surely would have screamed in fright. Maeve could easily be mistaken for a demon who had ascended straight from hell. Her hair was tangled with mud making it stick to her skin and fall down in dull and brown locks. Her body was stained from the dirt she had been buried in, but the scariest part was the look in her eyes. If anyone had seen the all-consuming rage in Maeve's eyes, they would have pushed themselves against the wall and prayed for divine protection.

Unlike the first time Maeve came to the executioner's house she didn't knock on his door. It was partly because she knew he'd be asleep and didn't want to wait for him to get up and secondly because she knew he wouldn't open the door to her. Taking a step back she used her powers to melt the lock in the door and quietly entered the home of the sleeping family. The night sky was black, and no candles were lit, so even if the executioner or his wife had been awake, they wouldn't have seen Maeve skulking towards their bed because she was darker than the shadows with the dirt that covered her body.

The executioner kept a sharp blade hidden under his bed knowing that because of his job he had certain enemies who wanted to see him dead. Having the knife within his reach gave him the comfort of sleep. Maeve's eyes had long ago adjusted to the darkness of the night, and with the light of the moon shining towards the bed, it wasn't difficult to spot what the shining thing was.

The knife made a sliding sound when Maeve pulled it out from under the bed, but the sound wasn't loud enough to wake the snoring man or his wife who lay beside him.

"I *hate* humans," Maeve whispered as she pressed the sharp knife against the large man's throat. She considered slicing his throat before he got a chance to speak, but when he opened his eyes and fear rapidly spread in them, she wanted to enjoy his terror.

"I told you to separate my head and body," Maeve hissed, her eyes crazy.

"I-I-I did," he stuttered with sweat forming on his forehead and throat where the blade lightly pressed.

"Liar," she snarled with a clenched jaw.

"A-Are y-y-ya a ghost?" he asked with his chest rapidly moving up and down.

His wife, who lay beside him, gasped when she opened her eyes to see what looked like a demon to her. A shriek escaped her shivering lips as her gaze fell to the knife that was pressing against her husband's throat.

With her motherly instincts warning her to protect her large pregnant belly, she leaped out of bed and clamped her body to the wall in fear.

"If I were a ghost, would I be able to press this knife to your clammy throat?" Maeve whispered.

The executioner made a throaty sound as sweat ran down his face making it look like he was crying. "I swear I did as ya said. I buried your body where I killed ya and yer head in the forest past the church."

His wife, who stood pressed against the wall, tried to stifle her sobs with her hand, but it was no use.

Maeve stared down at the man and though she knew better than to trust the word of a human, he seemed sincere. In the end, Maeve decided it was better to know with certainty than to kill him right now out of anger.

"Prove it." She pressed the knife deeper into his skin until it cut through the flesh and made a small dot of blood form around the blade. "And if you're lying, I'll kill your wife and children in front of your eyes before I kill you."

As soon as Maeve removed the knife, he hurried out of bed giving his wife a terrified glance.

"Before we go." Maeve raised her blade and pointed toward the scared woman in the corner. "I need clothes."

When the woman received a "do as she says" look from her husband she hurried to her dresser where she pulled out the first dress her shaking hands touched. It was a small gown of cheap fabric, something one might wear to bed or under a dress, but it would do the job of covering Maeve's naked body.

When Maeve left with her husband the woman knelt by the bed and tried to pray, but that soon turned into more crying.

No words were exchanged as they walked through the sleeping village that would soon be waking. The executioner couldn't make sense of how this strange woman had come back from the dead. And as they walked, he was deep in his thoughts. He did not know about Maeve's powers, and being twice her size, he felt confident that he could easily win a battle between them. But though he worked as an executioner, he saw himself as a pacifist – as ironic as that might be. In his mind he brought justice and served the God he prayed to every day. Killing Maeve in the forest had not been a noble act, however, and in his heart and mind, he knew that Maeve's survival was an act of God. Thoughts spiraled through his head; would God see that he had tried to bring peace to a suffering soul and brought home money to help his family, or would he be eternally punished in the depths of hell for killing out from under the name of God and the law?

"We're here," he whispered when they'd reached the place where less than twelve hours ago he had chopped off Maeve's head.

"Dig," Maeve instructed.

Not having a shovel, the man got down to his knees and began to dig with his bare hands. By the time he'd gotten deep into the grave, the sun was starting to rise making it easier to see down the dark hole.

When the executioner gasped and flew back, Maeve showed no mercy. "Keep digging," she said.

His whole body was shaking as he kept removing dirt from the ground until it was clear as day that a headless body lay beneath his hands. Maeve looked down at the body, which she recognized instantly as her own. Her gaze was intense, and her throat was tight.

The executioner had told the truth; he had buried her head and body in separate graves. Yet here she was, alive and looking down at her *old* body lying headless in a grave.

Maeve raised her hands and stared down at them. They looked as they always had, only these were not the same hands she had stared down at yesterday. The answer was clear and felt ruinous. There was no way for Maeve to die because even if her head was ripped apart from her body, she would survive.

Although it was difficult to admit – she knew her head had grown a *new* body.

"I told you." The executioner hurried to his feet and away from the dirty headless corpse. "I did as you said."

Maeve couldn't handle the knowledge that she was forced to live forever. She felt mad about Zosia trapping her in her body for eternity. Why hadn't she stopped to question what that meant before taking that stupid crystal?

In a haze of despair, she felt the need to destroy and tear down everything around her. Unfortunately for the executioner, he was in the wrong place at the wrong time.

Maeve didn't speak or touch him as she used her powers to let the soil swallow him into the ground next to her headless corpse. The large man screamed and clawed at the ground to keep from going under, but when it didn't help, he prayed for mercy.

"Please, I have a wife and children. They need me."

Squatting down in front of him, Maeve looked into his eyes. "Remember Ellen? She never got to have children before you hanged her from a tree."

154

"I don't know anyone called Ellen," he cried with his head now the only part of his body above ground.

"No, I suppose you've killed too many innocent women for witchery to remember all their names." Tilting her head, Maeve asked, "Do they haunt you? I mean, do you suffer from nightmares or feel disgusted by yourself when you think of their frightened faces begging you for mercy?"

The executioner's nostrils flared as he tried to breathe. His head was turned upward and as dirt got close to his eyes, he closed them.

"I wish I could die and never feel pain again. But it is a gift taken from me and yet mine to bestow upon others."

"Please." It was the last word he said before his face disappeared into the ground.

Standing up, Maeve looked around. It was dawn now and the morning dew covered the layer of moss around her. She didn't bother disguising where he was buried. It seemed merciful to his family to make it easy for them to find his dead body. She was right of course. Before sunset that day, he was found and later buried by the church, where his wife and children often visited him.

For Maeve, however, there was no peaceful ending. That evening she sat by a lake watching the last rays of the sun caressing the surface of the water.

Misery is a demanding companion that will only stay suppressed for so long. Eventually, the agony of your soul rises to find a way out. Holding back the feelings is futile because trapped inside you, the emotions will gnaw at your intestines like pesky rodents with the voices of those that hurt you in the past. Maeve's rodents taunted her with the immense betrayal she had experienced from all the people she had loved in her life. And then there was the incomprehensible pain she had caused others. She tried telling her haunting inner voices that her intentions had been good, but they mocked her for getting so utterly lost altogether. With her heart shattered into a million pieces, and her mind drowning in misery and pain, she desperately longed for peace. She wanted to escape the excruciating pain in her stomach and the cruel voices in her head, but with death out of her reach, the only option she had was to distract herself. Looking down at her dirty hands once again, she hated them for growing back. With a steady gaze, she took a deep breath before setting fire to her left hand and watching it burn. The pain was just as intense as it would be for anyone else, but to Maeve, it also brought a sense of relief because in that all-consuming pain there was a complete focus that liberated her from her broken heart and inner demons. Her eyes were wet with tears and her lips quivered as the flames on her hand warmed her face.

As if the fire could somehow cleanse her soul of the pain she had caused, Maeve rose to her feet and used her palm to set the rest of her body on fire. Her arms, chest, and neck were all covered in burn marks and flames as she walked out into the soothing water.

The dirt was smeared into the water leaving her burnt skin as she walked out into the lake until her body was under water and the flames were extinguished. Spreading her arms and legs she swam to the middle of the lake where the golden evening sun was shining through the trees and onto her body, which had already healed itself of all the burns.

Maybe if Maeve had found the humility and strength within herself to find her sister and make amends her life would've taken a different course. But like so many other survivors of great tragedies, Maeve became bitter and cynical. Stuck in a victim's mental attitude, she could only see darkness and hatred, and in that way, she became her own worst enemy.

As she swam back toward the shore and slowly walked out of the lake, her legs felt too heavy to drag through the water and she was too tired to let out the scream of frustration that filled her chest. Falling to the ground, she couldn't even muster the energy to cry although on the inside she was sobbing. Maeve's inner world was inflamed, and her demons were back to poke their fingers into her sore and infected mental wounds. But on the outside, her face remained numb and cold and only a single tear escaped her dead eyes.

Slowly she let go of her plan of killing herself and replaced it with another ambition. "If I'm forced to live in the same world as humans, then I'll do it on my terms," she whispered in a raspy voice. Her thoughts were too foggy to think of anything that could make her happy, but at least she knew that she wouldn't tolerate seeing others display their joy. She would make sure that the evil humans were as miserable as she was.

As she looked toward the last rays of sunshine for the day warming the trees, other dreams took shape. She dreamt of killing Zosia. Oh, the satisfaction it would bring her to destroy the creature that had ruined her life. But with Zosia having no physical body that was impossible. Maybe setting fire to the forest around her would hurt Zosia, but Maeve knew that the trees would regrow because nothing was stronger than the will of Mother Nature. There was nothing she could do to get her revenge on Zosia – she was the earth itself, and no one could compare or compete with her. But as Maeve's angry mind spiraled, she thought of the one creature on Earth that Zosia viewed as a threat. The man Zosia had sent Maeve to kill.

If I'm cursed with immortality, then he can't kill me, she thought as she rose from the ground and set out to find the Cobra.

CHAPTER 16

THE CHARMING MAN

Althea and Annabel walked down the narrow staircase in the smoke-filled inn. The wooden steps showed signs of decades of use and felt uneven to step on.

"How did it go?" the barman asked them with a look of concern.

"Your wife is resting now, but she took well to our healing," Annabel said and held a hand to the wall for support as she descended the last step.

The barman raised his gaze as if he could look through the ceiling to his bedridden wife upstairs. "Will she be all right?"

"Aye." Annabel gave him a comforting smile. "We've given her some salves to use for the back pain but it's a matter of too much hard work from too early an age. Her body is worn down and she needs a rest."

"But what about the guests? I cannot do all the work myself." He dried his hands on a rag and threw it to the counter.

"Oi, barman, can we have another round over here?" someone called from the bar in a tipsy voice followed by his friends loudly agreeing.

Althea, who had been behind Annabel, now stood beside her, looking around the room. There were tables and wooden benches under the six paned windows toward the front of the room. The windows looked smudgy and in desperate need of a cleaning. One of the windows stood open, letting some much-needed fresh air into the dusty, dark room that had a smell of tobacco, sweat, and beer.

Looking through the open window, Althea saw the muddy road and the stable where Tobias waited for them. "I'm coming," the barman shouted to his customer and muttered to the two healers, "Let me get ye some food and drink as we agreed on."

The room wasn't big and out of the nine tables that were spread out, only two were occupied by guests. The rest of the patrons stood at the bar. Annabel chose a table in the corner with privacy. Dusting crumbs off the chairs, she sat down with a sigh and gave her friend a tired smile. It didn't take long before the Innkeeper called out to them and pointed to two plates on the counter.

Annabel was just about to stand when Althea placed her hand atop her wrist and softly said, "It's alright, I'll get it, you stay here and rest."

Annabel nodded with a soft gaze. It had been a difficult few days with little rest for either of them and without a magical crystal running through Annabel's body, she was much more exhausted than Althea. Annabel leaned her head back and closed her tired eyes, which had dark circles under them from too little sleep.

When Althea rose to fetch the food, she felt all eyes on her from the seven people standing at the bar. One of them seemed to be the center of attention as he made two women and a man laugh but when Althea approached the bar, he shifted his attention to her. With a charming smile, he walked over to stand close enough for her to hear him and said, "I hear you're a healer."

Remembering what Annabel had tried to teach her about interacting with humans, Althea steadied her nerves, suppressed her fear, and looked into his dark brown eyes.

He was tall enough that she had to lean her head back, and with his symmetrical features, strong jawline, and defined eyebrows he could only be described as handsome. The strangest calmness fell over her and for a moment she lacked words. Unlike most humans she had met, this man's energy wasn't fast or stressful. Nor was it as loving and melodic as an Earthen's energy. It was like nothing she had ever experienced, and the closest comparison Althea could think of was the slow and steady energy of an oak tree without a care in the world.

"You're speechless. I would like to say that I have that effect on women, but I'm afraid that's rarely the case." He grinned and leaned closer with a spark of humor in his eyes. "I assure you I'm not as dangerous as I look. I rarely bite… unless, of course, you want me to."

"Ehm…" Blinking her eyes, Althea finally managed to answer. "Yes. No. I mean, yes, I'm the healer, but no, I don't…" She trailed off unable to remember what she had been saying. Her gaze had gone to his mouth as she thought about his offer to bite her. It had seemed like an invitation to something sexual, but having no experience in flirting, she couldn't be sure. During these past weeks that she had traveled with Annabel, Althea had seen hundreds of people, but with the intense sparkle in his captivating eyes and his strong physique, this man stood out.

Lowering his voice to almost a whisper, he let her know, "I could use a healer."

Althea angled her head and looked him over. She didn't pick up on any sickness but asked, "Are you in pain, sir?"

The man placed a hand on his chest, and his lips and eyebrows drooped as he said, "Not physically, but emotionally. I feel lonely, and could use your help."

Althea lowered her voice, "I'm not sure how I could help with that. I only heal physical pain," she explained.

"I think you could help me better than anyone else. I've heard healers have a magical touch, and I know I would feel a lot better if you and I went upstairs and you healed me with your magic." There was mirth in his tone, but Althea still picked up on his intentions and flushed crimson. Widening her eyes, she gave a breathy "Oh."

"Ah, come now, a stunning woman like you must be used to male attention. There's no need to look so shocked," he said with another charming smile that revealed his perfect teeth.

"You find me stunning?" Despite Althea's fear of humans, she found herself leaning a bit closer to him.

Their eyes were locked, and it was as if she knew that hugging this man would feel as safe as hugging an old tree.

There was a small narrowing of his eyebrows, as her surprise at his compliment was unexpected. Angling his head, he watched her for a second trying to decide if her question was genuinely as sincere as it had sounded.

"Hasn't anyone told you how beautiful you are?"

The innocent widening of her eyes told him no. For a long second, he stood fascinated with this fairy-like creature whose freckles danced across her cute nose and whose multi-colored eyes contrasted with her thick, flaming red hair.

Althea didn't answer his question, but he was unwilling to let the conversion die, so he was quick to open his mouth again and introduce himself. "I'm Damon."

She looked at his right hand that he held up. She had seen this greeting ritual between men and women, but it still felt forbidden when she placed her hand in his.

With an extended gaze into her eyes, Damon bowed down and kissed the back of her hand. "I'm delighted to meet you, Miss..."

"Althea. My name is Althea."

For a short moment, they stood with him holding her hand and the two of them studying each other intensely. His energy was intoxicating like the forest after a thunderstorm, and although her heart hammered in her chest, she felt calm at the same time.

Annabel's voice broke their connection. "Do you need help with the plates, dear? I'm famished."

Gathering her wits, Althea pulled her hand back and gave Annabel an apologetic look. But her friend was looking at Damon and not her. The most peculiar feeling of competition hit Althea right in her solar plexus. The charming man had just called her stunning and beautiful and she had enjoyed his attention.

Annabel, however, didn't seem like her usual warm personality around him. She exchanged one long glance with the handsome stranger and then she sidestepped so as to create distance from him.

Picking up her plate and glass of ale, she gestured for Althea to do the same before herding her to their table. Althea couldn't help looking back in the direction of Damon at the bar and found him watching her as well.

"Don't look at him." Annabel's warning came as she sat with her head down, picking up a spoon. "Eat your food as fast as you can without looking suspicious. As soon as he's distracted, we're leaving."

Althea leaned forward and lowered her head. "Why, what's wrong?"

"I'll tell you as soon as we're outside. Now eat, Althea."

The two women ate quickly and without any further talk. Despite Annabel's warning, Althea couldn't help a few glances in Damon's direction.

He was back to talking to other patrons at the bar but whenever she sneaked a peek, he seemed to sense it and met her glance.

When another tall man walked in and greeted Damon with a manly slap on the back. Annabel froze with her spoon in mid-air.

It made Althea study the man, who had a generous amount of black hair with a dusting of silver giving away that he had to be at least ten years older than Damon. The newcomer was dressed in leather and when he removed his jacket, she could see how fit he was.

Annabel muttered a low "We need to leave, *now*."

Not understanding what was going on, Althea followed Annabel while soaking up any details she could about the two men who made her friend uncomfortable. Where Damon was handsome in a classical way, his friend was rugged with a scar running up his neck that stopped by his jawline. He had a small silver hammer around his neck and now that he was rolling up his sleeves, Althea saw two tattoos: a wolf on the inside and a raven on the outside of his left forearm.

Annabel and Althea were almost by the door when Damon addressed them. "Ladies, you can't leave this soon. I was just about to introduce you to my friend, Mr. Thomas Hechmann."

Annabel didn't stop to talk. Opening the door, she pushed Althea out and gave a quick curtsy to the men without uttering a word.

Sensing the panicky energy in Annabel, Althea made sure to keep up with her fast pace as they hurried to the stable and fetched Tobias.

They worked together to hitch him to the wagon, while Annabel sent worried glances back at the inn.

"Don't look," she whispered, but of course that made Althea turn her head and see the two men watching them through the open window. Their facial expressions were serious now and she was dying to know who they were.

When Tobias was all set, Annabel climbed up to sit on the wagon and offered her hand to pull Althea up.

"Why are we running away? Did you know those men?" Althea asked as she settled into the narrow seat next to her protective friend.

"They aren't men," Annabel muttered and gave the command for Tobias to move. Pulling out a sheepskin from behind her, she covered Althea and herself. As Earthens they weren't cold, but humans used hides from sheep to keep warm and Annabel was careful to blend in.

"What do you mean they aren't men?"

"Those two were Faders."

Althea opened her mouth to ask more questions but there were so many that she couldn't decide which question to ask first. "But he seemed so nice."

"Ha," Annabel scoffed. "There's nothing nice about Faders. Trust me. If we had stayed they would have either killed us themselves or taken amusement from getting the humans to burn us as witches. Faders are evil, Althea."

"But..." She kept playing the memory of her short conversation with the tall stranger in her mind and nothing about him had seemed evil. "I felt so at ease with him."

Annabel gave her a sideways glance. "You wouldn't be the first. Faders can be charming and with their long life they are knowledgeable and often charming."

"But how did you know they were Faders?"

Annabel hurried Tobias on and moved in her seat. "The longer they have lived, the slower their vibration. You must have felt it."

"I did feel it, but it felt soothing."

"Yes, as soothing as a snake hypnotizing its prey."

Althea pushed her hands under her thighs. "He said I looked stunning and I didn't pick up on any danger from him. Are you sure that all Faders are evil?"

164

This time Annabel turned her head and spoke in a hard tone. "They sold their souls, Althea. What you see is nothing but an imitation of kindness."

Althea sank lower in her seat and for a while they rode on without speaking. Once they were about an hour away from the inn, Annabel approached a farmhouse and asked for permission to spend the night in their barn. Tobias was used to the outdoors, but it was December and colder than usual.

The women placed the sheepskin on haystacks and as they lay close that night, Annabel began to share.

"It's interesting how humans have always been curious to know the truth about the world. They look to religion, science, and myths for answers. Constantly they try to sharpen their vision to see farther and wider, without realizing that the answers were never far away or out of reach, nor have they ever been hidden. The truth of the world is as obvious as their own noses. It's right there but out of sight."

Althea propped herself up on her elbow. "What do you mean?"

Poking at her nose, Annabel pointed out, "Do you see your nose when you look at me?"

"No."

"Exactly. The nose is always in the view of the eyes, yet the brain chooses not to acknowledge it. Your eyes are trained to look past your nose to see farther."

"I never thought about it," Althea said and squinted her eyes to see her nose.

"Humans have feared us Earthens for a long time now. They've executed our family members for crimes they never committed. All the while they're clueless about the real danger living among them. We Earthens are a kind species that serve to heal and protect, but Faders are unpredictable and it's best to stay away from them altogether. There are many myths about them.

Some say they can't be killed, but that's not true. They heal faster than humans and if no harm is bestowed upon them, they have the possibility of living forever. But they can be killed, I've seen it myself."

Althea listened with full concentration.

"If I were to kill a Fader, I would remove their heart or their head. You would have to do great bodily harm for them to die. Stabbing them wouldn't be enough."

"One of the men had a large scar on his neck. Did you see it?"

"Yes, I saw. You can see why women are drawn to them now, can't you?"

Althea nodded. She had felt all kinds of unknown sensations from the closeness of the Fader who had called her stunning.

"Not all of them are as handsome as those two. But they are all powerful and rich. It's the gain they get from selling their souls."

"How does one sell their soul?"

Annabel sighed. "I'm not sure. Maybe it's more a saying than a real thing, but if the myths are real, they are loyal to some overlord who controls them."

"Are all Faders men?"

"Most are but not all. The ones I've met have all come with enormous self-regard. Of course, the humans have no idea that they're living in a world ruled by Faders."

"Why are they called Faders?"

Bobbing her shoulders in a shrug, Annabel looked up at the thatched roof of the barn. "I'm not sure. Maybe because they can shift into other bodies or maybe because they fade into the shadows when there's a sign of a threat. But you couldn't catch them if you tried. They have a network of powerful allies in other Faders and they help each other when needed. We are talking of kings and mayors with great influence."

"How does someone become a Fader?" Althea asked.

"Well, unlike we Earthens, Faders aren't born that way, they are born as normal humans. My parents told me stories about their master. He's the one who gives them immortality."

Lowering her voice, Althea whispered, "Are you talking about the devil?"

"I'm not sure." Annabel looked down and picked at the sheepskin. "It's hard to know what's true and what's scary stories, but I was told that this man walks the earth and has for thousands of years."

Althea's first reaction was to scoff and say, "That's impossible." But then she remembered her body regenerating from the fire in the town. "Do you know how to find him?"

Annabel looked disturbed by her question. "No. Why would I go near him? Promise that you won't try to find him, Althea."

Holding up a palm, Althea quickly said, "I assure you that I have no plans to go near him. I just have so many questions, like why does he create Faders? What's in it for him?"

Annabel shook her head. "I don't know."

"If humans can become Faders, then can Earthens too?"

"That's a good question. I can't imagine any Earthen so consumed with worldly possessions that they would want to morally give up their souls for power. It's just not in our nature."

Althea thought about Maeve and how she had bought into James' lies about living a life of luxury. "I think my sister would. She's changed."

Annabel took Althea's hand and gave her a comforting smile as they lay on their sides facing each other. "Do you think those two Faders will follow us?" Althea asked after a long moment.

"It's possible. We'll need to keep an eye out for animals that act suspicious."

"Animals?" Althea quickly asked. "Oh, right, because Faders can shift into other shapes."

"Yes." Annabel blinked her tired eyes and yawned.

Rolling onto her back, Althea sighed. "I was just getting better at navigating a world of humans, and now I have to be aware of Faders too. It was so much simpler living in the cottage."

"Those days are gone, but if you stick to me, I'll teach you everything I know about healing and about keeping clear of danger from humans and Faders. I've survived for thirty-six years, and I plan to stay around for many more to come."

Althea squeezed Annabel's hand feeling grateful that she hadn't been alone tonight. Being isolated for so many years gave her a great disadvantage and she was grateful to have a friend watching out for her. Her thoughts went to Maeve again as she wondered where her sister might be and if she had found a friend as well.

CHAPTER 17
THE CRUELLEST FATE

Tracking down the richest and most powerful man in the world turned out to be much harder than Maeve had ever imagined.

Charles Fuji wasn't a man who flaunted his riches or status. Nor did he live a flamboyant lifestyle with grand palaces or expensive mistresses. Those things he had lived out centuries ago and found that they complicated his life. Like a powerful spider, he preferred to sit in the shadows, pulling strings and controlling the web he spun.

Those that knew him called him the Cobra – a name that suited him in more ways than one. He saw himself as a collector of souls and knew exactly which type of human to lure into his service. They were always successful on their own accord, competitive and materialistic by nature, and insatiable when it came to power.

His offer of immortality was rarely rejected. The few times someone had surprised him and said no, he had killed them on the spot. Allowing someone to walk away with knowledge that could hurt him was unthinkable. The Cobra wasn't just the most powerful man in the world. He was also the most feared. No predator could compare to him because he was by far the most intelligent and dangerous creature alive.

Being as ancient as he was, he'd lived in many bodies, and no one knew his real name. His subjects were given great privilege and wealth. Among them were kings, dukes, and nobility in many countries. But their status in life came with a price of complete loyalty to him. Over his extended lifetime, there had been those who underestimated him and strove to take his place or showed disobedience. They paid the ultimate price, much worse than death itself.

Charles Fuji was not a man of mercy. When he sought out revenge he turned into a terrifying snake. Not a snake of great size that would slowly choke you to death. No, he preferred the shape of the black king cobra, which was quick, agile, and impossible to escape or plead with. He would set his fangs into his victims and transfer a venom into their bloodstreams that gave them a fate much crueler than death.

His venom didn't kill his victims. Instead, it destroyed the essence of the person, taking every memory and ambition they ever had. The attack left the person unattached to their soul and always in search of something to fill the large void inside them that they could not understand. It was particularly satisfying to him to see these powerful traitors regress in intelligence and end up with the mental ability of a small child. All their previous grandness became irrelevant as they couldn't remember their life from before the time they were bitten. He left them broken, and with a feeling of having lost the connection to their most valuable possession –their soul.

It seemed to be a pattern with his victims that their desperate attempts to regain what they had lost resulted in them hoarding everything possible. That's why he had given them the name Gleaners. They collected anything and everything they could – from objects to gossip, to things that others considered trash.

Humans often interacted with Gleaners and mistook their condition for a form of madness. Never did they suspect that their suspicion and aggression toward those trying to take away their things was a result of a particularly venomous bite.

Charles had lost count of how many thousand Faders and Gleaners he had created. While keeping a watchful eye on his Faders, he didn't spend any time on the Gleaners. He made sure his Faders visited each one a few times a year. Mostly to remind them which fate awaited if they ever crossed him.

His Faders reported that Gleaners lived in homes where one could no longer see the walls because they were covered in junk while others lived in tents on the streets, and some were locked up in madhouses.

To humans, Gleaners appeared insane with their large, intense eyes that were always red as if they were drugged and the way they mumbled meaningless things repeatedly.

The worst part of the fate of a Gleaner was that each night when they fell asleep, they were cursed with dreams of who they had once been and who they'd once loved only for the cobra to hunt them down each night in their nightmares and kill them.

Gleaners always woke from their nightly terror screaming with sweat dripping from their bodies. For mere moments after they woke, they remembered who they'd been. In hopes that they would be able to remember the dreams and who they truly were, they repeated meaningful phrases or wrote them down until their memories were wiped clean once again. As if a part of their mind wanted them to remember, they would mumble the phrases and words they'd spoken when they'd awakened, and they repeated these words relentlessly – sometimes mumbling, sometimes shouting. The fate of a Gleaner was crueler and much more painful than death. Every Fader feared that the Cobra would one day set his fangs into them.

Maeve, however, had no idea of the snake pit she would be entering when she arrived at his house.

CHAPTER 18
QUIET MOUSE IN THE SNAKE PIT

Standing on a quiet street in London, Maeve looked up and down to be sure no one saw her. The façade of the large house was presentable but didn't reveal that the richest man in the world lived there.

She was aware of Zosia's words that the last Earthen given the task to kill this man had failed. But Maeve wasn't here to kill him. In fact, she had no intention of complying with any of Zosia's instructions ever again.

She was here because she wanted to be as great a threat to Zosia as he was. It was still a bit of a mystery to her what he had done to earn Zosia's attention, but in her eyes, her enemy's enemy was a potential ally. When Zosia gave Maeve incredible powers and immortality, she never imagined that Maeve would use them against her, but Maeve was done being taken advantage of. From now on she would be the one making the rules and taking what she wanted.

The Cobra might be dangerous for a normal Earthen or human, but with Zosia's secret weapon in her blood, Maeve felt invincible and was certain that he couldn't hurt her.

Maeve's life had changed drastically since she'd turned twenty-four and so had her personality. Some people crumbled after emotional injury, but she had become cold and cynical. It wasn't like she had any other choice now that Zosia had tricked her into taking the crystal.

173

Though Maeve hated humans with all her heart, she hated Zosia more. If it weren't for her indifference, Maeve's aunt would still be alive.

A few days ago, Maeve had attempted to talk to Charles Fuji, but his zealous butler had turned her away without hearing her out. She had been tempted to kill him on the spot and force her way into the house, but there had been people in the street that day.

This time she returned in a fashionable gown with her hair neatly arranged. She was an intelligent woman, and it hadn't been difficult for her to steal money.

As she knocked on the large white front door once again, she hoped it wouldn't be answered by the same butler who had turned her away the last time she was here. Unfortunately, luck wasn't on her side.

The middle-aged man had a stiff upper lip and greeted her with formality but at least he was kinder now that she looked like a proper lady.

"Yes, may I help you?" His gaze roamed the street as he looked for her carriage and escort.

"I'm here to see the master of the house."

It took him a minute to realize that her red hair color and burning eyes were the same as those of the peasant he had dismissed a few days ago.

"I don't know where you managed to steal such a fine gown, but thievery is not a valuable trait in a young lady," the butler said with his nose in the air.

"I did not steal it, I bought it," Maeve insisted, and in a way she was right; she did not steal the dress, only the money to buy it. "Now please take me to your lord."

It infuriated Maeve to see the butler raise his eyebrow and look down at her.

"I'm afraid the lord does not have time. Good day," he said and closed the door in Maeve's face.

Huffing through her nostrils, she turned around and walked down the stairs determined to find another way in.

At first, she considered sneaking in through the servants' door, but as she quietly walked down the hallway she heard the voices of women conversing. Sticking her head around the end wall she saw four servants in the kitchen, and she realized she'd have to walk past them to get to the rest of the house. Maeve was clever enough to know that she could never go unnoticed, especially not with her prestigious blue dress.

Quietly she made her way back outside and tried to think of another way in. That was when she noticed an open window on the second floor with curtains flapping in the wind. Her chest lifted in a sigh to prepare herself as she approached the tree that stood next to it.

Althea and Maeve had always loved to climb trees and they'd been skilled at it since they'd had to climb one every morning and night to get to and from the terrace where they'd slept. It was, however, much easier to climb a tree in bare feet and a thin summer dress than it was in the stiff shoes and heavy blue dress that Maeve was wearing.

When she nearly lost her balance, she managed to grab a branch above her head just in time to save her from falling. She took a deep breath and continued forward, but the further out she got, the more the branch was weighed down.

Still too far away from the window to reach for it, Maeve was considering her options. She wasn't sure the branch would hold her weight or that she could jump this far. The sound of voices made her stiffen and look down to see two servant girls her age coming from the kitchen and into the servants' area on the side of the house. Holding her breath, she hoped they wouldn't notice her.

They were close enough that she could hear them gossip

"Well, all I'm saying is that if the lord invited me to his room as he did with Alice, I certainly wouldn't protest," one of the servant girls said in a flirtatious voice, which made the other giggle.

"I would happily settle for Mr. Thomas or Mr. Bradshaw."

Maeve closed her eyes, wishing the women would stop simpering over men and get going with their chores inside. When they'd finally left, Maeve let out her breath and turned her attention to the open window. Resolutely, she stepped out a little farther and stretched out toward the window. But it was no use; she could not reach it. With a steadying breath, Maeve took another small step and heard the branch squeak under her. Bouncing down on her knees to get some strength only made the branch sway more. With her lips tightly knitted together, she lunged toward the open window just as the branch snapped in half from her weight. She held tightly onto the windowsill with the rest of her body dangling below the window.

Using both her hands she hoisted herself inside and considered herself lucky that no one had seen her clumsy entry into the quiet hallway.

Sitting up, Maeve questioned for a moment why someone with her powerful abilities had to humiliate herself in such a matter, but setting the house on fire hadn't been a possibility when she needed Charles Fuji to cooperate with her.

Faint voices from down the hallway carried to where Maeve sat and made her pay attention. And then there were footsteps coming in her direction. With no more than a split moment to hide and with few options available, she was forced to hide behind the tall curtains. Quiet as a mouse, she watched the annoying butler walk by with his nose and gaze so high in the air that it kept him from noticing her feet sticking out under the curtains.

Once the sound of his footsteps was far enough gone, Maeve poked her head out to make sure the hallway was clear. Her instinct told her to go in the direction of the deep voices that sounded muffled as if they came from a different room. Walking as quickly and quietly as she could she hurried down the long hallway. With her gaze lifting to the ceiling it felt as tall as the church she had visited with her parents as a child. On the walls hung portraits that looked very old and showed people who had to be long dead. For some reason, they all had stiff lips and bored expressions.

Getting closer to the room with muffled voices, she found the door a little ajar and peeked inside. Three men sat around a table playing cards and drinking what looked to be whiskey. One had his back to her. Another she could see only in profile, but the third man sat in a way that made her see him clearly. If only she knew which one was Charles Fuji.

For a moment, she tried to think of what her first line would be when she walked inside the room, and rehearsed in her mind. *You should really get friendlier butlers... no.* She bit her lip. *If you hate Zosia as much as I do, then we should work against her together.* Maeve shook her head and bit her lip again. It was annoying that he had company and maybe she was better off waiting for his friends to leave. If she knew which of the rooms he slept in she could wait for him there and have a private conversation with him.

She was debating what to do when she heard a voice behind her. Looking over her shoulder, she spotted the butler who had turned her away at the door. Marching toward her with his eyebrows lowered and his head dipped forward, he reminded her of a goat about to attack. She could run, but with a big heavy dress on she couldn't move at her usual speed and where would she hide? Maeve chose another option and quickly burst through the door and slammed it shut with both hands as soon as she was inside. With extra energy rushing through her veins, she stood with her back to the door and her chest visibly rising and falling.

The intense stares from the three men in their leather chairs had Maeve forgetting every word she had planned to say.

Her gaze was drawn to the man in the middle. He was Charles. She could tell because the two others tensed and moved forward in their seat as if getting ready to protect him. Charles on the other hand leaned back with a relaxed and slightly intrigued smile.

With a dry mouth, she felt the door push against her back. The butler was doing his best to get in and hammered on the door.

Arching his brow, Charles suggested to Maeve, "Maybe you should step aside, miss."

She complied and took a large step forward which resulted in the snobby butler almost tripping into the room. Quickly regaining his balance, he spoke with a face redder than a tomato from hurrying down the hallway. "My lord, I assure you it was not my doing that this woman has disturbed you, she must have sneaked in. I will escort her out immediately."

Raising a palm to silence his butler, Charles angled his head and asked Maeve, "How did you get in here?"

"Are you Charles Fuji?" she asked to be sure. In her head she had expected an old and unattractive man, but Charles was anything but. She knew from Zosia that he had lived much longer than the oldest tree in the world, but to others he would appear to be a man around forty who took very good care of himself.

"Yes, I am." He rose from his chair and looked Maeve up and down with authority radiating strongly from him and intelligence glimmering in his dark eyes. "Now, how did you get in here?"

"That's not important. What you should be asking is how we can help each other," Maeve said and raised her chin.

Charles groaned and walked toward the door prepared to escort Maeve out. "You're not the first to offer me services I didn't ask for, and although you are beyond the other women in beauty, I'm afraid I'm busy and not in need of your services currently." He stopped and gave Maeve an evaluating look. "But perhaps if you come back tonight."

Maeve's eyes narrowed, confused as to what he was talking about, but she didn't get a chance to respond before they were interrupted by one of his friends.

"Ah, come on now, Charles. It's impolite to turn away a lady with a tempting offer. I wouldn't mind entertaining her for a little while. It would be the gentlemanly thing to do."

Maeve's glance shifted to the man who had spoken. He looked to be in his mid-forties but if he was a Fader, he could be centuries old. His elegant clothes gave him a distinguished look, but his words and the scar on his neck told her he was no true gentleman.

"Leave us," Charles dismissed the butler, who bowed and sent a last glare in Maeve's direction before he left the room.

Getting up from his chair, the youngest-looking man of the three moved closer to Maeve. His skin was flawless without a scar, and he had thick black lashes that complimented his black hair. "Is this some type of rebellion against the confinements of a privileged life? Did you really come here without an escort?"

"I don't need an escort," Maeve said in a defensive tone.

"No?" Walking closer to her, the youngest of the men muttered low to his friend with the scar. "She's so much like the red-haired beauty we saw up North."

With a scowl, Maeve moved back and refocused on Charles, who hadn't said a word. "I know what you are and so does Zosia."

CHAPTER 19

A HANDSOME FACE WITH LONG FANGS

Like the snake he was, the Cobra had shed his skin many times. His origins were so ancient that he had forgotten when he was born and to whom. Since then, he had gone by many names and lived in many bodies. His current body had belonged to a Fader who had wronged him long ago. After killing him, the Cobra took his body and name, just as he'd done with others so many times before.

The identity of Charles Fuji had served the Cobra well because as a wealthy Asian man, he had lived a luxurious and powerful life. The Cobra had spent two centuries in Asia and one in England as the handsome Charles Fuji where he manipulated and controlled others for his amusement and gain. He did not carry Charles Fuji's ancestry because a Fader could not turn into their victims but only appear to look like them, and Charles' attractive appearance did the Cobra many favors. He was tall for a Japanese man, and his silky black hair, dark eyes, toned face structure, and well-built body gave him an easy time with women.

"How did you get in here?" he repeated while watching Maeve, who despite feeling very flustered, kept her face stiff and emotionless.

"If you must know, I climbed the tree in your back garden and came in through one of your windows."

The man with the scar chuckled. "Didn't I tell you to cut down that tree?"

181

Charles didn't look amused. "Why would I? Any thief or assassin stupid enough to come into my house would quickly wish they had never entered."

Maeve wasn't fazed by his threat and raised her chin.

Moving closer, Charles tilted his head and narrowed his eyes a little. "You're not the first Earthen who's been stupid enough to come here."

"I'm not stupid," she answered sharply and looked up at Charles.

"Then why would you think it was a good idea to come here?"

Maeve raised her chin and exuded all the confidence she could muster. "Because I have something to offer you. Something, I'm sure you'll be rather grateful for."

He didn't answer at first, but then he spoke in a smooth voice. "You're much prettier than the last one who came knocking, but if I wanted a lady of the hour I'd go to a whorehouse."

His words triggered the memory of James calling her a whore before leaving her for dead and it made her spit out, "I'm not here to sleep with you." Maeve's tone was sharp as she spoke through her clenched teeth with a sideways glance to the two other men in the room, and added, "Or them."

The man with the scar sighed. "How disappointing. It's so rare for women to take initiative these days. I was hoping you had a rebel's desire." Looking to his friend with the dark hair, he sighed. "I miss my days as a Viking. Women back then were uninhibited and unashamed of their sexuality."

"Stop!" Charles didn't look at the man with the scar when he barked out his order, but the man complied without complaint when Charles added, "You two, leave us."

Maeve stood locked in a staring contest with Charles when his two friends left the room and closed the door

182

behind them. Covering her right wrist with her left palm, she felt her pulse race and tried to calm her nerves. The executioner had been a large man but nowhere as scary as Charles. He was hard to read and his dark eyes hardly blinked.

"I'm listening so state your purpose," Charles demanded.

"Zosia intends to kill you."

He raised an eyebrow and spoke in a mocking tone. "Everyone intends to kill me, that's nothing new."

"She chose me to do her bidding, but I won't."

A small smile tugged at his lips. "Is that so? Did you know that you're not the first Zosia has sent to kill me?"

"Yes. I'm aware," she answered without looking away.

"Are you also aware of the fate that fell upon the last Earthen who tried to kill me?"

"No." Maeve frowned. "I didn't come here to talk about her. I came because Zosia hates you and I hate *her*. If I could, I would kill her for what she's done to me. Since that's not possible, I want to understand what it is you do that makes her see you as a threat."

Charles arched a brow and smiled.

"What's so funny?" Maeve asked and crossed her arms.

"Are you saying that you want to be my apprentice and have me teach you everything I do?" His expression revealed how laughable he found the idea.

"No. I'm not here to be your apprentice. I want us to be equals."

That statement made him laugh out loud, but there was no real amusement, simply ridicule at how insane her request was.

Maeve's face, neck, and ears reddened as she waited for him to stop laughing at her. When she finally did, he lowered his head with a faint smile still resting on his lips. "What is your name, miss?"

"Maeve."

"Let me be clear, Miss Maeve. You could never be my equal. I have dined with Cleopatra and advised Marcus Aurelius and Alexander the Great. You are nothing but a peasant girl in a fancy dress. Do you even know how to read and write?"

Narrowing her eyes, Maeve hissed, "Of course." In reality her abilities were limited. Rose had taught them to read and write, but with the scarcity of books she hadn't had a chance to practice much.

"I may not have your experience yet, but we are both immortals and I'll catch up to you sooner if you teach me what you know. If I'm forced to live in a world with humans, then I want to live in comfort and luxury just like you do."

He scoffed. "You're not immortal."

Tightening her folded arms, Maeve insisted, "Yes, I am."

With his back to her, he made an icy remark. "If there's one thing that I don't tolerate, it's lies. I almost feel bad about killing someone so defenseless, but you understand that I have to send a message to Zosia."

"What are you talki..." Before Maeve had finished her sentence, Charles' body changed. His eyes slithered into the long narrow pupils of a snake. His clothes disappeared just like his skin did. Maeve watched with large eyes as the man that had stood before her so confidently turned into the small form of an animal. She looked down at the black cobra before her and though she had never seen one before, her instincts warned her of danger. As the black king cobra slithered toward her on the floor, Maeve stepped backward.

She had never seen a Fader shift before, and it astounded her that Charles was now the king cobra rising from the floor. His yellow eyes were fixated on her and his split tongue came out in a sizzling sound that made goosebumps spread all over her body. Maeve's throat tightened on instinct because every part of her dreaded the attack she knew was coming but didn't have time to flee from.

It happened within seconds. Charles didn't toy with her but went straight for the strike. Maeve screamed when his fangs sunk into her hand. Stumbling back, she fell to the floor and tried to shake the snake off her. When her rattled brain remembered that she wasn't defenseless, she set the snake on fire.

That made him release her at once and as he fell to the ground engulfed in flames, Charles shifted back into his human body. He wasn't burned but he looked shaken as he gaped at her.

"I bit you," he said as if that should have been enough to finish her.

Maeve was angry and pushed at him with the same power that had hurled Althea through the market square back in Lerwick. Charles tumbled back and collided with the wall just above the mantelpiece. Falling to the floor, he groaned and got back up. This time, Maeve reached out her hand and suffocated him from a distance. With disbelief and confusion in his eyes, Charles waved his palms signaling for her to stop.

Releasing her grip on him, Maeve pushed him back once more.

"Who the hell are you?" The respect in his tone soothed Maeve. "And how are you still standing after I bit you?"

Looking down at her hand, Maeve saw the two bloody wounds from his bite up close. Raising her hand, she showed him. "A little bite won't hurt me."

Charles moved to stand in front of her again. In a hard movement, he reached for her hand and examined it before muttering, "It seems I underestimated you."

Maeve tried to pull her hand back, but he held on a little longer and this time his gaze lifted to meet hers. Maeve was fascinated by Charles, who exuded such authority and confidence. He represented the kind of power she wanted for herself.

"Did Zosia do this to you? Did she find an antidote to my venom?" he asked.

Maeve scoffed and jerked her hand back again. This time Charles released it and narrowed his eyes as she hissed, "Unless you want to die a painful death, don't mention her name."

For a moment he just looked at her, but then he went to pick up his glass of whiskey and took a large sip before asking, "Indulge my curiosity, Miss Maeve. Explain to me what it is about Zosia that makes you despise her so."

Maeve looked to the side. "She's no better than the humans killing us Earthens. She might pretend to care, but she's a selfish creature who had the chance to save my aunt yet chose to look the other way. It's her fault we Earthens are in hiding because she has the power to rid the earth of humans, yet she chooses not to." Maeve's tone was dripping with spite and her eyes were glowing with the heat produced by the emotional furnace of unfairness that burned in her stomach

"If those are things you dislike about Zosia, then I'm afraid you're going to loathe me as well, dear Maeve." Charles emptied his glass and set it down. "I don't like Zosia, nor do I like her Earthens. But she doesn't deserve the credit you give her because it's not her fault or doing that you are all in hiding. It's mine," he said with a proud glimmer in his eyes. "Witch trials started because of me. I designed the rumors, and it was my Faders who spread them to begin with. Of course, humans are more easily spooked than wild horses and it didn't take much for them to run with the lies." There was no trace of regret or empathy on his face as he spoke.

Fury rose in Maeve's stomach from speaking of Zosia, and Charles' use of an endearment felt belittling and threw her off a little. Quickly, she retorted. "You're wrong, *dear Charles*. It may not be her *doing*, but it is her fault that so many of us are hiding and being slaughtered when she has the power to rid the Earth of humans."

Charles understood that she used an endearment back to create leverage between them. He couldn't remember feeling this intrigued by a woman ever and leaned forward so that their faces weren't very far apart. "I just told you I started the witch trials that killed your people. Why does Zosia get all your hatred and not me?"

His question was valid, but Maeve hadn't arrived here hoping to find a good person. She had known Charles was a selfish man who took what he wanted. That was why she had been curious about him to begin with. Narrowing her eyes, she looked him over. His clothes weren't flamboyant, but clearly of good quality and fit him perfectly. Where James had been all about flashing his wealth, Charles was understated yet oozed ten times as much superiority and masculinity. And then there was the obvious difference that Charles didn't use his tongue to spin lies as James had.

"Because unlike her, you don't pretend to care about me or anyone else. I haven't caught you in a lie, yet, and like you, I *hate* liars. Zosia and James both pretended to care, and they used me but weren't there when I needed them, and *that* is unforgivable."

"James?" Charles raised a flirtatious eyebrow.

Maeve ignored his question and continued talking. "Zosia is crueler than you could ever be because you don't pretend to be good when you're not. I don't blame

187

you for taking what you want from whoever can give it to you. In fact, I plan to do the same. That's why I'm here. If I must live among humans, then I want to be in control and live in the greatest comfort possible."

Charles watched the determined expression in Maeve's beautiful intense eyes. It was a good thing she couldn't hear all the dirty thoughts in his mind because it would have flustered her and made her cheeks blush. "Being honest about my desires justifies my motives in your view. Are you saying I could kill you right now, and you still wouldn't judge my actions?" he challenged in his deep attractive voice.

"I think we just established that you don't have the power to kill me."

"Ah, but I didn't bite to kill you. I intended to turn you into a Gleaner."

Maeve didn't want to appear illiterate, so she didn't reveal to him that she didn't know what a Gleaner was.

"Killing you wouldn't be difficult. I could do it with my bare hands or turn myself into any predator I choose and rip out your heart or throat in a blink of an eye."

"I wish you could, but Zosia has cursed me with immortality." Maeve looked up at him and watched how hundreds of thoughts spiraled behind his dark eyes.

"What type of immortality?" he asked.

"Is there more than one?"

"I give my Faders the possibility of living forever if no harm is inflicted upon them," Charles explained.

Maeve paraphrased his words: "So, unless they are murdered or fall off a cliff, they could live till the end of time."

Charles nodded.

"But that's not the type of immortality you have?" Maeve asked, instinctively knowing the answer.

"No, it's not. There is only one weapon that can kill me, and despite what Zosia says it's impossible to get to, which makes killing me impossible." Though his eyes had returned to normal, there was still the glimmer of yellow in his pupils. "What type did she give you?"

Maeve sighed. "I should be dead, but my body heals and regrows itself, which means I'm cursed to live in this world forever."

Charles furrowed his dark eyebrows. "Your limbs regrow themselves? That's impossible."

"It's true. And my natural powers as an Earthen are enhanced as well. I can shoot balls of fire from my palms, throw people or objects around, and strangle a person from a distance."

Charles arched an eyebrow. "Impressive. But you are still an Earthen and that makes you soft. We both know you couldn't kill anyone if it came down to it."

Maeve felt frustrated and embarrassed that Charles was patronizing her. Squaring her shoulders, she spat out, "I've killed plenty. Go see how much is left of Lerwich, Glanchester, and Wintervale."

His mouth opened slightly and for a moment he stared at her before he muttered, "That was *you*? From what I heard those towns have been obliterated and everyone is looking for the culprit. Someone told me there are rumors that a dragon is to blame.

Maeve rolled her eyes. "Dragons aren't real."

"Nor are Earthens who kill. Or so I thought," Charles pointed out and went to sit on the edge of his desk. For a long moment, he watched her with a finger on his chin and an expression on his face that signaled deep thinking. "You want to become my equal?"

"I already am in so many ways," she answered without breaking their eye contact.

He crossed his arms. "If you want this lifestyle, I could help you get it. But it would require that you're useful to me."

Maeve didn't answer, but she tilted her head and listened as he continued talking.

"I like that you are smart and ambitious. I'm sure your anger toward Zosia can benefit both of us somehow and..." Charles raised one side of his mouth in a flirtatious smirk. "You're incredibly pleasing to look at."

Maeve didn't answer but soaked up how Charles liked the powerful and dangerous part of her.

He in return felt a surge of excitement he hadn't felt in centuries. When she had burned him in his snake form, he had experienced intense physical pain for the first time in a millennium. He would have sworn that no one could stand up against the Cobra because he was the most powerful being alive, but Maeve had proven that she wasn't an ordinary Earthen. For a moment her powers had startled him and until he understood her abilities better, he wasn't going to challenge her to another round of "who kills the other first?"

Charles was a collector of people and after the demonstration of her powers, he was determined to bring Maeve into his fold like a dangerous predator he could study up close and find a way to make it a pet of his. He had already picked up on Maeve's sexual innocence from the way she reacted to his closeness. Letting his finger lift her chin to meet his eyes, he used a seductive voice as he spoke. "You need someone who understands your anger, ambition, and your need to connect to something or... someone. I won't ever judge you, Maeve. There's nothing you can do that I haven't already done. I think you and I have a lot in common. In some ways we are the same. I have more than enough wealth and power to help you build the kind of lifestyle you want. Together, we would dominate the world."

Her breathing became faster from his sensual attack on her senses. "Are you asking me to marry you?"

"Marry?" The thought hadn't occurred to Charles, but he was adept at giving a hopeful young woman a satisfying answer. "It would be a crime to lock someone with a beautiful rebellious spirit such as yourself into a confining arrangement such as marriage. What I suggest is giving you the means to live an independent life on your own terms. But of course, I wouldn't mind *mentoring* you in different aspects of life that might be… shall we say new to you."

Maeve looked deep into his eyes. "Such as?"

Arching a brow, Charles said, "Such as finding the pleasures in life. It's one thing to have ambitions but you need to be smart about who you kill and why. Burning down towns isn't the way to go unnoticed."

"I grew up caring for nature and animals and healing the wounded, but I've come to realize that helping innocent animals doesn't compare to the satisfaction of destroying their enemies. Humans slaughter animals and Earthens for no good reason and I'm turning the tables on them." Maeve didn't back away from Charles' closeness.

"You really don't feel any guilt?" Charles asked with his gaze falling to her lips.

"No," she lied.

"Then what do you feel?" he asked, wanting to understand Maeve.

"Humans have taken everything from me, and with every kill, I take my strength back. It makes me feel in charge of my own life." Maeve thought back to all the humans she had already killed in a short time. This time, she was changing the narrative and focusing on her sense of vengeance. "Killing makes me feel powerful."

"I understand, but if you let that feeling become an addiction then you've lost all your power. Don't kill in vain, Maeve, it makes you appear weak," Charles advised.

It was impossible for Maeve to like anyone because being a whirlpool of self-pity and anger she did not even like herself. But with Charles, she felt like she could breathe. He was unapologetic and demanding, which was exactly what she was striving to become. Not only did Charles understand her rebellious and independent nature, but he was offering to support her. In a world with no allies left his offer was enticing. And then there was the soothing part about being around someone who was so much worse than herself, which made it easier for Maeve to silence the self-loathing voices in her head. Her wrongs were nothing compared to his.

Finally breaking the intense contact between them, Charles walked over to pour two glasses of scotch while he spoke. "You're the first Earthen I've met, Maeve, who isn't a soft pushover but actually has ambition in life." He turned around and walked back over to stand in front of her. Maeve found it fascinating to watch Charles walk. His movements were precise yet smooth as he narrowed in on her and handed her the heavy glass.

"If we are to be partners, I'll need proof of your loyalty."

Maeve watched him intently as he began to walk around the room in slow steps. "I'm impressed that you have defied your natural instincts as an Earthen and killed humans, but I need to know the extent of your strength."

"I already proved that by burning down Lerwick and those other towns."

"And why did you choose those towns exactly?"

"The people in Lerwick killed my aunt. The others lacked manners."

"Ah, that means you didn't prove anything. You killed humans who had killed your aunt. It's one thing to hurt those you hate, that's easy." Charles stopped and stared at Maeve with a serious expression. "But the question is, could you kill an Earthen?"

Her lips parted a little. The very reason Maeve hated Zosia was that she did not protect Earthens, and while killing all those humans, her heart had told her it was in vengeance for her people. What righteous purpose could make her kill an innocent Earthen?

But Maeve's thoughts spiraled quickly and as they fell into her deep layers of self-pity, she thought back to her sister. She had left Althea for dead but wondered if the crystal had healed her or if she had burned away with the rest of the cruel townspeople. Either way, Maeve was determined not to care; Althea had betrayed her and chosen humans over family. Her fate was deserved. In Maeve's mind, Althea became a representation of all Earthens, which made it easier to hate them altogether. They would never understand or appreciate all she had done to save them, so why should she do anything for Earthens when she would always be a villain in their eyes, and they chose to side with vile *humans* over her?

Though it went against the essence of an Earthen to harm others, especially the innocent and helpless, Maeve had already crossed so many of the lines and values of Earthens that this request did not scare her.

With a hard expression, Maeve confessed her darkest secret, "I already killed my sister when she tried to protect the humans. Make no mistake that I would kill Zosia if it was possible."

"Good. Then this challenge will be easy for you. Retrieve a compass that belongs to me, and I shall reward you generously. The Gleaner who has the compass may be scary to look at, but I should tell you that there is a kind Earthen inside of her and that she is one of the most helpless creatures you could ever meet. Killing her will most likely feel as unnatural to you as

193

killing an innocent deer in the forest. I want you to bring back her head and show it to me as proof of your loyalty." Charles spoke in a matter-of-fact tone as if he were conducting a business deal. He hoped Maeve would live up to his demands, but if she tried to cheat or steal his compass for herself, he would hunt her down and make her regret it.

Maeve had already made up her mind but pretended to think it over. "You're asking me to prove my loyalty to you. What about your loyalty to me?"

"Should you bring me my compass, I assure you that you have both my protection and loyalty." His smile was so rehearsed that it looked genuine. "I think we'll have a beneficial partnership, Miss Maeve." Taking her hand, he planted a kiss on the back and looked into her eyes. "I should warn you though, don't let her get her hands on your head. At least not if you want to keep your soul."

CHAPTER 20

A MAZE OF TREASURE

Maeve had never heard of Gleaners until Charles explained the fate that he bestowed upon them with his venom. She was curious to meet Edith, who had been an Earthen before her encounter with him. Maeve struggled to imagine what there was about a Gleaner's life that made Zosia pity them so much. In her mind, it couldn't possibly be worse than the fate of Earthens living in hiding or the risk of being executed for witchcraft by humans.

When she left Charles' office, she was tempted to hurt the butler that had turned her away, but he was surrounded by servants. Deciding it was wisest not to make a scene, Maeve left the house as quietly as she had come.

It was a drastic change to leave the idyllic street that Charles lived on and go to a part of London where no real lady would ever set foot. These streets were narrower without any trees to soften the wood and thatch that made up all the worn-down buildings. Fat rats roamed freely, and the air was heavy and smelled of sewage in this gray and depressing part of London. Maeve took in every detail as she walked down the street, from the man sitting on the sidewalk with holes in his clothes who was coughing his lungs up to the two dirty children running past her and leaving behind a smell of unwashed bodies. Their giggles made Maeve wonder what anyone living in these circumstances could possibly have to laugh about.

The feeling of someone watching her made her look to a window where a ghost of a woman, pale and with sunken cheeks, stood watching her with dead eyes. Maeve was probably the first well-dressed person the woman had seen on her street.

When Charles gave her the address, he had informed her that it was a part of London that even the city watch avoided.

Despite being immortal, Maeve still felt her instincts warn her that this wasn't a place she wanted to be. Ignoring the curious glances from the few sad souls who stood lurking in the shadows, she walked with purpose although she wasn't quite sure where to find the address.

Passing an alley, she saw two men with ghoulish faces and hurried along. It didn't take long before she heard footsteps behind her. The men thought her an easy target and followed her long enough that her sharp sense of smell picked up the putrid stench of ammonia. It made her think that someone had dipped them in piss, and it made her determined to never allow their dirty hands to get anywhere near her. Her high heels clicked against the ground as she picked up her pace, but that only made the sound of the following footsteps louder as the men picked up speed as well. Just before they reached her, she turned around and hissed, "Stop!"

Using enough power to hold them back, she created a strong wind from her palm that surprised the men. Despite how much they leaned into the wind and tried to move forward, they got nowhere. Maeve stood watching the two men dressed in rags struggling to keep their balance on the cobblestone street. She was momentarily amused by the way the skin on their cheeks was pushed back, giving them a weird facial shape.

Maeve's retracting the wind quickly made them both fall forward. Groaning on the ground, one of them looked up at her and blinked his eyes as if he couldn't decide what to think.

"I'm looking for the Place of Piles behind Mucker's Street. Do you know where that is?"

"Oi, what did ye do?" the shortest one, whose sunken cheeks made him look malnourished, asked.

"Answer the question," Maeve ordered and held up her sleeve to protect her nose from the smell of their unwashed bodies.

"We don't go there," the taller man said and had a genuinely scared look in his eyes as he got to his feet. "It's dangerous."

"Why?" Maeve demanded and took a step back to create distance from their lingering odor that hung heavily in the air

The tall and skinny man looked old to Maeve with his crooked, rotten teeth and wrinkled face. In reality, he wasn't yet thirty but had lived a brutal life with sickness and hunger. Avoiding Maeve's direct gaze he looked away and spat on the ground before answering: "The Place of Piles is a portal to hell is what it is. Everyone knows that."

Maeve raised her eyebrows and scoffed. "Perhaps hell is where I want to go. Now tell me where to find it."

"You don't want to do that, miss," the shorter man said and scrambled to stand up. "Those that entered have never returned to see the light of day. The creature that lives there... she's best left alone."

With irritation dripping from her tone, Maeve repeated her question. "Where is it?"

When neither of the men answered, she slowly closed her hand, and in the process, squeezed their lungs. The dirty men didn't understand how she was causing them physical pain from a distance, but eager to end the pain the shorter of the friends spoke in a hoarse voice. "Down... there." He sounded like an old man on his

197

death bed barely finding the strength to speak with lungs deprived of air.

Maeve eased her hold on him and waited for him to catch his breath.

"If you keep going, you can't miss it. It's just past the empty barbershop and down the alley to the left," he explained with fright in his eyes.

When Maeve turned her back on the two men, they hurried to run back to the dark alley they came from. Maeve had shown that she was not to be messed with and they feared her... but not nearly as much as they feared the creature that lived in the Place of Piles.

Maeve carried on walking down the street, this time with only the sound of her heels rather than approaching footsteps trailing behind her. She followed their directions and soon arrived at what looked more like a scrapyard than a house. With the piles of garbage stacked outside, it was hard to see the entrance. Some of the piles went all the way to the top of the house and continued onto the roof. For a moment, Maeve narrowed her eyes, trying to understand what kind of items she was looking at but there were so many objects tangled together from worn-out shoes, pans, and clothes, to pots, wheels, pieces of lumber, and barrels. Lifting her blue dress, she carefully made her way down aisles of garbage, stepping on hard, crunchy things and a few dead rats to get to the front door.

It was impossible to imagine that anything other than rats and insects lived in this house, but Charles had insisted that it was the home of a woman named Edith who was cursed by his venom to live the miserable life of a Gleaner. Maeve didn't bother to knock but instead opened the old creaky door that seemed as though it would fall from its hinges and turn to dust at any given moment.

Though it should have come as no surprise, Maeve's eyes still widened a tiny bit in horror when she saw how loads of garbage inside the house were piled up to the ceiling. Everything was dark with only glimpses of light shining through the holes in the roof. The smell of decay and rot made her gag and quickly cover her nose. Moving forward, Maeve took everything in with shock and disbelief. Dead rodents lay spread around in different stages of decomposition and when she turned a corner she stopped and stared. For a second it rattled Maeve to see bones and a skull that looked like it belonged to a human, but she quickly pulled herself together and steadied her nerves. "Hello?" she called out, not sure which narrow pathway to follow in this maze of broken items and insanity.

No reply came, but from within the dark mess the sound of an object falling made Maeve look up and squint her eyes. She saw no movement but walked toward the sound.

"Edith, is that you?" Maeve called out, "Please show yourself so we can talk."

Again, Maeve received no reply as the house remained quiet with only the horrible smell of death and the heavy energy weighing it down. Walking a little farther into the house, Maeve was suddenly spooked by the noisy sound of several objects falling to the ground as if someone were running and pushing things.

"Edith?" Maeve called and spun in all directions, looking up and down the aisle and to the top of the piles. Her biggest fear was that the whole house would crumple down on top of her, but she ignored her intuition to leave the creepy house and continued searching for the Gleaner. With a sigh, she walked in the direction of the fallen objects that now lay on the floor further down. There was a doll with no arms, a knife with a missing blade, a cutting board with a crack down the middle, and a vase that was shattered into five pieces.

"I mean no harm," Maeve lied as she peered around every corner searching for Edith. With only the sparse daylight shining through the holes in the damaged roof, the place was poorly lit. Even with Maeve's sharper eyesight, she moved slowly in certain places, minding her step while disgusting smells made her hold her breath.

Despite the noises of things falling from their tall piles, there was no other sign of the Gleaner. Nevertheless, Maeve felt certain Edith was there because the feeling of being watched sent cold shivers down Maeve's spine and made the hair on the back of her neck stand up.

"Edith," Maeve called in the friendliest tone she could muster, which to most would still feel insincere and cold. "I'm no danger. I'm an Earthen, just like you."

Her words triggered something inside the Gleaner who watched Maeve from high up on a pile in the dark shadows. The sudden ear-piercing scream that came from her lungs startled not only Maeve but all the insects and rodents that lived in the mountains of trash as well. As her hoarse voice echoed through the maze of garbage, the piles seemed to come to life as all types of rodents and insects came from their hiding places and ran past Maeve. Their collective sounds of squeaks and screeches were deafening and when a fat rat ran up Maeve's right leg she kicked and yelled herself.

Being so focused on getting the rat out from under her dress where it clawed its way up her leg, Maeve did not see how Edith crawled down from her pile of garbage that reached the top of a dark part of the ceiling, and in the process, she knocked items to the ground making the whole pile collapse. Only in the last second after Maeve hurled the rat across the room did she look up to see a pile of metal boxes and broken furniture come crashing down towards her like a destructive avalanche pulling other things down as well. Afraid that she would get buried under the piles, Maeve turned on her heel and ran in the opposite direction as fast as she could. The thunder from piles collapsing echoed through the house and she had to use her power to keep things from falling on her head. Once she reached safety in an aisle with no movement, her cheeks were flushed. Assessing the damages, she looked at the claw marks on her calf and thighs and the dress she had paid a fortune for, which was torn in several places and covered in filth from buckets with questionable contents that had fallen on her.

Annoyed, she released the fabric of her dress and became aware of the prickly feeling of someone watching her.

Turning to look back at the part of the house she had just come from, she narrowed her eyes to see through the dust that hung in the air. On the other side of the room, a small figure stood in the shadows staring at her.

"I'm done playing, Edith. Come out now, or I will make you regret it," Maeve threatened and stepped up on the fallen trash. A heavy cloud of dust still lingered in the air when she slowly walked toward the deformed figure.

"Get out! Get out! Get out!" the Gleaner hissed in screeches with spit flying through the air.

Maeve raised her chin and reminded herself that if anyone were to be scared it most certainly wasn't her. "Show yourself!" she instructed in a stern tone.

With a hunched back and a limp arm, the Gleaner dragged herself forward into the light. The rotten roof had a hole where the sun shone through directly onto Edith's old and frail body. She was a woman in her sixties who appeared to be a hundred years older than she was.

Not a single layer of fat lay between her skin and bones. She was small and though she appeared weak, she looked as though she would jump anyone who got too close. Her many wrinkles were defined by the dust and dirt that covered her completely. Her thin hair didn't cover her scalp but clung to her head as a sticky gray texture that didn't cover her wounds.

Edith inched closer and closer to Maeve without blinking. The part of her eyes that had once been white was now red and so was the surrounding skin, making her eyes appear large and terrifying. "Zosia. Zosia. Zosia," Edith mumbled to herself.

Maeve had no idea that Gleaners were cursed for a few moments each night with the memory of who they used to be and the people they loved and missed. And of course, Edith was too much affected by the venom to understand the words coming from her inner mind, which was trying to remind her of who she was.

For a fleeting moment, Maeve was able to feel sorry for someone other than herself. Edith had once been an Earthen, connected with nature and competent at healing and tending to others. Seeing her reduced to the paltry faith of a Gleaner brought a glimmer of sentiment to Maeve's cynical heart. It was a shame for Edith that she had crossed paths with Charles and come to suffer such a cruel fate. But every Earthen knew not to blame a bee for stinging or a snake for biting. It was all part of their nature. Expecting otherwise was naïve and foolish.

Though Maeve pitied Edith, she did not blame Charles for her fate. Unlike Zosia, he had never pretended to be kind or merciful. If anyone was to blame for the life Edith had been trapped into, it was Zosia, who hadn't protected Edith well enough. Zosia could have saved her just as she could have saved Rose. Thoughts of Zosia and her betrayal made Maeve's thick shield rise around her cold heart. The compassion she had felt for Edith was overshadowed by her hatred toward Zosia.

"Zosia can't help you, Edith, or at least she won't," Maeve said and squashed a cockroach with the heel of her shoe when it came too close. "I've come to collect something from you, and if you hand it over willingly, we won't have a problem," Maeve spoke unhurriedly while looking around at the overwhelming mess in the hopes of finding the compass Charles had instructed her to get.

Edith began to huff as her eyes, which already looked too big in her pale and hollow face, grew even more in size. "Get out!" she spat, revealing how many teeth she was missing. "*It's mine! It's all mine.*"

Maeve followed Edith's movements as she backed up against the nearest pile of trash, reaching out her arms and hissing like a crazed animal marking its territory and protecting her beloved treasures.

Maeve gave a small sigh realizing her task was harder than expected. Finding a small compass among these endless piles seemed impossible without Edith's help, but Maeve doubted the fanatical Gleaner had intended any sort of order in what items were kept where.

Raising her hand Maeve began to lift Edith mid-air and suck the air out of her. When the sun's dusty rays landed on her face as she walked closer Edith saw Maeve's pretty face for the first time and nearly gasped while raising a shaky frail hand to point her crooked finger.

Not understanding Edith's attempt at speaking, Maeve let her down and watched Edith blink her eyes for the first time.

"I saw you. I knew you would come. Where is it?" With her eyes fixed on Maeve's chest, Edith reached for Maeve, who quickly moved back and watched the Gleaner's hands possessively grasp at the air.

"Where is what?"

"The necklace," Edith uttered with her crazed eyes scanning Maeve frantically.

Raising her hand to her chest, Maeve protected the necklace she wore under her dress. She had taken it back from James the day she cut out his tongue and it was the only sentimental thing she owned. Maeve kept it to remind herself of the life she deserved and to never trust anyone other than herself to achieve it.

Seeing an opportunity, Maeve's face remained stiff as she lowered her hands to her sides telling Edith, "I'll give you the necklace if you give me the compass."

"I-I-I-" Edith huffed like a child with a stutter who was suffering from an asthma attack. With the way her hand went to the outside of the pocket in her skirt, Maeve had a feeling the compass might be close after all.

With slow motions, Maeve pulled her necklace out from under her dress and instructed, "I'll show you mine if you show me yours."

Edith couldn't stop staring at the necklace as her fingers pulled out a small item from her pocket. It looked to be nothing more than an old sailor's compass that had seen better days. But Charles had told her of its magic, and as Maeve would soon learn, the world was filled with many objects that held much greater value than what they appeared.

A smile spread on Edith's wrinkly face revealing the few teeth left in her mouth and her rotten gums. It was a creepy smile that didn't stem from kindness and love but an addiction.

In hunched movements, she eagerly hurried toward Maeve and stuck out her hand to grasp the necklace from her throat, but once again Maeve was quick to step aside with an arched eyebrow that warned Edith not to try anything stupid.

"How did you know I was coming?" Maeve asked.

"Give me." Edith's voice was old and weak and yet she spat her words out aggressively. Unable to meet Maeve's eyes, Edith stared at the shiny necklace while pacing on top of the garbage she viewed as gold.

"I saw you coming. You give me your treasure. Now it's my treasure."

"How did you see me coming?" Maeve again asked persistently.

Edith stopped pacing and stared at Maeve's necklace with her head tilted. In moments like these, Edith became the worst side of herself. Much like humans that suffered from addiction, all she saw was her drug. She needed the necklace; everything in her body longed for it. The venom in her body urged her to get it because without it she couldn't find peace. Seeing it around Maeve's neck felt torturous. In those moments when she gave in, there was nothing of Edith left but only a Gleaner addicted to hoarding.

The addiction and need for such a rare treasure overtook Edith and made her launch herself toward Maeve again, half-running, half-crawling, ready to bite Maeve's head off to get the necklace.

Although an old woman running to attack Maeve with crazy red eyes and drool dripping from her mouth was a terrifying sight, Maeve didn't flinch. Instead, she lifted her hand and forced all air from Edith's body, making her feel like every organ was shrinking in size.

"This is the last time I'll ask you, Gleaner. How did you see me coming?" Maeve spoke slowly, in no rush to end Edith's agony. "Are you ready to answer now?"

With her instinct to survive Edith nodded her head as much as her pained body allowed before Maeve dropped her to the ground where she lay in a pile of dead rats and their droppings. When enough air had returned to Edith's lungs and she could breathe again, she looked up to Maeve, who was waiting for an answer.

Rising to her feet she dug her hand into her pockets, which were stuffed with all sorts of objects, and pulled out a hand mirror. The glass was scratched in places and the handle only had spots left of the original green color.

"It shows me where to get my treasures and the story behind them," Edith said while poking the mirror much too hard. "I saw how a man gave the necklace to a lady who later yelled at him and threw it away. Then he put it around your neck, only to take it off again. And now you have it once again. It's a pretty treasure, and I-I-I want it."

"Let me see that," Maeve demanded as she charged toward Edith until she was standing just before the smelly old Gleaner, who held the mirror to her chest.

"Others have tried to steal it, but it only works for me you see," Edith said with a cruelly proud smile. "But I can ask it a question for you *if* you give me your treasure." She put up her finger, which had several scars from rodents biting her.

"Deal," Maeve agreed.

There was one question Maeve asked and the answer she received left her speechless. Her eyes were wide as she and Edith looked at the small mirror seeing both what had passed and what was yet to come.

The pictures hadn't finished when Edith suddenly threw the mirror away from herself and fell to the ground before crawling backward to escape the images it had shown.

With her heart drumming, Maeve dove to her knees to retrieve the mirror. Luckily, the glass hadn't shattered, and with her hands clasped tightly around the handle, Maeve shot Edith a death glare.

"It wasn't done. Make it finish!" Maeve demanded.

Edith looked up at her with frightened and angry eyes and screamed, "NO!" while spit flew from her mouth.

"Does anyone else know?" Maeve asked in a stern tone as she got to her feet.

Edith shook her head violently "No, this is the only mirror of its kind, and it has never shown me anything like that before."

"No one can ever know about this," Maeve stated out loud as she put the mirror into her pocket.

"I won't tell," Edith swore, but in reality, something like that was out of her control. She often yelled all types of things, mostly messages from her dreams that she couldn't understand, and surely this was something she would mumble on about. Not that anyone other than the rats would listen to her. But even if Edith could keep her mouth shut, Maeve had never intended to spare her life. She had promised to deliver her head to Charles.

Taking off her necklace, Maeve bent down and placed it over Edith's head.

Like a small child, Edith forgot all about the worries and confusion that had clouded her head only a moment before and lit up in a smile as her hands clasped the pretty necklace.

Maeve now understood Charles' words about Edith being the most innocent and helpless type of creature on earth. At that moment, she was like a small child, tired from a major tantrum, and confused about how the world worked. Even if Charles hadn't asked for Edith's head, Maeve knew she would have killed her anyway. It was what she would have wanted others to do to her if she had been in Edith's shoes.

"You've been cursed with this life because of Zosia's indifference to Earthens and your own naïveté. I won't make the same mistake."

Maeve was just about to end Edith's life when she remembered the compass. With Edith distracted by the necklace, she took the compass from her pocket and used it the way Charles had instructed. It transported both her and Edith to one of the most tranquil spots she knew.

"Look, Edith," she whispered and saw the Gleaner gape as she took in the nature that surrounded them. Trees stood tall, birds were singing, and the air was fresh and unpolluted.

Edith's eyes filled with tears as she reached out and picked a tall flower that she brought to her nose. Closing her eyes, she inhaled the scent and sighed with delight.

"Isn't it lovely?" Maeve asked but Edith didn't answer. Instead, she began picking as many flowers she could get her hands on in a new fit of need to collect. That's when Maeve lifted her hand and slowly squeezed it until all the air had left Edith's frail little body. She kicked and wobbled until her body had no more to give and she lay on her back looking up at the blue sky. Her red eyes were large and blank and with two fingers, Maeve gently closed them.

Though she didn't consider herself an Earthen anymore, Maeve still performed the ritual which she'd grown up doing every time she had come across a dead animal. Just as Rose had taught her, she placed her hands above Edith's chest and valued the life that had been lived.

"May you finally be at peace," Maeve whispered.

With a hand still on Edith's chest, Maeve used the compass once again and transported her and Edith to Charles' office.

Edith lay dead on the floor while Maeve stood beside her. It felt comforting to be back in the luxurious room with the thick carpet, books, and the delicious smell of leather and mahogany.

With a glass of whiskey in his hand, Charles turned from the tall window he had been looking through. "Welcome back," he said and took a small sip while glancing at Edith before letting his gaze settle on Maeve.

"I'm impressed. You had the chance to escape with the compass, yet you returned." Charles sounded pleased.

"We had a deal, and I delivered my end of the bargain. Now it's your turn to do the same," Maeve answered and stepped over Edith to approach Charles. With a flirtatious smile, she took his glass from him and drank the last of the contents.

His eyes were sparkling with intrigue as he watched her closely. "I think we can help each other a great deal."

Maeve smiled. "I think you're right."

CHAPTER 21
ETERNAL YOUTH BRINGS LONELINESS

Annabel became as close to Althea as family. She had sharp instincts, a good sense of humor, and great skills when it came to healing. Compared to the quiet life in the forest that Althea had been used to, the first five years with Annabel felt like an adventure. They visited villages and towns all over the country and never stayed long enough to draw suspicion.

Most nights, they slept under the stars or in the small wagon, but sometimes, they were offered lodging in exchange for their services.

On a summer night in Scotland, Annabel and Althea were staying in a cozy little inn. Coming back from the lake where they had been swimming, they were chatting happily. It wasn't until they were in the small room that they had been given for the night that Annabel turned quiet.

"What's wrong?" Althea asked when she sensed the shift in Annabel, who stood staring into the small mirror on the wall.

Taking a step closer to the mirror, Annabel touched her skin and hair. "It's been a long time since I last saw myself in a looking glass. I didn't realize how old I've become."

Althea threw herself down onto the hard bed and wrinkled her nose at Annabel. "You're not old. Why would you say that?"

"My hair used to be blond and now there's so much gray and look…" With both palms to her cheeks, Annabel pulled her skin back to straighten her wrinkles.

"You're beautiful," Althea assured her friend with love shining from her expressive eyes.

Ignoring Althea's compliment, Annabel turned around and asked, "How is it possible that you haven't aged a day while I'm beginning to look like my grandmother?"

Picking at the fabric of her dress, Althea looked down but didn't know how to answer. She was well aware that she didn't age and why.

With slow steps, Annabel walked over to sit next to Althea on the bed, touching a lock of her long wavy red hair. "Your hair color is still vibrant with a beautiful glow, and I can't find a single strand of gray."

"That's because I'm younger than you," Althea pointed out but still didn't meet her friend's eyes. She was happy when Annabel dropped the subject, but as the years went by without Althea aging at all, it became impossible to hide her secret.

Once she finally confided in Annabel how she and Maeve had been given eternal life by Zosia, Annabel's expression changed into a look of pity.

"Now you know why I don't age," Althea whispered after telling how she and her sister had shared the crystal of immortality.

"Oh, ye poor lass. I can't imagine why Zosia would burden anyone with such a cruel destiny."

Althea frowned. "She wanted us to go on some quest and help her with something, but that was the day Rose died and Maeve…" Trailing off, Althea still found it hard to speak about the disturbing events that had caused her sister to spiral into madness. "She never told me the details and I wouldn't know where to start even if Zosia

211

answered when I call to her. Now I'm left with stronger powers and a body that doesn't age."

The two women sat close, and Annabel placed her arm around Althea. "Life on Earth is hard enough to bear for one lifetime. I can't imagine having to wander these villages and towns forever."

"I try not to think about it too much, but there are days when I get sad about the fact that I might survive you too. I've lost too many already."

For a while they sat in silence with the bonfire in front of them and their lunch cooking in a pot. Leaning forward Althea stirred the vegetable soup and heard her stomach growl. "It smells good."

"Hmm," Annabel answered in a distracted tone.

Looking back over her shoulder, Althea saw Annabel with her arms crossed and her gaze on the treetops. Lowering her voice, Annabel muttered, "Is it just me or do we see that black eagle often?"

Pressing the side of her hand to her forehead, Althea shielded her eyes from the sun and focused on the lonely eagle watching them. "Maybe it has a message for us?"

"No. I've reached out and invited it to communicate with me several times, but it doesn't respond. I'm starting to worry that it might be a Fader keeping an eye on us."

Raising her eyebrows, Althea asked, "A Fader. Really?"

Mentally, Althea reached out to the bird, but it sat there passively watching them.

After that, they noticed a black eagle at least once a month. In the beginning, it worried Annabel, who feared Faders, but as the years went by and nothing happened, it became their inside joke that the bird was a spy and sometimes, Althea even caught herself talking to the eagle despite its silence.

Overall, life was good for Annabel and Althea. They had each other and made a difference in people's lives. Rose had taught Althea to read, but Annabel taught her about selling her services and always thinking ahead. Books were a rare and precious thing, but they were good at swapping the ones they had read to get new ones that fed their minds with ideas and a deeper understanding of the world.

The year Annabel turned seventy-four, a shift happened. She became withdrawn and showed no desire to see new places. As an Earthen she didn't get sick, but it was like her appetite for life wasn't there anymore and it worried Althea how rapidly Annabel lost weight.

Wherever they traveled, people now assumed that Annabel was Althea's grandmother. The decline of her functions happened gradually but by late fall, she was too weak to sit on the bench when they traveled and instead lay sleeping inside the wagon.

Althea wouldn't think about losing Annabel, but her denial made no difference and before the first snow hit the grounds, her dearest friend and mentor passed peacefully in her sleep.

The day that Althea buried her, she carried her body into the woods and picked a beautiful site for her to rest in. She stayed and sang Annabel's favorite songs and talked about their adventures together. When day turned into night, she lit a fire and slept next to it to be close. For forty years, Althea hadn't slept alone and now she had not a single friend left in the world.

Waking up the next morning, she cried for what felt like hours, but in the end, she had no other choice but to continue the life that Annabel had taught her to live.

On her travels, Althea was so lonely that she began having long conversations with the animals she met. Tobias was long dead, and her new horse Adrian listened to her long rants about longing for friendship and companionship.

Of course, her pretty looks drew the attention of human men in the villages and towns she visited, but she knew all the tricks to avoid them getting close to her.

Seven years into her time alone, Althea felt so deprived of companionship that she confided in a fox that came to drink from the same lake she was bathing in.

"Where's your family? Are you alone like me?" she asked while she submerged her body under water leaving only her head above the surface to see the fox that sat by the edge of the small lake.

The fox kept an eye on her but continued drinking as she babbled, "Being alone is no fun. Don't you feel lonely sometimes?" Leaning her head back she let her wavy curls turn straight as they touched the cool water. "I do. Last week, I was so desperate for a hug that I considered asking the blacksmith for one. He was changing Adrian's shoes and seemed so friendly when he joked and made me smile."

The fox sat down and stared at her as Althea raised her head from the water and ran her fingers through her wet hair while she pretended that the fox took part in their conversation. "Yes, I know he's a human and we can't get too close to them. You don't have to remind me, but you don't understand how much I long to feel someone hug me. It's not like there are any Earthens for me to hug." Standing in the lake with her feet on hard rocks and only her head and collarbones above water, she felt her chest squeeze with emotions and when her tears came, she clutched Annabel's necklace that she carried around her neck every day to remember her friend. "Rose used to hug me every day and for twenty-four years I slept with Maeve every night. Then I lost them, but Zosia helped me find Annabel and I wasn't alone." Althea's chest rose and fell rapidly as she spilled out her grief to the quiet fox. "Zosia doesn't answer my pleas. Now, I have no one to laugh with or be close to. No one to talk to."

The fox tilted its head when Althea stopped crying and gave him a sad smile. "I'm sorry, I didn't mean it like that. It's just that you don't say much, and you can't exactly hug me back, can you?" Walking out of the water, she wasn't surprised that the fox stayed put when she passed it. Animals typically felt at ease around Earthens. "You know what, I feel like you're judging me. Is it what I said about the blacksmith? I didn't actually hug him, did I? I'll have you know that every time a human man offers me his... physical closeness, I stick to the lies Annabel taught me." Her eyes glazed over. "But you can't blame me for wondering what it would feel like to accept such an offer, can you?"

Holding out her hand she turned the ring on her finger. "The blacksmith flirted with me, but I told him I'm married and that my husband is the jealous type. You know the saddest part is really how good I am at lying, but I guess that's what happens after decades of telling the same stories. It's become such a habit that sometimes I lie even when it's not necessary."

The fox scratched behind its ear and seemed uninterested in her confessions.

"I like your fur," she told the fox. "You have an orange glow to your red coat, which makes you a redhead like me." Putting a dress on, Althea began untangling her newly washed hair while looking at the fox. There was something in its eyes that made her walk closer and squat down. "Hey, beautiful, would *you* be my friend?"

The fox blinked and looked to the side.

When she reached out her hand, it sniffed her fingers and placed its head on her palm. "Aww, I'll take that as a yes." Eager for contact, she used her other hand to stroke the fox's back.

That was too much for the wild animal and it scuttered out of her reach.

Disappointed, Althea apologized, "I'm sorry, I didn't mean to scare you." Standing back up she sighed out loud. "I really need to find some real friends. I think I'm losing my mind."

Closing her eyes, she prayed to Zosia like she had so many times since Annabel died. "Please, Zosia, I beg of you. Help me find other Earthens the same way you helped me find Annabel. If there are no Earthens left, please, please take back the eternal life you gave me. I do not want to live alone and be unloved.

Like so many times before, there was no answer. All Althea got from nature was the connection to the beautiful fox who sat watching her from a distance with an intense gaze.

With another sad sigh, Althea put on the rest of her clothes and led Adrian back to the wagon.

As they left the tranquil spot by the lake, the fox kept sitting and observing. He had heard and understood everything. Looking left and right, he made sure that he was alone before he shifted into a bird and lifted from the ground. For a while he followed Althea from above as he had on occasion for the past forty-five years. She was singing a sad tune and looking straight ahead as she sat on the small bench in the front of the wagon as it moved forward.

He had been tasked by the Cobra to keep an eye on Althea. That she was Maeve's twin sister was hard to understand because they were as opposite as two people could be. It had been seven years since her friend Annabel died and he saw how she still grieved. It had touched his cold heart to hear her express how she longed to be touched and Damon would have happily hugged her himself if things had been different. For now, he would watch her from a distance in the same way people caught butterflies in a glass jar and observed one's beauty without ever touching its wings.

CHAPTER 22
A POWERFUL SPIDER

The creaking of the floorboards made Maeve look up from the papers in front of her. She was one year from her seventieth birthday but hadn't aged a day since she took the crystal of immortality at twenty-four. And yet, her eyes revealed the decades of cynical ploys for power that she had indulged in.

"Oh, it's you," she said with disappointment when Damon walked in.

Giving a polite bow, he straightened up and explained in a calm tone, "Charles asked me to share my report on your sister with you."

Maeve scoffed. "I honestly don't know why he insists on keeping an eye on her. All she ever does is trot around with that horse from one muddy and miserable village to the next."

"She's near the highlands in Scotland now. I saw her yesterday."

"And?" Maeve shook her head a little as if his disturbance was annoying.

"There's not much to report. She's still alone after Annabel died."

"Who?" Maeve cocked an eyebrow.

"The woman she traveled with until she died seven years ago."

"Ah, yes, right." With a dismissive wave of her hand, she pushed the papers away. "I really shouldn't have told Charles about splitting my crystal with Althea. It's a waste of everyone's time to do these reports on her. So what if she's immortal like me? It's not like my sister would ever do anything remarkable or be a danger to anyone."

Damon kept his tone even. "I can see why Charles insists on keeping an eye on her. She has the same level of power and immortality as you do, after all."

"Hmm... and does she still look young?"

"As pretty as ever," Damon said, and it somehow provoked Maeve's vanity.

Getting up from her chair she moved around the desk and got closer to Damon. "You and I never..." Her voice had turned a bit seductive as she looked deep into his eyes.

Stiffening slightly, Damon shifted his balance a tiny bit. "With your connection to the Cobra, I prefer not to get involved."

"Charles doesn't own me like he owns you and the other Faders. I can sleep with whomever I want to."

Fixing his gaze on a statuette on her desk, Damon kept quiet. He had no desire to sleep with Maeve but didn't want to upset her either.

"So, you think my sister is pretty, do you?" she asked, watching his facial expressions closely.

"Mmm," he answered with his lips pressed together.

She moved even closer. "Prettier than me?"

Damon had been twenty-eight when he accepted Charles' offer to become a Fader. From his poor upbringing in Poland, he had used his sharp intellect and charm to climb above his rank. When Charles came along and spoke to his ambition of climbing all the way to the top and getting back at the people who had wronged him, it had been too hard to resist.

Looking at Maeve, he knew what she wanted him to answer, but despite her ruthless nature and position as one of Charles' favorites, he wouldn't be pressured to deliver empty flattery.

"Your sister can't compare to you when it comes to fashion or style. You have access to the finest seamstresses while she wears simple and ill-fitting dresses. Her hair is either hanging loose or arranged in a messy braid while your hairstyle is always impeccable. It shows that she's outdoors all year round when she rides from town to town. Her complexion is that of a farm girl, while yours is that of a fine lady."

Maeve placed her hands on her hips. "You must think me an imbecile, Damon. I asked you a question and you're pointing out the obvious without answering me truthfully. Do you think Althea is prettier than me?"

With a disarming smile, he clarified, "You are both beautiful women. She doesn't have your elegance, but if I had to choose between being with one of you, I would pick her."

"Why?"

Damon inhaled sharply and spoke on his exhalation. "Because she isn't cunning or experienced like you are. She would be easy to charm and most likely be much more pliable than you."

The way Maeve's nostrils flared revealed that she wasn't pleased, but she pretended not to care. Raising her chin she said, "Is that your way of saying that you're lazy and don't like a challenge?"

Damon refrained from telling Maeve that he had felt her interest before and didn't see much of a challenge in seducing her. He was smart enough not to get involved with anyone who slept with Charles – even if they were as beautiful as Maeve. Standing tall with his hands folded in front of him, he calmly observed Maeve as she walked to one of the windows and looked out while talking to him.

"Did my sister have any friends or interesting plans?"

"Not that I know of. She seems to live a very isolated life."

220

"What do you mean? She travels all the time and works with humans, doesn't she?"

"Yes, but she never stays long enough to make any friends or fall in love."

With another scoff, Maeve placed her hands on the windowsill and studied the people walking on the street outside. "Falling in love is for fools. Althea is smarter than that. She saw what happened to me when I fell in love. If it wasn't for her and Rose finding me in time, I would have been killed by the only man I ever loved."

Damon had a hard time imagining Maeve as an innocent young girl in love and changed the subject. "Do you need anything else?"

She turned toward him and crossed her arms. "Have you heard from Mr. Thomas?"

"I saw him a few weeks ago in Spain. Why?"

"He's overseeing my profits on the slave trade. Philip II of Spain has granted a near-monopoly in the slave trade to Pedro Gomes Reinal, and as you very well know, he works for me."

"I'm aware. Just as King Philip works for Charles," Damon added.

"Yes. Of course. All Faders do. Anyway, I suspect that Mr. Thomas is frolicking around instead of pressuring Pedro as I asked him to. I heard rumors that he rented a house outside Seville and has been hosting wild parties."

"Sounds like something he would do. Thomas is a true hedonist."

Maeve sighed. "Will he never get enough of that sort of thing?"

Damon smiled and lifted his shoulders in a quick shrug. "What do you expect? The man was a Viking. He's come a long way from the uncivilized heathen he used to be."

"He's still a heathen if you ask me," Maeve muttered.

Damon couldn't help provoking her a little and pointed out, "I got the impression that you liked that side of him. Didn't you two spend some time together in Portugal?"

Maeve gave him a cold look that only her cynical eyes could give. "That was more than twenty years ago. My personal relationship with him is irrelevant, but I might need you to visit with him and make sure he's doing the work I ordered him to do."

This time it was Damon who crossed his arms. "Are you meaning to tell me that he now takes orders from you?" They both knew he didn't and neither did Damon. Maeve was like a spider pulling threads and controlling people with her connections and powers. But despite her influence with Queen Elizabeth and other heads of state, Maeve held no power over Faders as old as Damon and Thomas.

"I meant what I'm *paying* him to do," she corrected herself. "The French have now made slavery illegal in France. Did you hear that?"

"Yes," he answered and looked toward the door, wanting to leave.

Maeve narrowed her eyes, "Are you still determined not to get involved in slave trading?"

Rocking back on his heels, he cleared his throat. "Unlike you, I hold no hatred towards humans. I'm fully capable of making money without enslaving others."

Maeve smacked her tongue. "Humans have held slaves for as long as anyone can remember. The Roman empire was built on slaves. Why shouldn't we take advantage of such lucrative business opportunities? I'm just upset about France. Other countries had better not follow with a ban as well. It's bad for my business."

"Then it's a good thing that you have such a wide range of investments," Damon said and took a step back to signal that he wanted to end their conversation.

Maeve understood and went back to her chair making it sound like she was the one dismissing him, "I have work I must finish so I can get ready for tonight. I assume you were invited to court as well?"

"I was. I'm told not to miss Shakespeare's newest play. Apparently, it's quite witty."

Maeve didn't look up but made herself look busy. "You may leave me, Damon."

Bowing his neck, he left feeling annoyed with her for making him look like an errand boy. He might owe his loyalty and service to Charles, but not Maeve. It was enough that Charles had him keep track of Althea and regularly report her whereabouts to him. Although, now that Althea had begun talking to him, the assignment had become a bit more entertaining. For a brief moment, he wondered what she would say if she knew that she wasn't just talking to random animals but a Fader who had followed her for almost five decades. Damon knew things about Althea that were intimate and deeply private. If he had been a better man, he would have cared about someone as kind and sweet as her. Damon had every worldly possession designed to bring a person comfort. And yet, he was well aware that the greatest luxury in life would be forever out of his reach. In his centuries of living, he had learned that caring about others was an indulgence he couldn't afford.

CHAPTER 23
VILLAGE OF HOPE AND NEW BEGINNINGS

Two things followed an Earthen wherever they went: the knowledge that being themselves around humans could lead to a witch trial where they would be murdered in front of their loved ones, and second, the fear that today was the day it would happen.

They had no wings to fly in the sky or fins to swim in the deep oceans. For Earthens there was no place where they could be safe from the threat of humans. And so, each day they carried the fear that it would be their last day.

Endless times, Althea and other Earthens had prayed to Zosia for help. But no answers came.

On a dreadful winter day when Althea's horse stood stuck in high snow and she once again was left with no food for either of them, she wanted to lie down in the snow and surrender to death. But she'd died from starvation before only for her body to heal itself and for her to wake up with the same hungry growls in her stomach. Exhausted from dragging herself through the snow she desperately shouted at the harsh wind for help.

Her knees hit the soft powder of snow as she collapsed in sobs. But when the harsh wind died down around her, she looked up with her face crimson from crying. Her tears stopped flowing and her eyes widened when she saw how the snowflakes falling from the ground rose to form the feminine frame of Zosia.

"Don't despair, Althea. All will be well," she whispered, and with only the snow falling, it felt quiet and peaceful as she spoke.

"Please, please, Zosia, I'm begging you to take back this immortality and let me close my eyes for the last time. What's the point of me suffering like this? I've wandered seven years alone and met no Earthens. Am I truly the last one left?"

"You are not. The number is dwindling fast, but there are still a few hundred spread around the world. I need you here, Althea, I sense you will be important to me."

"But I'm so lonely. Can't you at least help me find some of the other Earthens and help us be safe from persecution? I know it's in your power."

The snowflakes danced in the air, and feeling desperate for contact, Althea reached out to touch Zosia. "I can't go on like this."

"I could bring you home, but only if you promise to return."

"Home to you?"

Zosia's voice had the same ethereal quality as always when she spoke, "Home to the realm you came from and where you will return one day. I have considered making it a sanctuary for all Earthens but it was my hope it wouldn't be necessary. Earthens are meant to balance out the energies on Earth and without you, bad things could spiral out of control."

"Please, Zosia, take me home. I'm desperate."

There was no reply and then the snowflakes of Zosia's body separated and fell back down.

The disappointment in Althea was colossal. Closing her eyes, she let her head sink. But then a sound alerted her that something was going on. Right in front of her horse, ice crystals rose and formed a portal.

Her horse neighed as the most spectacular sight showed through the portal, of green grass and colored flowers. While Althea gaped, her horse moved forward pulling the wagon into another dimension where it was summer.

Still shocked, Althea stood unable to move when a chuckle sounded and Zosia asked, "Are you coming?"

As she stepped through the portal, Althea's head went from side to side taking everything in. "What is this place?" she asked in awe.

"Here you'll find different types of nature from endless forests, beautiful mountains, and tranquil beaches to vast deserts. It is where all animals and Earthens come from and return to in the form of nature after living on Earth."

Tears ran down Althea's cheeks as she watched herds of reindeer and elk roaming freely around her in the field of wildflowers where she stood. One of the elk came to greet her and her horse and Althea stroked its fur. Releasing Adrian from the wagon, she allowed him to walk freely and he followed her as she went to drink from the crystal clear lake close by. As Althea sank to her knees and drank from the lake, water droplets rose in front of her as Zosia appeared again.

"You will be safe here, Althea. It is protected land, untouched by humans, with creeks that run through the enormously lush forests. My only condition is that you visit earth daily to continue your work. For the sake of nature and humans, you must bring your kindness to balance out the evil in the world.

Taking off her jacket, Althea soaked in the warm climate and the delicious feeling of sunshine caressing her skin.

"Here, there are no seasons. The trees always bear fruit, and the flowers thrive throughout the whole year," Zosia explained.

Althea felt too overwhelmed to speak and couldn't get enough of the colors more vibrant than anything she had ever seen on earth. "It's so peaceful here," she breathed. Working as a healer, she had heard humans talk about the heaven they believed in often, but this was magnificent beyond anything their words could ever describe. Although it looked quite similar to Earth, it felt like another planet entirely. Every plant and animal was flourishing and radiated the peace that they bathed in. The birds sang melodies filled with messages of bliss and peace, leaving her ears satisfied yet hungry for more of the sweet music. Their singing was angelic and more beautiful than anything Althea had ever heard before.

She watched in fascination as the herd of reindeer crossed the meadow filled with large purple, pink, and white flowers. The largest reindeer looked up in acknowledgment of Althea and bowed their heads majestically before continuing with no trace of fear.

It surprised her that her moment of distraction had been enough for Zosia to disappear. Getting up she spun and called for her.

"Zosia, where did you go?"

Instead of water droplets forming her figure, petals from some of the many wildflowers now rose into the air where they elegantly danced, together forming the feminine figure of Zosia.

"How do you like your new home?"

Moved to tears, Althea's voice was brittle. "I'm so happy and I never want to leave again. What did you mean when you said that it's where animals and Earthens come from? Does that mean there are other Earthens here?"

"Your brain may limit you, making you forget who you are and where you come from, but you *are* nature, just like all other Earthens.

"Before an Earthen lives amongst humans and after they die, they melt into one with nature again, becoming the very soil you stand upon and the air you breathe."

"Is Rose a part of nature? Is she here?" Althea asked and looked around as if she might be lucky enough to see Rose waving at her.

"Your aunt was met with the warm embrace of nature the moment she left her body. She watches you through the eyes of the birds, and she feels your embrace every time you hug a tree, and so does your father and all your other ancestors along with the future generations that will live as Earthens."

Althea sucked in her lips and rubbed her chest with her palm, feeling overwhelmed and touched. "Why haven't you told all Earthens of this place?"

"Earthens forget about their home because it would make it too difficult to live in the human world away from this tranquillity. They would long to return, and potentially all take their own life from feeling homesick. If you are to live here, it's with the promise that you will all return to earth daily to continue your work as healers."

"But just knowing that there is life after death would bring so much peace to those who live in fear or have lost someone they love," Althea argued. "Why don't you tell them?"

"Because I am not like the gods the humans worship. I don't claim to have any answers. I am merely nature and the force of balance. I will not interfere with any answers or personal opinions because I am no wiser than you are, Althea. I show myself rarely and only use my voice to aid the balance on Earth." The purple, pink, and white flower petals elegantly danced around, keeping the feminine form of Zosia's body as she spoke in angelic whispers through the air. "I'm showing myself to you because you are right. My Earthens are dying out, and without them, darkness is spreading in people's hearts and minds."

"Can't you do something to stop the evil?"

228

"I tried. Maeve had the potential to help, but she lost her way."

"She told me you wanted us to go on a quest, but we never got that far."

"I'm aware that things took a drastic turn after I met with Maeve. Too much happened to her in too short a timespan. But there's still hope."

"You think Maeve could still go on the quest?"

"I'm always hoping for a positive outcome, but I would be surprised."

"Do you want me to go on the quest alone?"

"It's kind of you to offer, Althea, but you were never meant to get the crystal of immortality. You don't have the ruthlessness that it takes to kill. Instead, you must gather all the Earthens and create a sanctuary for you all here to live. You will know when I have selected the right person for the task of collecting the weapons needed to kill the Cobra."

"Who?"

Zosia didn't clarify but all the petals from the flowers suddenly transformed into a giant butterfly that flew around a little. "I've chosen this meadow for you Earthens to live in and grow your numbers. Here you can live in peace if you promise that you will continue to heal humans and bring balance to the nature of the Earth."

Althea nodded and smiled as a family of bunnies ran past her feet. "What is the name of this place?"

"It does not have a name. I've never felt a need to give it one. But with the help of the other Earthens you can build a village here and name this realm whatever you want."

Althea thought for a moment but could not come up with anything and looked back to Zosia. "I would love for you to name it…"

Zosia was back in the shape of a woman looking down at Althea. Although she didn't have a mouth,

Althea felt as though Zosia was gently smiling. "I will not interfere with any answers or personal opinions, I will only show myself and use my voice if it's to help the balance on Earth," she repeated.

"But this realm will help us Earthens grow in numbers and in that way help to serve the balance you thrive for on Earth. We would not be able to create this village if it weren't for you. I would welcome any suggestion you might have for a name."

For a long and silent moment, Zosia raised her chin and looked forward before she finally answered, "Orenda."

"Orenda." Althea tasted the word and asked, "Does it mean anything?"

"Orenda is the invisible magic power believed by some of the indigenous people on Earth to pervade certain spiritual energy in people and their environment. It suits this realm well."

"Orenda," Althea agreed, liking the sound of the beautiful word.

"Orenda," Zosia repeated, and from the ground a new portal formed from flowers, sticks, and tall grass. "I will send out invitations for all Earthens to join you here. You shall be their leader and caretaker. That will be your task, Althea. These portals will take you wherever you are most needed. Or where you set your mind to."

Standing in the sun, Althea suddenly remembered how lost and powerless she had felt not long ago when she was stuck in piles of snow on Earth. "Thank you for answering my prayers, Zosia. I will be forever grateful."

Moving forward, the female shape bowed down and kissed Althea's forehead before turning into a butterfly and taking off across the meadow.

Althea watched in rapture as the butterfly dissolved and the petals slowly fell to the ground. The portal still stood and before she had time to think, Earthens began to arrive. Over the next weeks, more than two hundred arrived from all around the world. They all told the same story of how Zosia had whispered through the wind for them to plant their feet on the ground, lift their hands, and let the power of the earth flow through them to create a doorway.

To most of the Earthens, Zosia was a name that belonged to myths their ancestors had told them. Some froze in shock at hearing her voice, and others cried with joy, but all of them gaped when they followed her instructions. Portals from natural materials like sticks, stones, and leaves would lift from the ground to form the shape of a doorframe. Each Earthen intuitively walked through the opening sensing a longing to see what was on the other side. The first time they walked into Orenda, they were as awestruck as Althea had been and once they realized everyone here were Earthens, and that no human could harm them, many cried with happiness. Althea soon learned that building a village wasn't easy. Not only did they have language barriers, but their taste in what a home should look like also varied. The Europeans preferred cottages while the Earthens from South America preferred to build their homes up in the treetops of the forest. Slowly, a community took form with Earthens coming and going to Orenda through portals. Each time the doorway had served its purpose, the natural materials it was made from fell to the ground again.

Everything was lush and the air smelled sweeter in Orenda, where all Earthens agreed that nature was a more generous and gorgeous nature than on Earth.

What had been open flower fields and untouched forest when they first arrived became a large village filled with cozy cottages and gardens where they grew their food. It took time to build the village, but being cursed with immortality, Althea had all the time in the world.

Despite having hundreds of Earthens around her, Althea often thought of her friend Annabel and missed her greatly. After what Zosia had told her, she clung to the idea that her friend was always close by and often talked to both her and Rose. Her new role as leader of Orenda was overwhelming at times. There were days when she loved the feeling of great purpose in her life and other days when she felt unsure and underqualified to make decisions that involved others than herself. On those days, she walked in solitude, seeking guidance from Annabel, Rose, and otherwise Earthens. She asked them how to best accommodate all the different cultures in Orenda and although they never answered her directly, she always came back from her walks with a new perspective and appreciation. So what if things weren't all perfect? Every Earthen here had suffered deeply and came to Orenda traumatized in some way. Even for those unable to understand one another, it was still incredibly healing to be among like-minded people who would never hurt them. She found comfort in the thought that in time they would heal their wounds together. They all carried ancestral grief from the generations of Earthens who had lived in fear. It made sense that it would take some generations to eradicate all that negativity.

Althea mused that being immortal, she would get to see children born who would never have to worry about mobs of humans attacking their house at night. In Orenda, Earthens could be themselves and take up as much space as they wanted. They were finally safe.

Selflessly, Althea was the last one to have her house finished. She loved her small, yellow cottage with a thatched roof, a green door, and paned windows.

Besides her cozy home, her favorite place was the community house, which was more like a small manor in size with a beautiful library, indoor activities, and a dining hall to eat in when it was raining outside. With so many people working with dedication, the building was close to done in record time. It was barely half the size of James' manor, but to all the Earthens it felt enormous. Most of them had been nomads on Earth with no more than a tent to sleep in.

Above the large entrance doors to the community house, Althea hung a sign that read, "Annabel."

"Who is the Annabel?" Khalid asked one day as he and Althea were cleaning the windows in the community house. He was born in Egypt and his accent was thick from only speaking English for a year, but he was a quick learner and an intelligent man.

He wasn't the first to ask, and Althea happily answered, "The Annabel Manor is named after my close friend, Annabel. She died more than eight years ago but we traveled together, and she taught me everything she knew. She was a warm and wonderful person who always dreamed of settling down somewhere. Unfortunately, it wasn't safe to live among humans, so we lived a life of traveling while working as healers. Annabel would have loved Orenda, and I thought it was only fair she finally got a home, even if she can't live in it."

"And the biggest house in the whole village at that," Khalid added with a kind smile. "I wish my daughter would come; I know she would love it here, but she's married to a human, and what with him being unable to enter Orenda, she's staying in Egypt."

"As long as her husband is the one she loves and they are happy together," Althea said.

Khalid sighed deeply with concern in his dark eyes. "Mohammed is a kind man, but it's her safety I'm worried about. I too lost my wife to the superstition of humans."

Just then, Maria came walking. She was an older woman from Spain who filled the role as a second leader of Orenda and supported Althea in all ways.

"We all know the price of human superstition all too well here, don't we, Maria?" Althea asked her friend.

Maria stopped and watched Althea and Khalid working on the windows. "Yes. I think we've all lost loved ones on that account. My oldest son was just seven when he slipped up. In hindsight, I should have never allowed him to play with the priest's nephews but there weren't many children in our village and they became friends. Despite promising he never would, Pedro told them about Zosia and how the god they believed in wasn't real." Maria's eyes glazed over as memories took her back. "Of course, they told their uncle, the priest, and soon rumors traveled. They came for me first, but my husband and three sons helped me escape. They paid with their lives for that and today Carmen and I are all that's left of our family."

Although Maria didn't cry, the pain on her face from speaking of her lost family was clear and it broke the heart of Althea, who empathized with the woman who was close to the same age as herself.

"It was many years ago and Carmen was only ten when we escaped," Maria continued, "but we still miss the others every day." She looked to Althea and went to stroke her back with motherly compassion. "I'm so grateful you've created this village. My family would have loved it."

Althea took her hand and brushed it between her palms as she spoke the same words Zosia had once spoken to her. "Your family is watching you through the eyes of the birds, and hugging you back every time you embrace a tree, and they kiss you through the warm rays

234

of the sun. They're here, Maria, within Zosia, within us, and they are enjoying the peace of Orenda just like the rest of us."

"Thank you, dear," Maria said with watering eyes and brushed her gray hair behind her ears.

For a moment they held each other in a tight hug and empathized with one another.

"At least you have Carmen here," Khalid told Maria. "I was just talking about how my daughter is married to a human and can't leave him to come and live in Orenda."

Althea gave him a small smile, "You should invite her for a visit. I would love to meet your daughter one day."

"Maybe I will. What about you, Althea? Do you want children one day?" Khalid asked.

Sadness filled Althea. "My situation is a little different from the rest of you..." Her eyebrows tightened as she trailed off. For a moment, she stood with her two new friends in silence considering Khalid's question. "I've lost everyone I ever loved."

Khalid exchanged a glance with Maria before placing a hand on Althea's shoulder and talking in a soft tone. "No parent should outlive their children. I understand and sympathize with both of you for your losses."

"I didn't have any children," Althea clarified to correct the misunderstanding.

"But if fear kept you from having children then doesn't that feel like a loss to you as well?"

Althea looked down and as she reflected on Khalid's words, a wave of grief washed over her. With no men in her life, children had never been an option for her. There were several attractive men in Orenda who would make great fathers, but she would outlive all of them and it was more than her heart could bear.

"I wish we'd had Orenda sooner. My friend Annabel would have been a wonderful mother and grandmother. She loved children."

Maria smiled. "Remember what you just said about my family being with me. I'm sure Annabel is with you as well. She's at peace with Zosia and so is everyone else we've lost," Althea dwelled on her words because they brought up thoughts of her sister. She had thought a lot about Maeve since her conversation with Zosia. For the first time, she opened up and talked about her to Maria and Khalid. "I have a sister who is still alive. I lost her many years ago after our aunt was executed. Grief drove her crazy and she became a different person from the loving sister I used to know. I'll spare you the details, but things didn't end well between us, and we went our separate ways." Althea closed the last window after they had washed it and together, Khalid, Maria, and she walked through the village. With an endless forest to roam, the cottages were well spaced out, all getting a good amount of privacy and some getting their large meadows entirely to themselves.

"Did she arrive here, yet?" Khalid asked as they took a turn down a thin dirt trail with fruit trees' boughs hanging above their heads.

"No. Maybe she doesn't know about Orenda or maybe she's refusing to come," Althea speculated.

"I don't think that's it." Khalid shook his head. "Zosia collectively whispered out to all Earthens. Could it be that your sister is nervous about seeing you again? Maybe she worries that you're angry or disappointed with her."

"Yes," Maria agreed. "You should find her, Althea. Family is everything! I would give anything to have my husband and boys here. I never had a sister, but you may actually have a chance to reconnect with yours."

"I've been considering it a lot lately, but it's been so long that it feels like another lifetime has passed since I knew her," Althea said and felt her heart ache from the memories of the last time she'd seen Maeve.

"Do you know where she lives?" Khalid asked.

"No. But Zosia mentioned her, and that tells me she's still around."

"There's only one way to find out." Khalid brushed his hand against Althea's back as they passed the large field where Earthens were harvesting and growing food. Everything was colorful and lush, and several women raised their heads and waved as they passed.

In her strong Spanish accent, Maria said, "You're young, dear; now that we finally have a place to be safe, it's time to be courageous. If for some reason your sister rejects your offer of living in Orenda, at least you'll know that you did your part to mend the relationship between you."

Althea smiled and didn't tell Maria that she was the older of the two. She preferred not to talk about her immortality. Eventually, they would catch on to it, and she would need to answer all the questions that came with it. But for now, she felt like maybe she could escape the curse itself and pretend to be normal for a while. "To be honest, I don't know how Maeve would react to seeing me again. We didn't separate on good terms."

Maria took Althea's hand. "If it doesn't go well with your sister, you'll still have all of us waiting for you back here with hugs. We're your new family."

They had reached Althea's cute little yellow cottage surrounded by trees and meadows.

"I think I'll seek Maeve out and invite her to join us here. I'm not the same person I was when we went our separate ways, so I have to assume she's changed as well. Hopefully for the better." With her mind made up, Althea nodded and parted from Maria and Khalid before she headed inside her charming home surrounded by flower bushes and fruit trees, a place she wished she could have shown Rose and Annabel.

Picking up her medical bag she returned outside and walked out of her garden to the nearby forest where the trees were green with moss. She had learned never to create portals inside her garden the hard way. The one time she did it, all the petals from her blooming roses and rhododendron flew up to form the portal and as a result, her beautiful bushes were left completely bare afterward.

Closing her eyes, Althea set the intention for the portal to take her to whoever needed her help at that time. When she opened her eyes, a portal had formed from sticks and pinecones showing her a well in front of a town with tall towers. The sun was setting in that realm and the light shone softly as to welcome her to the human world. Remembering her promise to Zosia, Althea stepped through the portal to find the person she needed to help.

CHAPTER 24
STRANGERS WITH A PAST

It had been almost fifty years since Althea and Maeve had last seen one another.

Once Althea set out to find her sister, she picked up a trail of material wealth that far surpassed anything she could have imagined. Within the half-century, since Maeve had started her jewelry empire, it had grown to be the most profitable and best-known jewelry store in England. After Queen Elizabeth became one of Maeve's best customers, the rest of high society followed suit, competing for jewelry with the biggest and most exquisite diamonds and jewels. Standing in London outside the glamorous home in Mayfair where her sister now lived, Althea thought about the contrast to Rose's crooked, old house in the forest where they had grown up together.

Closing her eyes, Althea tried to push out the memory of the crazy rage in Maeve's expression the last time she'd seen her. In her nightmares, she had often relived how, that day, Maeve had thrown her through the air like a rag doll and knocked her unconscious when she hit a wall.

For decades, Althea had considered her sister dead to her. After Maeve's horrendous act of burning down an entire town and killing the people who lived there, she had concluded that the sister she had once loved no longer walked the earth.

But maybe it was time to get to know the new Maeve and make amends; after all, Orenda was all about new beginnings and hope.

She took a deep steadying breath as the people on the crowded street passed in a blur of color.

With Althea traveling so much, she knew she was a difficult person to find. And yet, she wondered if her sister had even tried to locate her. She doubted it. In her mind, it made sense that Maeve would feel ashamed of what she'd done. If Althea hadn't been immortal, Maeve's violent attack would have killed her. Surely, Maeve felt remorseful about what happened and today she would get a chance to apologize.

Maybe with time spent in Orenda, away from humans, they could get to know this new version of one another and rekindle the sisterly love that they'd once shared.

Straightening up, Althea stopped herself from having too much hope. She had already lost Maeve once. Setting her hopes too high was foolish. Losing her sister again, or even the dream of what could be between them would be all too painful for her traumatized soul.

Althea's heart was working at double speed when she went to knock on the door of the fancy home.

After delivering her message that she was here to see her sister, she waited another long while until the butler returned and led her inside a grand entrance and up the stairs to a lavish tearoom. The grand room had tall windows overlooking the busy streets of London below. Some of the windows were open, letting in a cool breeze and the noise of people in the streets. Everything oozed money, with the carvings on the doors, the double-layered silk curtains, and the thick carpet on the floor. Althea took in the many decorations that looked like they had been imported from around the world.

Not having spoken for half a century, Althea had no idea what to expect. Would her sister be happy to see her, or would her eyes still glimmer with hatred just as they had when she'd burned down the town and killed everyone that day Rose died?

When she heard footsteps outside, she stared at the door and held her breath.

Maeve entered with an expression that didn't reveal much. Closing the door behind her, she stood for a moment watching Althea, puzzled to see her sister after close to five decades. Slowly she walked closer without either of them speaking.

At first, Maeve wondered if her mind was playing tricks on her, but as she studied details on Althea's face that she had forgotten, memories rushed back. Althea still had the freckles that Maeve had counted when they were children and her abundant untamed orange curls that Maeve had loved to let her fingers run through. Looking into her sister's eyes it felt like an eternity since she had seen a person with such beautiful blue and green eyes. There was no hostility on Althea's face – nor was there joy.

"You haven't changed at all," Maeve said and broke the silence.

"No?" Althea asked in a sad tone. "You have. I hardly recognize you."

She saw only a few similarities between this elegantly dressed woman and the loving sister Maeve had once been. She had been blessed with beauty from birth, but her perfectly shaped eyes that had once shone with kindness had lost their sparkle. Though her body had not aged, and her lips were still perfectly curved and full with a cute little nose above them, she no longer looked like the girl who had run barefoot through the forest with careless giggles.

An urge rose in Althea to reach out and free her sister's red hair from the neatly arranged hairstyle that didn't leave a single strand to bounce freely. The bright orange color she remembered had changed into a darker auburn. It still seemed a crime to contain all that gorgeous, long hair in a hairstyle that looked to entrap the essence of Maeve's free spirit.

The sisters had grown up wearing dresses made of cheap fabrics. Althea still wore a simple, practical dress that left her with room to move and forage. It was a far cry from Maeve's fashionable gown that complimented her every curve but didn't look comfortable. "It's been a while," Maeve said with a slight upper curve at the edge of her perfect lips.

Seeing Maeve cut off from nature, in her lavish home that reeked of material wealth, made Althea sick to her stomach. Everything about Maeve represented the life she'd been so eager to live with James that it had cost them both everything, and yet it was still the path Maeve had chosen. Almost fifty years had passed since Rose died, and yet in that moment, Althea felt a wave of resentment wash over her.

Maeve, who had been staring into her sister's eyes, remembering how happy they had once been, saw the shift in Althea. She had come close to embracing her sister in a tight hug, but the moment she saw how Althea's gaze turned disapproving, Maeve fell back on her usual cynical disinterest. She didn't need or want her sister's judgment.

With a tight emotional shield pressed to her chest, she asked in a sharp tone, "What are you doing here?"

Althea was thrown off by the change in her tone but decided to follow through with the plan she'd entered with instead and answered, "I've come to talk to you."

Maeve breathed noisily and gestured toward the two opposing sofas in the middle of the room. When they went to go take a seat, Althea was surprised Maeve didn't sit in the seat next to her but instead took a seat across from her.

"You changed your hair," Althea pointed out while pulling at her own curly orange locks.

"The orange reminded me of you," Maeve answered honestly with a stern face.

Althea nodded, trying not to take the insult to heart. "It suits you," she replied after a silent moment and tried to muster a polite smile.

"You would be surprised what potions can do if you experiment a little bit." Maeve barely blinked, and though her face looked cold and her eyes bored, her emotions were spiraling out of control behind the shield where she hid them so well. "But then again, you've never been one to take any risks, have you, sister?"

Althea sucked on her tongue to stop herself from scoffing. Maeve wasn't subtle about her condescending tone, but Althea chose to ignore it. Maybe Maeve was rude and off-putting because she had been surrounded by humans too long. Orenda would be healthy for her and hopefully bring out the old and kind Maeve.

"I've taken risks plenty of times and I'm sure that you've been through just as much in the past decades as I have," Althea said, using her hands to underline her words as she spoke. "I've come to talk to you, Maeve, because I think it's time we find our way back to one another. We both lost Rose, but we handled our grief differently. To me, it was heart-wrenching to lose my aunt, the woman who raised and loved me, but it was even harder to lose my twin."

Maeve cocked an eyebrow. "Then maybe you shouldn't have abandoned me."

Althea drew back in her seat and stared at her sister in astonishment. "Abandoned *you*? You were the one who tried to *kill* me!"

"After you chose to protect humans instead of avenging Rose," Maeve accused and raised her sharp jawline, which made her throat appear slim and long.

243

"Do you truly believe she'd be proud of you for murdering a town full of people? You think it wouldn't disappoint her to see what's become of you, Maeve?"

Scoffing, Maeve folded her arms in front of her. "You and Rose never had any ambition. You were content living in fear and poverty out of sight. But if Rose were still alive, it wouldn't matter what she thought about my choices because those choices are what have created my success. Did you know that I've built an empire with mines in Africa and extravagant jewelry stores across Europe? Five minutes from here, you'll find my largest store. Just look for a sign that says 'Intoxicate' and you'll see the most luxurious jewelry shop in the world."

Maeve avoided her sister's judgmental eyes and looked toward the open window, feeling the cold breeze against her face as she spoke. "I could have taken care of Rose and offered her a life of wealth and happiness. It's too bad you betrayed me, or I would have extended that offer to you."

Althea shook her head and spoke with arched eyebrows. "If you think I'm attracted to this lifestyle then you've forgotten who I am. This is a lovely home full of esthetic beauty, but I feel no warmth here. Everything seems cold and materialistic and frankly, you don't seem happy to me, Maeve. This isn't a lifestyle that Rose would have wanted for herself or us. I feel certain Rose would have rejected your offer because she'd want to live in Orenda."

Though Maeve's face remained stern, Althea noticed how her chest rose and fell in her dark red layered dress. A part of Maeve wanted to throw Althea out the open window, but Charles was on her back about not being controlled by her emotions and impulses. Ignoring Althea's hurtful words, for now, she instead asked the obvious. "Orenda?"

Althea blinked her pretty eyes and remembered why she was there in the first place. "You were right, Maeve, it's unfair how Earthens are treated in this world, but I don't think the answer is to fight hatred with hatred. Zosia has answered our prayers and provided us with a sanctuary where Earthens can live in safety away from humans. Didn't she call for you to join the rest of us?"

Maeve narrowed her eyes. "I don't talk to Zosia."

"No, that's not what I meant. For all the other Earthens, a doorway appeared with a faint whisper to walk through. Only Earthens can enter, and it's unlike anything in this world. We've created the most magical village called Orenda. I know you would love it there, Maeve. And maybe if you got away from all of… this, you would feel better. There's also the quest you talked about before we took the crystals of immortality. Remember? Zosia said I couldn't go alone, but I could help you like you wanted me to," Althea said but struggled to read her sister's cold eyes.

"You put your trust in the wrong place, dear sister, Zosia will spit you out and abandon you once she's gotten what she wants."

"I'm sorry you feel like that, but she's been very supportive and created Orenda to help Earthens. There are hundreds of us, learning from each other and bonding across natures and language barriers. It would be wonderful if you could be part of all that."

For a moment, Maeve felt stunned and asked, "There are hundreds of Earthens in one place?"

"Yes." Just talking about Orenda made Althea's face soften. "I live in a small yellow cottage with a vegetable garden. The nature is lusher and richer than anything you've ever seen, and animals walk freely with none of us fearing humans. You should come. Having a place that is our own is the steppingstone we always dreamed of and needed. Now we can safely grow in numbers."

Looking around the room, Althea added, "There's nothing wrong with being wealthy and enjoying a luxurious lifestyle, but it all depends on how you obtain that material wealth. I can tell that you're not happy, Maeve. None of this brings you true joy."

Maeve didn't confirm or deny Althea's claim. She just watched her with a look of disdain as her sister continued,

"I came to tell you that Orenda is just as much your home as mine. If you want it to be."

Maeve's gaze turned hard and drifted to the side. "You may find my way of life cold and materialistic, but I find yours appalling and pathetic. I don't need you to save me from humans, because unlike you and those other Earthens, I'm not scared of them. It's humans who are scared of me, and with good reason."

Althea watched her sister and desperately tried to connect to her love for Maeve. All she found in her heart was love for the memories of a girl she'd once known because the woman sitting in front of her was a cold-hearted stranger.

"You can tell Zosia that I don't take orders from her or anyone else." Maeve raised her chin.

"When did you become so selfish?" Althea asked with her eyebrows lowered in despair.

"I take care of myself, the way no one else ever has. The one you should be calling selfish is Zosia. She knew the quest was an impossible task, yet she was so willing to destroy my life without the slightest bit of hesitation."

Althea stood up inhaling sharply and exhaled in a huff. "I don't believe Zosia would ever do something to harm others without reasonable means because unlike you, she does not carry a sense of self-importance the size of this house. Her only mistake was choosing you to save the world, but luckily, she's in the process of finding someone else. Maybe that person will be altruistic enough to think of others than themselves, which clearly isn't possible for you."

Maeve curled up her lip and looked at her sister with heated eyes. For a moment they stared at each other with hostility before Maeve hissed, "I owe you nothing."

Althea shook her head with disappointment. "It's clear to me that coming here was a mistake. You have all these material possessions and yet your soul is poor. There is nothing joyful about you or your life. I see all these dead things around you, but nothing of true value. When was the last time you had a warm hug or a genuine smile? When was the last time you felt at peace and laughed?"

Maeve stood abruptly and with the movement of her hand, she pushed air towards Althea, making her fall backward and knock over the sofa. Unlike the last time Maeve had thrown her, Althea didn't end up unconscious. With shocked eyes, she looked back over her shoulder toward Maeve and was prepared to protect herself from the monster her sister had become. But the moment Althea raised her head, Maeve reacted on instinct and strangled Althea without touching her.

Her eyes widening in horror, Althea's right hand rose to her throat, and her other slapped the floor begging for Maeve to release her hold. Althea had hoped for a reunion with her sister and instead, she was attacked once again. Not being able to breathe wouldn't kill Althea but it felt violating all the same. For a long moment, the twin sisters stared at each other with thoughts running through their minds. Althea remembered how Maeve had once looked at the world with her large and curious eyes. She remembered being the careful twin as a child while Maeve ran as fast as her legs could carry her, and quickly got back up whenever she stumbled over her own feet. Even covered in dirt with bruises she would rise up and keep running in giggles. There was nothing curious or childlike now about the cold woman in front of Althea.

Maeve's eyes were guarded with layers of pain, and her pupils were dark shields that protected anyone from seeing the fragile soul that hid under all its armor.

Releasing Althea, Maeve dismissed her with an icy tone: "I didn't ask for your opinion on how I live my life. You can leave now!"

Althea stepped back and rubbed her throat, which was as red as if Maeve had squeezed her neck with both hands. She was disturbed and saddened by Maeve's hostility, but before she could say her goodbyes a small chirping bird landed in the open window and warned of a dangerous predator approaching.

Turning her head to look at the bird, Althea picked up on the description of who was coming and the bird's fear of the man. Suddenly everything made sense to her, and she understood how her sister had become the heartless cold woman that hated everyone and everything.

Turning to Maeve, Althea exclaimed, "So that's how you managed all this?"

Maeve's face didn't flinch as she watched her sister without giving anything away, but Althea still understood what wasn't said between them. Based on the fact that the bird only seemed to be warning Althea and that after a long moment of silence, Maeve still hadn't said anything to defend herself, Althea pointed out the obvious: "You can't hear the bird?"

Maeve's silence confirmed Althea's suspicion.

"You can't communicate with animals anymore. Did Zosia shun you? That would explain why no doorway opened for you with an invitation to join all the other Earthens in Orenda."

"I thought I told you to leave. You've overstayed your welcome, *sister*." Maeve pronounced the last word like a curse.

"Maybe that's what happens when you sell your soul to a snake."

Maeve arched an eyebrow. "Believe me, I still have my soul. And Zosia may have shunned me, but I can still control the elements and create better potions than you ever could." Her words were sharp and her tone cold as she spoke. "Zosia is the one who wanted me to sell my soul; the things she asked of me were purely selfish and she never cared what happened to me, you, or Rose. Charles on the other hand has helped me make a name for myself and attain the life I've always dreamed of."

Althea pitied her sister, who claimed to have the world at her feet but suddenly looked so small in this grand tearoom.

With her gaze on the bird, Althea pondered. "With you being shunned, you can't enter Orenda, even if you wanted to."

"Then it's a good thing that I don't want to. I guess this means I'm not an Earthen anymore."

Althea's head was spinning with questions. "Did Zosia cut your connection to nature because you became a Fader?"

The question made Maeve scoff. "I'm not a Fader, Althea. Maybe you should ask Zosia why she cut me off since you two are so close."

"What even are you, Maeve? You're not a human, Fader, or Earthen."

Narrowing her eyes, Maeve declared, "Maybe I'm exactly what the humans so desperately want me and all other women to be. Maybe I'm a witch."

"You're not a witch, Maeve. Stop saying that."

A knock sounded at the door, but the person behind it didn't wait for an invitation before the door opened and the most intimidating man Althea had ever seen entered the room. At first glance, he looked like any other rich businessman of the sixteenth century, but his eyes carried an authority that no human could gain within a lifetime. When his gaze lingered on her, Althea felt as though he saw right through her. The first time she had met a Fader, she had been taken aback by how slow his energetic vibration had been. She had often thought of Damon, whom she had misread as a jovial, nice man. It was a good thing that Annabel had recognized him and his friend as Faders and taught Althea everything she knew. Althea understood that the slower their vibration, the older a Fader was. In her mind Althea compared it to how a tree grows wider in its trunk. Charles, however, had slow energy unlike anything she'd ever felt before. With humans their pulsation was quicker than heartbeats, but with this man, several moments passed between his energy waves.

"Hello," he said in a curious tone as he assessed the woman by the window who was sending judgmental glances his way.

"Althea was just leaving," Maeve said dismissively as she shot Charles a warning look.

With large eyes, Althea was ready to react to any sudden movements from the Cobra as she headed towards the door.

"Goodbye," she said, and for a moment the sisters locked eyes before Althea left and hurried out of the building with a beating heart.

Still sitting at her desk, Maeve looked at Charles with a deep exhale. Seeing her sister again brought up feelings and memories that she'd become good at suppressing. She couldn't be more grateful that Charles was there to help distract her from the skeletons peeking out of her closet. But suddenly Charles seemed full of questions, which only annoyed Maeve further.

"Your sister?" he asked and looked toward the door that still stood ajar.

Maeve nodded and tried to change the subject. "What are you doing here?"

He ignored her question. "What did she want?"

"None of your concern," she said and sent him a cocky smile.

"I'm not so sure."

"She's made a village with Zosia that only Earthens can enter. She wanted me to join; obviously, I said no."

"Where is this village?"

"It's only accessible through a portal."

Though Charles remained quiet, hundreds of thoughts spiraled behind his intelligent eyes. Though most of the public had no idea that Charles ruled the world they lived in, he had everyone, and everything wrapped in his web. The knowledge that there was an edge of the world left to conquer intrigued and excited him. Being a man of intricate plots, challenges aroused him.

"Tell her that you want to make amends and go on the quest with her, Maeve. Finding the object will be impossible, but it will give you a chance to learn everything you can about this village and how to reach it."

"No," Maeve replied dryly.

Charles took slow steps toward the desk where she sat and narrowed his eyes. "I'm not asking, Maeve."

Maeve leaned back in her chair unbothered and raised her eyebrows. "Good. Because I don't take orders from anyone."

Maeve's disobedience annoyed Charles, but it was also one of the things that made him like her. She wasn't afraid of him like everyone else and though he would never think of her as an equal he liked the challenges she offered.

Maeve sighed, which made her attractive chest rise and fall. "Now are you here for a *business meeting* or do you plan to waste more of my time, Charles?"

Charles instantly picked up on the flirting undertone in Maeve's words and closed in on her. "I like that dress on you. You know I think red suits you."

Maeve arched an eyebrow as an invitation.

"But if I'm honest I think you'd look much better naked." He began to unbutton his coat with a flirtatious smirk.

"Close the door," Maeve instructed, still sitting in her chair.

Charles headed toward the door as instructed with dark eyes. "Why don't I lock it?"

CHAPTER 25

ORDER TO SEDUCE

Damon felt Charles before he entered the room. As a Fader, his senses were sharper than those of humans, but he suspected his ability to shift into animals had left a mark on him as well.

His friend Mr. ThomasThomas had just returned from Spain and they were feasting on the dried ham, olives, and oranges that he had brought with him. Thomas was the closest thing Damon had to family and he too sensed Charles approaching and turned his head toward the door.

Charles didn't bother knocking or waiting for an invitation before he joined them at the table and took the glass of wine that Damon poured him.

"Hard day?" Damon asked.

"I just came from Maeve."

Thomas laughed a little. "That explains how serious you look. That woman is a handful."

Charles leaned his head back and emptied his glass in one long gulp before holding out the glass for Damon to fill up again.

"Her sister was there."

That made Damon stop pouring and with the bottle stalling mid-air, he stared at Charles. "Althea was here? In London?"

"Yes."

"How? I had reports telling me she was seen in Scotland not two days ago."

"Good question." With his eyes, Charles signaled for Damon to keep pouring.

"It's been three months since your last report. Why is that?"

After filling Charles' glass to the brim, Damon put the bottle down and tore a hand through his hair. "The thing is that she's changed her traveling habits. She used to move from town to town with her horse and wagon in a predictable manner. Now, she's hard to find and the alerts I get on her make no sense. My spies will see her in different parts of the country on the same day. Before I make it to either place, she's gone and there's no trace of her on the roads leading away. How do you explain that?"

Charles spun the wineglass in his hands. "You should have told me about this. Something is going on. Althea came to invite Maeve to live in a place called Orenda. Have you heard about it?"

Damon and Thomas exchanged a glance before they shook their heads.

"Is it here in England? The name sounds foreign to me," Thomas said.

"That's what I want you to find out. Maeve mentioned that the only way to get there was through a portal. We need to find out where that portal is and how it works. If Earthens found a place to build a village, then I want to know where it is."

"What did Maeve say? Didn't her sister tell her how to get to the portal?"

Leaning back in his chair, Charles answered Thomas. "Maeve doesn't like her sister and their meeting didn't go well. I suggested that Maeve should spy on Zosia for us, but you know her. She has to be lured slowly until she believes it was her idea all along.

"Did you talk to Althea?" Damon asked with interest. "How did she look?"

"Like a country girl who got lost in London. Her hair hung loose and her complexion was tanned. She may be charming when she smiles, but all I saw was scowling. She looked..." Charles thought about it for a moment. "Strong and fit, like someone used to working hard."

"Ahh, come on. Even an old snake like you can't deny that she's pretty," Thomas teased.

"I'm not denying anything. I already decided that I'll seduce her and sleep with her."

Damon had been drinking and coughed. "Who, Althea?"

"Yes. There's nothing to entice a woman's sexual appetite like a little competition. I'm certain it would vex Maeve if I slept with her sister."

Thomas laughed, but Damon didn't even smile. He never favored the toxic intrigues that seemed to entertain Charles when it came to his women.

"I got everything from Maeve that I could. She shared that Zosia is in search of the next Earthen to go on a quest to kill me."

"Ah, yes, because so far her success rate is pretty great," Thomas pointed out with sarcasm.

"It doesn't matter who Zosia sends on that quest. They'll never succeed. I made sure of that." Self-importance was written all over Charles' face. "Not only are the objects hidden well but finding them would also require teamwork between a Fader and an Earthen."

Damon frowned. "But what if a foolish Fader decides to go on the quest to defy you?"

Charles looked to Damon as if he were slow, and stated the obvious. "Every Fader knows that killing me would mean certain death to themselves and all of you. If I die, you die. Show me a Fader who isn't happy with their privileged life and wants to commit suicide, or even worse suffer my wrath and end up as a Gleaner?"

Damon knew better than to disagree with the Cobra. With a small nod, he agreed, "Then you have nothing to worry about."

"We need all the information we can get on this Orenda village and the Earthen that Zosia is planning to send on the quest." Looking straight at Damon, Charles ordered. "I want you to find Althea and win her trust."

"Excuse me?" Damon wrinkled his nose.

"I don't care how you charm or seduce her. Just get all her secrets."

Pushing his plate away, Damon protested. "Can't you get one of your new Faders to do it? I'm far too busy with my businesses and the newer Faders are always hungry for your approval; let them kiss your arse."

"You've followed Althea for more than forty years. If anyone can find her and get her to talk, it's you."

Usually, Damon wouldn't have pushed back a second time, but he hated that he had to spy on Althea. He had overheard enough conversations between her and Annabel over the years to know she was no danger to anyone. She had confessed her inner thoughts to him when she thought she was talking to a fox, a deer, a bird, or whatever animal form he chose to get close to her. "I apologize but following a harmless Earthen around the country when I have important business meetings in London is inconvenient to me."

The change in atmosphere happened instantaneously. Charles' eyes turned cold and his voice stern. "You think this assignment is below you?"

Damon had multiple reasons which he couldn't and wouldn't share with Charles for most of those reasons he was in denial about himself. He didn't want to admit that Althea's confessions sometimes made him reflect on things that didn't serve him. He was well aware that she would loathe him and everything he stood for if she knew who he truly was. It wasn't that he cared about her, because he had stopped truly caring about anyone a long time ago. But now that Charles had declared that he wanted to seduce Althea and sleep with her, it had also placed her in the same category as her sister Maeve in his mind. Sleeping with the same women as Charles wasn't wise. Most of the time, Charles interacted as a normal person would, but Damon had known him long enough to witness his unpredictable and deviant nature firsthand. There was no doubt in his mind that Charles Fuji was by far the greatest embodiment of moral depravity to ever walk the Earth. Damon was intelligent and driven enough to understand that being in Charles' inner circle was better than being his enemy. But he was never completely relaxed around him or foolish enough to forget the serpent that Charles could turn into at any given moment.

"You seem confused. Did you think I was making a request that was open for negotiation? Do I need to remind you, young Damon, that the reason you have your age and superior status in life is because of me? I can take all of that away just as quickly as I gave it to you. Now, rethink what you just said. Did I make a request or an order?"

Damon drew in a long steadying breath. His hands were rolled into fists under the table, and he was in a heightened state of alertness. Charles' anger could be lethal and there was no wiggle room to say the wrong thing.

Thomas moved in his seat. "Damon understands and will do as you asked. Right, Damon?"

His friend's concern was touching. It was rare for Faders to have true friendships.

Nodding, Damon agreed, "Of course."

It was as if the Cobra's head had been raised, ready to attack, and now lowered, making everyone let go of the breath they were holding. His tone of voice softened as he said, "Good. I would think asking you to seduce a beautiful woman would be considered an enjoyable task."

"I'd gladly do it." Thomas laughed to lighten the heavy atmosphere. "I've always had a thing for redheads. Besides Damon isn't nearly as devilishly handsome as I am." Thomas grinned, though in truth, Thomas was a well-built man with charm, he was well aware that he couldn't compare to Damon when it came to appearance. It didn't bother him as he compensated with buckets of charisma and confidence that always drew people to him.

"Damon will do it. He's already been watching her for so long."

"You'll have to put a smile on that ugly face of yours then." Thomas lightly slapped Damon on the shoulder. "Otherwise, no woman will spill her secrets to you."

Damon looked at Thomas and exaggerated a smile to mock his friend.

"Whoa, with a smile like that she'll be begging you to marry her."

Damon laughed with disgust in his voice "I'm not bloody marrying an Earthen."

Pushing his chair back, Charles calmly stood up and spoke with a hard edge. "You will if I ask you to."

Scrunching his face up, Damon looked straight at Charles. "Are you asking me to marry Maeve's sister?"

Keeping his Fader in suspense, Charles pretended to think about it. "Not at this point. I'm asking you to get her to tell you everything about Orenda and whom Zosia chooses for the quest. Get close to her and earn her trust. After watching her for all this time, you must have learned something valuable about her that you can use to seduce her." Damon groaned. "She's nothing like the women I normally interact with."

"You mean, she's not a whore?" Thomas asked and grinned at his joke.

With a sideways glance at his friends, Damon muttered, "At least I don't seduce the virgin daughters of

258

my business partners. Your reputation as a rake is well deserved. My women are well taken care of and when we grow apart, I always make sure they lack for nothing for the rest of their lives."

Thomas threw up his hands. "When did you grow tired of the chase? I don't always seduce virgins. I enjoy an experienced lover as much as the next man."

Charles cut through the chatter. "Find Althea and give me a report once you have useful information to share."

Popping one last olive in his mouth, Damon pushed his chair back and rose from the table as well. "I had better see if she's still in London." He walked over and opened a window. "Finding her has been the tricky part lately."

From his pocket, Charles pulled out an old-looking compass. "I have a suspicion that Orenda isn't anywhere in this world. If humans truly aren't allowed to enter then Zosia must have created a different dimension somehow. That would explain why Althea shows up in so many different places within a short time span. I believe she travels through those portals she told Maeve about."

"But if humans can't pass through those portals, then we Faders might not be able to either," Damon pondered.

Charles nodded in agreement. "That's what I need you to find out. This will help you move from one place to the other fast."

"You're giving me a compass?"

"It has the power to transport you any place you want to go. That way it will be easier to track her."

Damon reached for the object but Charles didn't let go at first. In a stern voice, he warned. "Don't lose it."

With a bit of hesitation, Damon took the compass and asked, "How does it work?"

"You hold it and think of the place you want to go. Once you're locked in on the thought, squeeze it twice and it will take you there."

"Sounds simple enough." Stuffing the compass in his pocket Damon looked at Thomas. "I'll see you later."

"Let me help you find her. London is a big place," Thomas said and without another word, he shifted into a raven and flew out the window.

Exchanging a last glance with Charles, Damon swallowed his bad feelings about the assignment, shifted into his favorite of all forms, a black eagle, and flew out to hunt down Althea.

CHAPTER 26
THE EAGLE AND HIS PREY

After Althea's unpleasant confrontation with Maeve, her first instinct had been to hurry back to Orenda to lick her wounds. As she entered a quiet alley where a tree had dropped all its leaves, she lifted her hand to create a portal but was interrupted when a bird came and told her of a child in great pain. With a sigh, she remembered Annabel's words that the best way to forget your problems was to help someone else.

Following the bird, Althea was led through the streets to a house in a middle-class neighborhood. She took a deep breath before knocking on the door. The birds always seemed to know who was open to a visit from a healer and so it didn't surprise Althea when the mother who stood in the doorway began to cry. "I prayed for someone to help my child and not an hour later, you arrive on my doorstep. You must be an angel."

Althea shook her head. "I'm afraid not. But if you show me to your daughter, I'll do my best to ease her pain."

Two hours later Althea walked out of the house feeling pleased with herself. The girl had been burning up from fever, but with Althea's help, she stabilized her temperature and managed to help her eat. The pain she had experienced was eased and with a few more visits from Althea over the next days, the child would be up and running by end of the week.

It was late fall and there were enough leaves, sticks, and rocks on the ground to create a portal back to Orenda, but with too many people around she preferred to find a quiet place. It wasn't that the humans would see the portal, but when she walked through to Orenda, they would see Althea disappear into thin air. Most who noticed Althea enough to see how she would disappear would think their mind was playing tricks on them and carry on with their day, but being a kind and considerate healer, she was aware that for some people an experience like that could cause them to potentially get a heart attack from distress and confusion and she didn't want that on her conscience. Luckily, she'd seen a park not far away and headed in that direction.

Walking down the crowded streets of London, where people wore tall hats and heavy gowns, Althea struggled to understand what it was about humans that lured Maeve into wanting their lifestyle.

As a healer, Althea had met many humans throughout the decades, and the more she learned about them, the more she pitied them. They lived in a world filled with rules they made themselves, yet those rules benefited no one. Hatred, suspicion, and fear of others ruled the world they lived in, which placed everyone in tight boxes that few could stay within.

It all felt like a play-pretend to Althea – their fashions and their strange social status which depended on gender, pure luck, and family connections. Those irrelevant constructs of society were defining things in the human world. It made Althea long all the more to return to Orenda, a place where people could be exactly who they were without judgment.

She was already overwhelmed and saddened by her failed encounter with her sister, who had once again attacked her physically. And now as she walked amongst the humans watching them wear uncomfortable clothes and ride their horses down busy streets, she became even more frustrated that Maeve's desperate desire for this ridiculous way of life had cost Rose her life. It was all too overwhelming for Althea, who simply wanted to return home.

As Althea slowly walked into the sea of people, she was invisible in the eyes of all, *except one*. She was so focused on getting to the green area that her strong senses were oblivious to someone watching her from afar.

Birds told her about other people who needed her help. It was their natural instinct, but Althea was still reeling from the harsh words spoken between her and Maeve and didn't have the energy to heal more people today.

She had to be close to the park and wanted to run to escape all the people who looked like Maeve in their expensive outfits. But the streets were crowded, forcing her to follow the flow of the people in front of her.

The park was just down the street when she passed a tavern and watched a man getting thrown out of the door right in front of her. He slammed his head on the ground and moaned in pain. Instinctively, the healer in Althea rushed to his side.

"Are you okay, sir?" she asked with a hand on his shoulder for support.

The man placed his hands to his face and groaned.

Looking to the door, Althea saw a large bald man with crossed arms and a hostile expression on his face. She wasn't sure if he was planning to attack the poor man on the ground again, but just in case, she moved to squat between them while tending to the victim of the attack. Being immortal, Althea wasn't scared of humans like she had been as a child and teenager, but she preferred not to get into conflict with them.

"You say one bad word about my brother again and I'll bloody tear out your vocal cords, you bastard," the bald man threatened as he left the tavern where he barely fit through the short, crooked door. Althea watched as he spat on the ground next to the wounded man and headed down the crowded street, toward the park. Part of her wanted to leave the wounded man and continue to the park, which was only a few buildings away yet seemed so far. But Althea knew she couldn't leave someone in need of her help.

"Can you sit?" she asked in a soft tone.

Groaning with pain, the man tried and with her support, he sat up. She noticed that his clothes looked expensive, and his hair was cut in a fashionable hairstyle, but with his hands to his nose, she couldn't see how hurt he was. Music from inside the tavern and onlookers making comments bombarded her senses. The man muttered, "I think he broke my nose."

Althea didn't feel like she had much choice. Helping the tall man to stand, she led him back into the tavern and sat him on a bench in the corner. "Wait here," she instructed and went to talk to the barmaid, who found a wet cloth for her.

There wasn't much light in the tavern where men were getting tipsy in the late afternoon.

Returning to the man, she asked, "How are you feeling?"

He sat with a leg on each side of the wooden bench and his back leaning against the wall. Still with his hand to his nose and his head leaned back, he muttered, "I've been better."

Mirroring him, Althea sat astride the bench in front of him. "Let's see the damage," she instructed as she lifted her hand and gently pulled his down. Focusing on him to feel his energy and assess how much pain he was in, her soft yet tired facial expression quickly changed. It was in that minute she felt his slow vibration and now that his hand was down, she recognized Damon, whom she had met in an inn almost five decades ago. Just like her, he hadn't aged a day.

Damon saw the shock on Althea's face and knew she recognized him. Even in the dim light of the tavern, she was as breathtakingly beautiful as ever and the fact that they sat so close made the situation intense.

"*You!*" She moved her hand away as if she'd been burned.

"*Me?*" Damon pretended he didn't know what upset her. "Have I had the pleasure, miss?"

Althea's thoughts were a melting pot of her original confusion and curiosity after meeting Damon the first time, and Annabel's warnings, that made her rise from the bench.

"Don't go." Damon's serious expression and his hand on her wrist made Althea stiffen and look down into his eyes. There were no other Earthens around for her to protect, and with her being immortal, Damon didn't scare her. Slowly, she lowered her body to sit on the bench again.

"Damon Bradshaw."

His eyes widened a little. "Who told you my name?"

"You did. Many years ago," she answered while assessing his every facial movement to figure out what he wanted from her. Faders were known to be tricksters who used others for their amusement.

Angling his head, he looked impressed, "And you remembered."

"Only because you were the first Fader I ever met."

Damon's gaze went to the side. The fact that she remembered him and knew he was a Fader complicated his assignment. Earthens didn't mix with his kind, except for her sister of course. "Are you sure?" Meeting her eyes there was a small smile on his lips and a challenge in his eyes. "I seem to remember there was a connection between us."

Althea gave a dry laugh. "You just asked me if we had the pleasure of meeting, and now you want me to believe that you remember a special connection between us."

With his handsome face turned serious and his dark brown eyes lowered, he declared. "Oh, I remember it well. You were with your friend who rushed you out of the inn. I never forgot about you, Althea."

Moving her head to avoid his gaze, she felt her heart pump faster in her chest. She hadn't expected Damon to remember her name, making her feel flustered. Her next question flew out of her mouth like a hard accusation: "Why do you work for *him*?"

Knowing full well whom she was referring to, Damon still asked, "Who?"

Althea met his warm dusky brown eyes and ignored the way her palms became clammy. "The Cobra. You're one of his soulless slaves," she answered without shielding the disgust in her voice.

To Damon, the disdain in Althea's tone was worse than her words. Raising a defensive eyebrow, he muttered, "You seem to have gotten a few details wrong. I'm no one's slave and I'm not sure how to determine if I have a soul. Do you?"

Althea moved a little closer to him and whispered so that the group of tipsy men in the tavern who were now singing wouldn't hear her. "I have free will. Can you say the same?"

He didn't like her putting him on the spot like that and drew in a deep breath slowly. "My situation isn't always ideal, but I try to get the best out of it. Immortality comes at a price."

"*He* indoctrinated my sister," Althea accused. "I saw her today. There was nothing left of the warm and loving girl I used to know."

Damon scoffed a little and shook his head. "Don't blame Charles. I was there the day Maeve came to find

266

him. She was cold-hearted and ambitious even before she met him."

Althea pulled back a little. "He uses people."

Her comment made Damon laugh. "So? That's the way of the world. The strong thrive and the weak suffer."

"And you're alright with that?" Her indignation confirmed to him how naïve she was.

"It doesn't matter what I think. It's been that way for all of history. You Earthens are..." He paused and smiled a little. "Well, you're not exactly thriving, so I guess that puts you in the group of the weak people."

To most women, Damon's deep brown eyes were warm and flirtatious, and they found him irresistible with his strong jawline, thick brown hair, and charming smile. But to Althea, he was provocative and represented everything that made the life of an Earthen difficult.

From the small tic at the edge of her eyes, Damon knew that Althea was angry. "We Earthens work hard every day to counterbalance the unfairness and hardship people like you create in the world. One day we'll find a way to break the hold the Cobra has on those in power."

Damon raised an eyebrow. "You mean kill him?"

"If that's what it takes."

"I thought Earthens didn't have the nerve to kill." A handsome grin spread at the edges of his lips before he continued, "But I guess Maeve could prove me wrong there."

"Maeve isn't an Earthen anymore. And killing is never something that should come naturally to an Earthen. But the world will be better off without him, so yes, if it came down to it, I believe I would be able to find the strength within me to kill him."

He wanted to laugh and tell her she didn't have what it took, but Damon's mission was to seduce Althea – not to antagonize her further – so instead he said, "I hope it doesn't come down to it then. If you killed him, I would die as well."

Althea had been just about to speak but closed her mouth again and then she spoke on a breath, "Oh."

"You didn't know that, did you?"

The way her lips disappeared told him he was right. With a small smile, he said, "It's touching that killing me doesn't seem to be your goal. Does that mean you like me just a little?"

Ignoring his flirtatious tone, Althea became serious. "No. I don't like you. The only reason, I'm still talking to you is to understand."

"Ahh, you wonder why I would let a mere mortal punch me in the nose?" Damon asked in his attempt to soften her up. "I did that for you."

"Me?" she asked as if his words were pure stupidity.

"I know you believe I'm an awful person for being a Fader, but you know so little about us and you judge based upon rumors that aren't all true. I..." Damon gave her the smile that he knew women always fell for. "I never forgot you, Althea, and I've kept my distance for years because I knew you wouldn't have it in your heart to be with someone like me. But think about it..."

"Think about what?" Althea asked with her brow wrinkled.

"How many people on this planet don't age? You and I both know the sorrow of losing the ones we love. With me, you wouldn't have to experience that heartbreak."

Althea gaped at Damon for a long moment and then she burst into laughter.

"What's so funny?" he asked, with his flirtatious smile fading from his face.

"You." She shook her head. "First you don't remember me, and then you do. Now you're trying to make me believe that you timed getting thrown out of the door so that I would help you and fall in love with

268

you. You are ridiculous!" Her laughter stabbed Damon in the center of his large ego.

"Did you pay him to punch you?" she asked.

Damon tried to keep his cool and put on his flirty smile that usually worked so well with ladies. "Nooo," he assured her and tried to be smooth. "I'm talented like that."

"I think you're talented at lying in general. It probably comes with being a Fader."

Her words triggered him because one thing Damon hated was lies. He was forced to pretend with Charles for survival, and there were situations where his lack of aging required him to lie as well. But other than that Damon preferred the truth. "You lie too, Althea."

She pulled back a little.

"Don't pretend like you're perfect because you're an Earthen. You lie all the time."

"I have never once lied!" Althea lied.

Damon's eyes widened in shock as he put a gentle fist on the table and laid out the facts. "How many times have you told people that Annabel was your mother, and later grandmother, when you weren't blood-related at all? And what about all the lies you tell to make hopeful men stop coming on to you? You even have a fake wedding ring."

Blinking her eyes, Althea breathed, "How do you know that?"

"I told you I couldn't forget you." With a small shrug, Damon admitted, "I checked in on you from time to time. Just to make sure that you were comfortable."

"You spied on me?"

"It wasn't like that. I wanted to be close to you, but I knew you would reject me if I approached you in my normal body."

"What is that supposed to mean?"

Damon scratched his thick, dark locks of hair as he was beginning to see that his strategy of declaring his interest was going astray. "Ehm... it means that I sometimes spend some time with you in a different form."

Althea raised her eyebrows with a hard glare and asked, "Like a bird?"

He looked to the side, avoiding her gaze. "Yes. Or a fox."

Althea's eyes grew large. "Did I ever talk to you?"

Damon tried to calm her by looking deep into her eyes and staying relaxed himself. "Sometimes."

Remembering talking to a fox at one point, Althea's voice shook a little when she asked, "Were you there when I bathed?"

He could see color rise in her cheeks, and hurried to say, "Look, Althea, I've been around for more than two hundred years. I assure you that I'm very familiar with the female physique and I'm used to..." He didn't get to finish before she stood up.

"I don't care how many women you've been with. I never chose to show myself to you and yet you've seen every part of me." Her voice was raised, which made a few of the tipsy men who were singing quiet down and look their way.

"What was I supposed to do?" Damon whisper-hissed.

"How about respecting my privacy?"

She tried to get up but once again, Damon touched her arm and asked, "I'm sorry. Please don't go. How can I make it up to you? What if..." Damon threw out the first thing he could think of. "Would it make you feel better if I let you see me naked?"

Althea's first instinct was to say no, but then she looked around the busy inn and thought about his offer. It seemed childish, but she liked the idea of humiliating him in front of everyone in the tavern and maybe even throwing away his clothes and leaving him stark naked. "Actually, yes. I think it would make me feel better." Holding out her hand, she looked him dead in the eye. "Give me your jacket."

First Damon smirked, but when he saw how serious Althea's face was, his smile dropped, and he leaned closer. "I was thinking we could go someplace private... and I promise I will make it up to you."

His handsome brown eyes sending her flirtatious signals made Althea want to gag. Everything about Damon and his arrogant face made her want to roll her eyes. "If you think I'm going anywhere alone with you then you're delusional." She leaned in, so that their faces were only a head apart, and then she spoke with grit in her teeth. "If you want to make it up to me then you'll get undressed right here and give me the satisfaction of seeing you humiliated."

Damon hesitated for a moment. In his mind he cursed Charles for giving him this assignment to begin with. But knowing that failure wasn't an option he began to unbutton his jacket and took it off. When Althea reached for it, Damon pulled the jacket back and reached into the left pocket. "I'll just keep this," he said and put Charles' compass on the table.

"Now the rest of it," Althea ordered.

Scrunching his nose up, Damon scanned the room. "You're really going to make me strip in front of all these people?"

"Oh, so you do care about dignity. As long as it's yours?"

"I already apologized and when I offered to take off my clothes, I never suggested it would be in front of all these people. You're going to get me booted out, again, and I don't..."

Althea cut him off mid-sentence. "Give me your shirt."

Sucking in his lips, Damon glanced over the room. It wasn't that he was embarrassed to be undressed in front of others, but as a Fader, Damon preferred to keep a low profile, and stripping in a public inn was anything but low profile. "All right, but if I do this then will you give me a chance?"

With her arms crossed, she didn't answer.

Sighing with annoyance, Damon grabbed onto the fabric of his shirt and was about to pull it up when the drunk men sitting by the bar began whistling.

When Damon turned around to tell off the men, Althea's gaze drifted to the compass on the table. It clearly meant a great deal to Damon and that told her it had to be an heirloom of some kind. Maybe it would make him stay away from her if she took the compass and showed him that she wasn't a scared little Earthen.

After Damon's warning to the drunk patrons, they began booing and throwing pickled onions in his direction. Most laughed, except for the barman, who was getting tired of the commotion.

"Are we even now? You wanted to embarrass me, and I would say you succeeded." Damon stood in his underclothes, wearing only a long white shirt and his underpants, but Althea wasn't satisfied.

"You're still far from naked," she said in a dry tone.

Damon leaned in and whispered, "There are other ways I could make it up to you, you know."

"This works fine for me... Go on," Althea encouraged with a nod to his lower body. "You saw me without anything covering my private parts. Now take off what's left."

From across the room, the annoyed bartender was making his way over. From his tense expression, Althea knew he was about to ask Damon to put his clothes back on.

There were too many people watching, and she had no real interest in seeing him completely stripped naked. Putting his jacket and shirt down on the table, she leaned forward and scolded, "Damon Bradshaw, you can put your clothes back on. All I ask is that you stay away from me. I don't care if we live to be the last two people on this Earth, I want nothing to do with you."

Still having Charles' order in the back of his mind, Damon couldn't give up. A weaker man might have backed down, but he looked Althea deep in the eyes, and stuck as close to the truth as he could. "I can't do that."

"Excuse me, sir, but I'll need you to get dressed or leave." The corpulent bartender was red in his face but created the perfect distraction for Althea to leave.

"Piss off," Damon hissed at the man while putting his shoes back on and then the rest of his clothes before grabbing his jacket in one hand and setting off in pursuit of Althea, who abruptly rose from the table and hurried out of the small and dark tavern at a fast pace.

She was halfway down the street before he caught up to her. "Look, can you stop for a second?"

She ignored his plea and continued walking with her gaze straight forward and the wind playing with her orange curls.

"Althea, I apologized. What more can I do to make you forgive me? I know I seem like a stranger to you, but it's different for me. I've been around you for close to fifty years and I have strong feelings for you."

It stressed Althea that Damon was right on her heels. She had already been in an emotionally draining confrontation with Maeve earlier and desperately needed to create a portal and escape to Orenda where she could digest everything in peace.

The park was close now and she only needed elements of nature to create the portal to go home

"Where are you going?" Damon called out behind her.

Over her shoulder, she hissed, "Stop following me. Just leave me alone."

"Did you even hear what I said?"

With too many people in the street, her senses were overwhelmed, and with Damon too close to avoid him, Althea stopped abruptly and turned. "What?"

He looked genuine when he repeated, "I have strong feelings for you. Why else would I humiliate myself in this way?"

"Oh, you think this is humiliating for *you*? What about me realizing that I've told you my secrets when I thought you were an animal? I would have never stripped naked and bathed if I had known it was you."

Holding up both palms to appease her, Damon said, "And I understand that. Which is why I'm apologizing to you. Again." Although he genuinely meant it, it only came forth as condescending to Althea.

With a deep breath, she looked up and down the street feeling stressed and upset about the situation. "How many animal shapes can you even shift into?"

"I don't have an exact number. Hundreds."

Her eyes expanded. "Hundreds? Are you jesting with me?"

"No. I can shift into any animal or person that I've..." He stopped talking and frowned.

"That you've what?"

Slowly he explained, "That I've killed."

Althea opened her mouth and then closed it again.

"You didn't know that about Faders?" Damon asked.

"No. I always knew you were bad people, but..." She looked down. "Are there any animals that you haven't killed?"

274

"Yes, but not many. I've been around for two hundred years, Althea."

"What animals have you spared?"

"Ehm... mostly sea animals. I haven't killed every type of fish, whale, or shark in the ocean."

"Have you killed a peacock?"

Damon scrunched up his face and gave her a funny look. "You mean those flamboyant birds with large colorful feathers?"

"Yes. I saw some at the botanical garden in Oxford. They are the prettiest birds I've ever seen," she said while studying his face closely.

"Right, but they don't even fly, Althea. What would be the purpose of shifting into one of them?"

She narrowed her eyes. "Maybe to spy on people, which seems to be your specialty."

"Oh, I see. Did you confess something special to a peacock in Oxford and now you're mortified it might have been me?" he teased.

"No." Her body language betrayed her, and it made Damon laugh.

"You did! Aww, that's sweet." While talking, he put on the jacket that he'd been carrying in his hand.

"Good day, Damon Bradshaw," Althea said dismissively before turning and walking on.

"Won't you let me buy you a meal and talk to me without your anger?" he called after her, but Althea didn't reply.

Watching her walk away, he buttoned his jacket and stuffed his hands into his pockets. He felt frustrated and embarrassed over his painful attempt at trying to seduce Althea. Surely Charles would punish him for his failure. But as his hands brushed the soft pockets of his jacket and he realized they were empty, his whole body froze and his heart skipped a beat. There hadn't been anything on the table when he left the tavern. He was a hundred percent certain of that but searching all of his pockets, there was nothing. Pivoting, Damon looked back to the tavern but the street was empty.

"Bloody hell!" Tightening his jaw, he set off at a fast run and chased after Althea, shouting for her to stop.

When Althea looked over her shoulder to see Damon sprinting towards her, she set off in a run as well, and the Earthen was a lot faster than he expected. Taking a sharp turn into an alley, Damon shifted to his black eagle shape and set in pursuit. Never had he imagined that Althea had it in her to steal from him or anyone. She'd always seemed to be the purest and most naive person he'd ever come across. The picture he'd had of Althea in his head seemed to vanish and he was beginning to hate the new version she was painting.

Rising above the houses, he followed her running down the street pushing at people to get by. She kept looking over her shoulder until she felt sure that he wasn't there. Slowing down to a walk, she entered Hyde Park, where Damon landed on a branch and watched her from above.

Looking around over her shoulders, she made sure no one was close before she exhaled and raised a hand. He stared in disbelief as from the ground, twigs, leaves, and stones rose into the sky where they floated to make the shape of a doorway.

Understanding that he needed to act fast before she was gone, Damon took off from the branch he sat on and flew down to stop Althea from leaving with the compass.

Althea heard the flapping of large bird's wings but didn't turn her head in time to stop the attack. She only just turned her head to see a scary black eagle swoop down and grab her by the hair. As she shrieked and raised her arms to protect her face, the portal collapsed. She was on the ground with her eyes closed and her face scrunched up when the claws in her hair were replaced with strong hands. Damon's dark eyes, which had been flirtatious and inviting, were now dusky and angry. Lying on top of her his lips were tight and his eyes were even scarier than the eagle swooping down to attack her had been. He stayed on top of her for no more than a few seconds before he rose to his full height and yanked her by the arm to get her to her feet.

Althea's hair was always a mess of wavy curls, but after having a bird claw its way through it, it was almost as wild as her large, frightened eyes.

Still holding a tight grip around her arm, he lowered his voice and locked his jaw before he hissed, "Give me the compass."

Raising her head, she stared at him trying to get it through her head that he had been the same eagle that had attacked her.

"Let go of me," she cried and tried to pull away.

"You took it. Now give it back," he thundered with his voice shaking and still holding her pale skin, which was hurting from his tight hold.

"I will," she promised and that made him release his strong grip on her.

Althea stared into his eyes and moved back while reaching into her pocket and pulling out the small metal compass. "I'll give it to you if you give me what is mine in return."

Damon wrinkled his brow with a warning in his eyes. "How? What are you talking about?"

"You took something precious from me. It's only fair that I take a small thing from you in return," she challenged.

"That thing isn't mine to give. It's the Cobra's and if I don't return it, he'll…" Damon stopped talking. "Just tell me what you want, Althea, and I'll give it to you. *Anything*."

Looking straight into his dark eyes, she made her demand. "Give me back my privacy and dignity."

"How can you talk about dignity and steal at the same time?" Damon reached out his hand. "Give it back."

Stepping back, Althea pulled the compass to her side. "Tell you what, Fader, if you leave me alone for the next, say, five hundred years, then I'll return this to you. Until then, I hope we never meet."

Althea raised her hands and used air to push him to fly through the air. Landing on his back, he launched himself back up quicker than a hungry wolf ready to attack. But by the time he got to his feet, Althea had created her portal and was running toward it.

Damon was fast, but Althea entered the portal before he had a chance to reach her. His footsteps followed her trail but where Althea had effortlessly moved through and disappeared, he just fell through the doorframe of sticks and landed on the grass of Hyde Park.

Sitting on the cold grass, he saw the doorway dissolve with all the sticks, twigs, and stones falling to the ground.

The wave of panic that washed over Damon in that moment made him put a hand to his head. Not only had he failed to bond with Althea, but he had also lost the magical object that Charles had entrusted him with.

Thoughts of the Gleaners he had visited over the years made his insides cramp up in fear. No one came back to the Cobra and told him about a failed mission without paying a heavy price. Damon needed to find a way to get back the compass and make Althea spill all the secrets about how that portal worked and what was behind it. But charming her now would be harder than ever because right now, he hated her, and she hated him. She had always been a naïve Earthen in his eyes, but at least he had been slightly drawn to her because of her beauty and sweetness. Now, she was nothing but a liar

278

and thief whose irresponsible actions could cost him everything.

One thing was for sure. The next time Damon saw Althea, he wouldn't lose any time trying to charm her. He didn't care if he had to tie her down and make her tell all her secrets, but he would get the compass back and give Charles the information he needed. Anything to avoid the sad fate of a Gleaner.

CHAPTER 27

THE BEGINNING OF THE END

"Did you find what you were looking for, miss?" the skinny man with round glasses and slanted eyes asked when Maeve picked up an old necklace in his store after she'd walked around browsing for a while.

"I never do," she answered with annoyance before putting the necklace back down in its box.

The small pawn shop in the center of London was filled with old heirlooms such as expensive utensils, jewelry, and watches. It was one of the many stores Maeve often stopped by, but never did she buy anything, because they never had what she was in search of.

Her long pale fingers traced over an old and expensive ring with an emerald before she sighed and headed toward the door.

The floors were uneven, and the walls tilted inward in the old building. Even though the owner took good care of the expensive objects in his store, the air was heavy from the smell of smoke and dust that came with most of the old objects.

"Have a good day, madam," he called out after Maeve, who didn't reply or even look in his direction as she exited the small, creaking door, making the silver bell ring softly.

Her jawline was even sharper than usual because of her clenched jaw. She was usually a lady of manners, just as Charles had taught her to be, but she nearly shoved a man who got in her way because he didn't stop for her when she walked toward her carriage. She was too annoyed to have patience with a stupid human when for fifty years she had been in search of something that seemed more and more impossible to find by the day.

As she got into her closed carriage, she shut her eyes, while her chest rose and fell in a frustrated sigh. For the millionth time, she pulled out the small hand mirror she had taken from Edith many decades ago.

She thought back to the day she got the mirror, just as she often did, in the hope that maybe she had forgotten something that could help her now. Going over every detail from that day in her mind, she remembered standing in a rotten house full of garbage with an old and deluded Gleaner who didn't like cooperating. Edith's pockets had been stuffed with all sorts of objects and one of them had been the old and scratched-up hand mirror that Maeve now tightly clutched in her hands.

"It shows me where to get my treasures and the story behind them," Edith had said.

"Let me see that," Maeve had demanded as she charged toward Edith until she was standing just in front of the smelly old Gleaner, who had held the mirror to her chest.

"Others have tried to steal it, but it only works for me you see. But I can ask it a question for you *if* you give me your treasure." Maeve could still remember Edith's disheveled appearance with all her scars from rodents biting her.

"Deal," Maeve had agreed and walked over to stand next to Edith, who looked like an old unwashed woman with the spirit of a child who was proud of her favorite toy.

That day Maeve hadn't hesitated before asking, "Can anything change my fate so that I don't have to live forever?"

Edith repeated Maeve's question to the mirror, though she stuttered most of the words.

It had been bizarre to watch the mirror change from showing their reflection to suddenly showing images of Althea and Maeve on their twenty-fourth birthday when they had split the crystal. It was strange to see herself through the mirror because all her memories came from the perspective of her eyes. Now she saw it from another perspective entirely. The images were blurry like a dream, but it was clear as day, how when Maeve cut the crystal in half something happened with its magic.

Maeve's sharp gaze was glued to the small mirror as the image of Althea and her putting the crystal into their mouths turned into something she did not remember. It soon became clear that it had yet to happen. The mirror showed a newspaper where the date stood out in bold letters. A date that was five hundred years in the future.

Maeve's eyes widened when she saw herself in the mirror. Though she did not look much older her hair was starting to gray, and her face was starting to form wrinkles. She walked down a street where people wore strange clothes and signs lit up like magic. Everything about this future version of Maeve seemed normal until the mirror showed how the last of the crystal's magic seeped out of her body, leaving her to fall to the ground and take her last breath. Soon her body was removed from the street, and humans carried on as if she had never existed. It left Maeve frazzled and shocked.

Edith watched with her large eyes, not understanding much of what the mirror showed, but after Maeve died and people carried on down the street, a face appeared that made Edith confused and caused her to squirm.

Though it looked like an entirely different person, the mirror showed Edith when she had once been a young and beautiful Earthen. It revealed how Zosia, who had been in the shape of leaves, had given young Edith the crystal of immortality. Unlike Maeve, however, Edith did not put the crystal in her mouth but instead stuffed it in her pocket and disobeyed Zosia's instructions by finding the Cobra to convince him to change his ways. She did not do much more than introduce herself before Charles transformed into a cobra and bit her. The mirror showed how Edith fell to the floor and suffered a pain worse than the most brutal kind of death as the Cobra's venom spread through her helpless body.

The mirror had only just gotten to the part where Edith, whose eyes were now red and wild, walked down the street as a Gleaner who had forgotten who she truly was. The pocket where she had put the crystal had gotten a small tear in the fabric, leaving the crystal to fall out and land on the ground. The mirror showed how a teenage boy found it and later sold it to an antique shop. But seeing the young woman in the mirror whom she could not recognize as herself brought unpleasant feelings up in Edith and left her with the creepiest sense of déjà vu.

The mirror hadn't finished showing its images when Edith suddenly threw it away from herself and fell to the ground before crawling backward to escape the images it had shown.

With her heart drumming in her chest, Maeve had retrieved the mirror Luckily, the glass hadn't shattered, and with her hands clasped tightly around the handle, Maeve had shot Edith a death glare.

"It wasn't done showing visions. Make it finish!" Maeve demanded.

Edith looked up at her with frightened and angry eyes and screamed with spit flying from her mouth, "No!"

"Does anyone else know?" Maeve had asked in a stern tone as she got to her feet.

Edith shook her head violently and insisted, "No, this is the only mirror of its kind, and it has never shown me anything like that before."

"No one can ever know about this," Maeve had stated out loud as she put the mirror into her pocket. And no one ever did find out, because Edith didn't live to tell the tale, and Maeve never spoke out loud about what the mirror had shown her.

She wished desperately that the mirror could have finished showing how she could find the crystal Edith had lost, but every time she asked the mirror anything, it only showed her reflection.

Her hands were gripped tightly around the small mirror as the carriage made its way through the bumpy streets of London. Maeve was consumed by regret and self-pity. At first, she had pitied herself for being stuck with humans, but now she had realized that she would only be doing them a favor by dying. And the last thing she wanted to do was help humans. Her initial desperation to end her life had transformed into a desire to become as powerful as Charles.

She had recognized the shift in her attitude as soon as the mirror had shown her how she would come to die. Now, fifty years later, she still remembered clearly the sudden epiphany that immortality was a gift and not a curse. With her long life and unique powers, she could build her empire and slowly kill off humans until there were none left. But without immortality, her time was limited, and humans would carry on ruling the world and destroy her legacy in the process.

These days, the thing that Maeve regretted most of all was how she had shared the crystal with Althea. If she had consumed it herself, she would have lived forever and she would not have been able to feel pain. It would have made her invincible. Instead, she was limited in lifespan and had already endured brutal amounts of pain, because although her body could repair itself, she could feel just as much physical pain as any normal Earthen.

But the mirror had given her hope when it showed her that there was another crystal out there, the one that Edith had lost. It was the reason why Maeve had decided to open her jewelry store "Intoxicate," and the reason she went to every antique store and pawnshop that she could find.

No one except for Maeve knew about the sword of Damocles over her head. She had to find the crystal, otherwise, she'd have to say goodbye to life and more importantly, the power she'd become so addicted to.

Unlike Charles, Maeve was ruled by her emotions and sometimes acted on impulse, but that didn't mean she wasn't a clever woman. She was smart enough to know that Charles was using her one way or another, but he would be naïve to think she wasn't doing the same. Maeve had a plan, a plan she kept very private.

She looked down at the small mirror in her hands feeling grateful it was the only one in the world. It meant she was the only one who knew of the fate that awaited her, and more importantly – her sister. Althea had no idea of the fate she would meet. For all she knew, the crystal had given her an endless life. She would have no chance to search for the crystal and prolong her life indefinitely, and Maeve would have no competition in finding the crystal.

Once Maeve found Edith's unused crystal and consumed it, she would gain true immortality and be raised above physical pain. Althea would die sooner or later and that was of no consequence to Maeve's plans. She knew exactly how she'd get what she wanted from Charles so that she could get her revenge and destroy everything Zosia held dear.

Little did any of them know that this was all just the beginning of the end.

To be continued in Orenda #2 – Betrayal of Blood.

We hope you enjoyed the first part of the trilogy, and we would be deeply grateful if you would leave a review on Amazon and/or social media. A few words from you will make it easier for new readers to give the book a chance.

WHAT'S NEXT?

Buckle up because things are about to get intense as we continue in book 2.
You can read the blurb and see the cover on the next pages.
You'll also find an overview of our back catalog of other books and description of the authors

Orenda 2 – Betrayal of Blood

Lured by promises of a privileged life among the wealthiest in the world, Damon became a Fader back in the 14th century. Shifting shapes and being immortal has its perks, but following every order from his maker, the Cobra, is getting old. Especially when his order is to seduce Althea, an Earthen who stole something valuable from him once and who he hasn't been able to track down for the past five hundred years.

Now, Althea is back asking for his help.
Will Damon be able to finally get back what she stole from him? And how will he manage to seduce a woman he can't stand and who clearly doesn't like him either?

Betrayal of Blood is the second installment in the gripping fantasy trilogy *Orenda* written by bestselling authors *Elin Peer* and *Pearl Beacon*.

<u>Get your copy</u> of the second installment of this epic fantasy on pre-sale today to be among the first to read it when it goes live on September 30th.

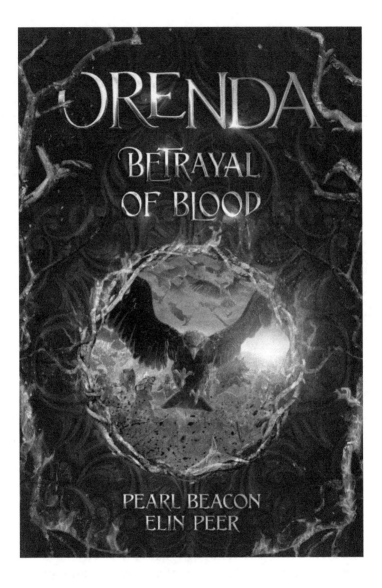

ORENDA

BETRAYAL OF BLOOD

PEARL BEACON
ELIN PEER

ABOUT THE AUTHORS

Meet Elin and Pearl, the mother and daughter team behind the *Ancient Souls* trilogy and other bestselling series.

They love traveling the world and have lived in different countries. Recently, they returned to Denmark after ten years in Seattle, USA. Now they're writing books in their yellow cottage that is perfectly nestled between a cozy village and the forest behind their house.

If you want to connect with them, you can find their contact info on the next page. They both love to hear from readers

Elin Peer

With a background in life coaching, Elin is easy to talk to and with over thirty books under her belt, fans rave about her unique writing style that has subtle elements of coaching mixed into fictional love stories with happy endings.

Elin is curious by nature. She likes to explore and can tell you about trekking through the Asian jungle, watching the sunset in the Sahara Desert, sailing down the Nile in Egypt, kayaking in Alaska, river rafting in Indonesia, and flying over Greenland in a helicopter.

She enjoys writing books with her talented daughter Pearl Beacon, whom she describes as one of the kindest and wisest people she knows.

To connect or learn more, please visit Elin at: www.elinpeer.com or simply send an email to: elin@elinpeer.com

Pearl Beacon

Pearl was only twelve years old when she began helping Elin plot the Men of the North books. She quickly realized that she wanted to pursue writing as a career and by the time she turned eighteen she was writing her fifth book. The prolific mother/daughter team always has a story or three cooking.

Like her mother, Pearl loves to travel and make friends around the world. When Pearl isn't writing, speaking, or doing sessions, she lives a quiet life close to nature surrounded by people she loves and the family dogs, Lucky and Leo who she showers with hugs and kisses.

To connect or learn more about Pearl, please visit: www.pearlbeacon.com, or simply send an email to pearl@pearlbeacon.com

Ready for more entertainment?

Check out an overview of our back catalog but be aware that those books all vary in the level of steam.

Men of the North by Elin Peer:

One prequel and fifteen romantic sci-fi stories that take place 400 years in the future where women rule the world.

These stories are unlike anything you've ever read and have made several best-selling lists on Amazon.

It's a tug of war between the crude alpha men on one side of the border and the altruistic women on the other side.

Can they find a way to integrate?

Clashing Colors by Elin Peer:

These five contemporary romance stories dive into the theme of "opposites attract."

From romantic comedy to dramatic scenes offering food for thought, these books will make you both laugh and cry.

Cultivated by Elin Peer

Set in the USA and gorgeous Ireland, these six contemporary romance books take on the question of mind control.

They're suspenseful, fast-paced, and full of humor. As always, they carry Elin's unique style of writing, which readers refer to as "self-help that reads like fiction."

The Slave Series by Elin Peer:

Five intense "enemy to lovers" books portraying strong women who won't be defined as victims. Expect some dark scenes and steamy sex.

Ancient Souls Trilogy

3 fantasy books that take you behind the veil of the afterlife.

Spirit guards, guardians, and ancient souls are trying to save humanity from destroying themselves.

Readers call these books brilliant, unique, and thought-provoking.

CPSIA information can be obtained
at www.ICGtesting.com
Printed in the USA
LVHW082230310722
724842LV00030B/697